Arboriginals

Peter Tiernan

DEEPWOODS BOOKS

This is a work of fiction. All of the characters, organizations, and events portrayed in these stories are either products of the author's imagination or used fictitiously.

Copyright © 2026 by Peter Tiernan

All rights reserved. Printed in the United States. No part of this book may be used or reproduced in any manner whatsoever without the express written approval of the author, except by reviewers who may quote brief excerpts in connection with a review.

Published by Deepwoods Books.

978-1-7325717-9-2

*To all the people
who keep circling
in my imagination
after 48 years of
life in this town.*

TABLE OF CONTENTS

Freshmen	1
1. Dooley's	5
2. Extremes	15
3. Fragels	19
4. Halfass	26
5. Blind Date	35
6. Spring Love	43
7. Collection	47
8. Pass/Fail	55
Graduates	63
9. Baptism	67
10. Voices	80
11. Masquerade	87
12. Revolutionary	101
13. $720,000	110
14. Luminaries	116
15. Justice	122
16. Top of the Park	131
Townies	143
17. Karma	147
18. Lost	153
19. Street People	158
20. Raven's Call	170
21. Visitation	176
22. Safe Arbor	179
23. Masks	184
24. Relics	190
25. Angell Hall	198
26. Forgiveness	202
27. Deciding	205
28. Odyssey	209
29. Authenticity	212
30. Last Advice	218
31. Heart of Jesus	224
32. Graffiti Alley	231
Arboriginals	237
33. Convergence	241
AUTHOR'S NOTE	265

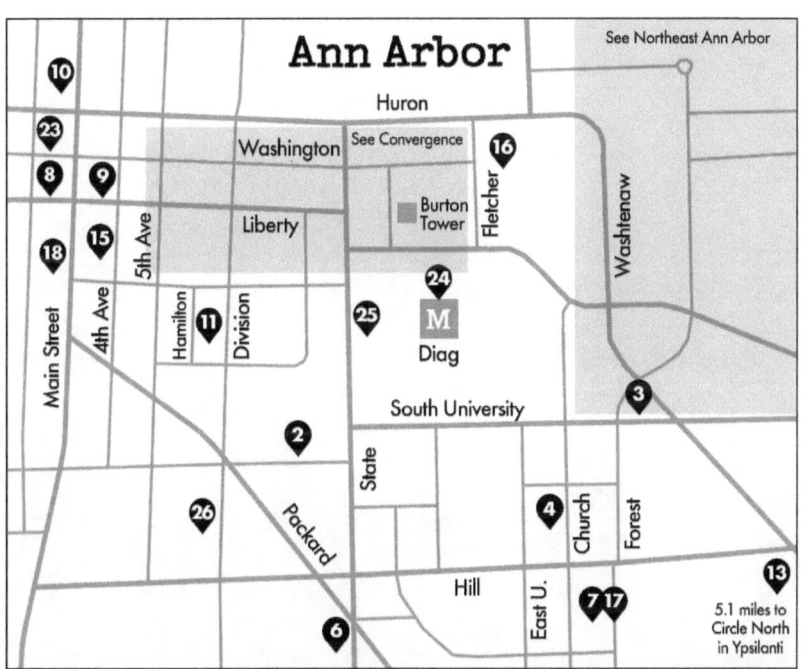

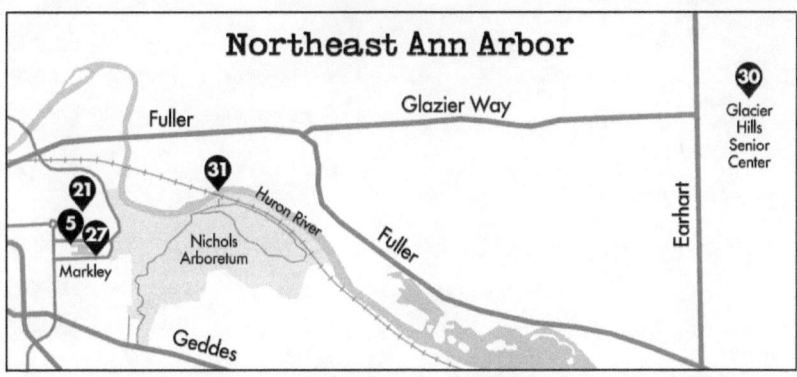

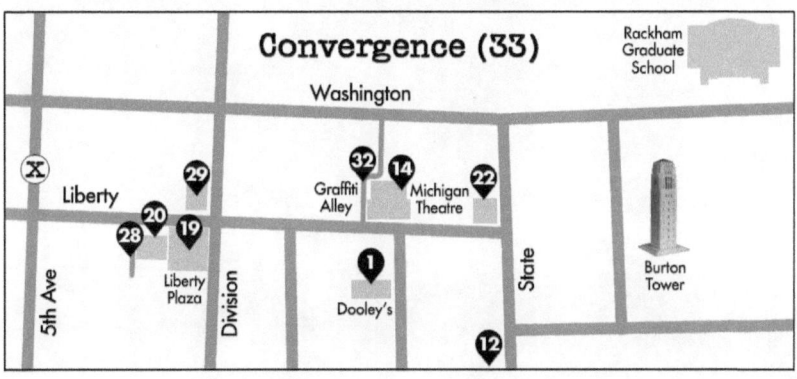

Cast of Characters and Chapter Appearances

Kip Knight	1, 4, 10, 15, 18, 24, 29, 32, 33
Reese Ward	1, 8, 10, 11, 14, 19, 20, 28, 32, 33
Kate Evermore	1, 2, 4, 7, 11, 14, 16, 20, 28, 30, 33
Hal McCallum	2, 7, 9, 12, 13, 20, 33
Chase Tyson	3, 7, 9, 12, 16, 17, 26, 33
Dean Harper	3, 6, 11, 15, 23, 33
Jeremy Baskin	3, 9, 10, 15, 16, 29
Cole "Clem" Emory	3, 7, 9, 16, 17, 21, 27, 31, 33
Leah Vogel	3, 7, 9, 12, 16, 22, 26, 33
Ben Hadley	4, 10, 12, 16, 19, 32, 33
Alec Bucksley	4, 7, 11, 14, 16, 25, 33
Grant Markham	4, 5, 9, 13
Jackie Johnson	5, 9, 16, 21, 27, 33
Carrie Asbury	6, 8, 11, 15, 18, 23, 33
Edgar "Boz" Boswell	7, 11, 13, 19, 27, 32, 33
Tom Whelan	8, 10, 11, 14, 20, 25, 30, 32, 33
Harvey Barlow	8, 11, 14, 30
Brandon Markham	13, 17, 21, 33
Maggie Bucksley	16, 17, 22, 25, 33
Max Tyson	16, 17, 22, 33

Freshmen

Ann Arbor is a college town, and like any college town, there's a rhythm to it. Every September, young people get deposited here, say goodbye to their families, and start finding out who they are. Thousands of new people, all at once, mix with older classmates, graduates, teachers, townies, vagrants.

If you could watch from high above, say from the belfry of Burton Tower, up where the bells chime every quarter hour, as if keeping the city's tempo, and if you could speed up those bells, compressing days to seconds, it would all look so dizzyingly predictable. Morning comes. People stream in. Their paths converge and snarl in the Diag, the center square of campus. The snarling untangles. Shadows grow. Night descends. Rogue lines streak through the night. It goes calm then starts to brighten. The rhythm repeats. After so many cycles, leaves fall. Snow comes. Campus goes spare and dark for the holidays. The bells keep stuttering their quickened cadence. The town greens and flowers, grows lush then shudders with yellow. It begins again.

Of course, those lines crossing the landscape aren't fixed vectors darting along undisturbed tracks. They're people. Going to classes or teaching them. Discovering freedoms, encountering obstacles. Enjoying success, suffering disappointment. Losing their way and finding it again—or not. If you could concentrate on one person and follow their journey, you'd find that, while they usually keep going when they cross another path, sometimes they pause, and occasionally they join that path. And if you could highlight the person they joined and follow them, you'd discover the same phenomenon. Do this enough, illuminating person after person, and you'd see them connecting over and over.

Why do you think when you come to town—to a football game or the Hash Bash or Sonic Lunch or the Art Fair or even just to run an errand—

you keep seeing the same people? They may be friends. They may be acquaintances. Maybe they're people everyone knows, like Shakey Jake or Doctor Diag or that chalk artist who draws flying pigs on the sidewalks. Maybe they're just random people you've noticed through the years. If you run into enough of them at the same time, you might call it a coincidence. And depending on your beliefs, you may ascribe the encounter to something more providential. But in a town like this, where the rhythms of the seasons vary so little and those who observe them are so abundant, what is coincidence but the accumulation of connection?

Take yesterday. Monday, April 23, 2012. You may have read about the two incidents downtown. Strange circumstances. You don't whether to laugh or cry. If you don't know the stories already, it's best not to hear them now. It doesn't really matter what happened. What matters is how? That'll tell you more about this town than anything, maybe even more about this world. The police said the incidents weren't related, but some of the people involved in the first event knew others involved in the second. The news reporter made a big deal out of that, but was it really so unusual?

Let's stop that time lapse we started in Burton Tower and rewind to the first contact among all the people named in that report. We can do that much. We can go back in time and follow anyone. But once we do, we're stuck where they are. We can't see any further ahead than they can.

So who met whom first? Watch the time lapse in reverse. Wait for the moment when all the people we've illuminated are gone. Now play the time forward again. Slower now. Wait for our first light to appear. Watch for when it crosses the next light's path.

There. Way back, 35 years ago. September 1977. At Dooley's, the town's most popular college hangout. Not around the bar or in that cavernous main room. Look up in the loft. See the two men in the corner, that unlikely pair?

Watch. Listen.

1. Dooley's

"I'm up for anything," says the one named Kip Knight. He looks too old for Dooley's. It isn't just that he's wearing a button-down shirt and creased slacks, like he's going to a job interview. It isn't even that his hair's more tamed than the day's trend. It's the squint of those eyes and the way he holds his mouth, lips pursed in a guarded frown, contained by parentheses of wrinkles already too deep to unset. He's used to keeping things to himself.

His friend holds a cardboard table tent in his hand. He's looking on the inside of it instead of the outside, where the drink specials are listed. The waitress makes a show of her impatience.

"Beer, shots, cocktails. Whatever, Reese," Kip says.

"Beer's good." Reese Ward sets down the table tent as gently as if someone sleeps inside it. He's been using the name Reese only since he got to town. The name on his birth certificate is Maurice, in honor of his mother's father. But even she never intended to call him that. He was always going to be Maury. The problem is that her husband quickly decided the name was too prissy for a son of his. So he shortened it to Mo. Too bad he hadn't foreseen how Mo's classmates might react. By the end of first grade, and all the way into high school, the boy originally named Maurice, then changed to Maury and shortened to Mo would be called Stooge, since the only Mo his classmates knew was the grumpy member of the *Three Stooges*. It was only in his junior year that he cut the nickname to Stu—and that was only because he'd earned enough renown on the gridiron in Bad Axe, up near the tip of Michigan's thumb, to reclaim control over his identity. "Stu" lasted long enough to make it into *The Detroit News* listing of third-team All-State football players, but died just three weeks ago, when one of his coaches turned "Stu Ward" into "Stewardess." Thus, Reese was born.

"Stroh's? Budweiser? Miller Lite?" the waitress prompts them.

Reese shrugs at Kip. "You're buying. You pick."

The parentheses around Kip's mouth twitch. Even if someone noticed the change, they'd have no idea what it meant. *Typical Reese*, is what Kip's thinking. *Always so passive, just going with the flow. No one would ever believe this guy was on the football team.*

It's true. Sandy blonde hair down to his shoulders, that patchy peach-fuzz beard, the grimy jeans jacket. Reese looks more like one of those hippie holdouts hanging around the Diag. And he's so scrawny. How *did* he make the Michigan football team? In a word: speed. He's a freshman, so he's getting more attention for his weaknesses—how small he is, how spacey—but some of his teammates have noticed he's been winning the sprint drills, beating even Harlan Huckleby. And he made a run today where he sliced through the line and accelerated past defenders. If you look for the strengths in him, you can see the lean muscularity. You might even read his indifferent manner as a kind of cagey vigilance, the performance of some wildcat ready to pounce—granted, the runt of the litter.

Kip sees none of this. He hasn't known Reese for long—just two days at orientation and this first week as his roommate. And Kip being Kip, his assessment of Reese doesn't go much further than self-serving: *Reese is an odd duck, but he* does *have connections.* "So did Leach say *when* he was coming?" Kip asks, to make sure Reese hasn't forgotten the reason they're there.

"Can't be much later. We got practice at six a.m." It doesn't matter to Reese whether Rick Leach shows up or not. He just wants to be done with this. He should've never told Kip he knew Michigan's star quarterback. It was a stupid boast. He never thought Kip would press him on it. But he wasn't making it up that Leach would be at Dooley's. He heard him tell his linemen he'd buy the first round.

Reese doesn't know Leach well enough to warrant a free drink, but Leach knows who he is—he handed the ball off to him on that one run. If Reese said hi to him, he'd say hi back. Then maybe Reese could introduce Kip, and then Kip would get off his back.

Kip peers over the railing into the crowd below. But the real action's directly beneath them, where the big horseshoe bar is. "He could be here already and we'd never know."

The waitress arrives with a pitcher and mugs. Kip pays her, fills the mugs, and slides one over to Reese. Kip downs his first glass in two swallows and pours a second. Reese sips the head off his beer. "Drink up. I don't want to spill this pitcher walking around." Reese takes a bigger gulp. "I just don't want to miss him, you know? That's why we came." Reese looks up at Kip for a second, then his gaze falls back into his beer mug. Kip notices. "We're having a good time, though. Right?"

Reese finishes off his beer in one long chug. "Let's go."

The main floor of Dooley's is more crowded than it seemed from above. There's no hope of finding a seat, but they're able to wedge in beside a cluster of coeds at the end of the bar. Kip figures them for sorority types. The pitcher's nearly empty by the time they claim the spot. Kip orders another. When it comes, he looks at Reese. "You got this one?"

Reese pats his jean jacket.

"Never mind." Kip lays down a twenty. "Get the next one."

Halfway through that pitcher, Kip gets enough courage to interrupt the coeds. "I find it hard to believe you're all alone here."

"Do we look like we're alone?" one says.

"You know what you won't believe?" Kip goes on. "You won't believe you're talking to a football player right now."

All the girls eye him. One says, "You're right."

"Not me. My buddy here. He's your football player." Kip leans back so the girls can see. Reese's eyes retreat into his beer. "You wouldn't guess it, I know. He's a tough little shit, though. Aren't you Reese?" He clamps Reese's shoulder.

The girl farthest away leans in. "He's not on the team. I'd know."

"Well, he is."

"Let it go, Kip," Reese says.

Kip throws his arms out wide. "Fine. Your loss, ladies." He scoops up his mug and finishes his beer.

"You don't have to tell people I'm on the team."

"Why not?" It's cool. It's your thing."

"My thing." Reese downs his beer. Now the second pitcher's gone. "I got the next." He fishes in his pocket and finds a folded-up five.

"You know what I mean. It's a claim to fame." Kip has a claim to fame, too, but it's by association—not that he's ever considered the distinction. His father discovered several bands around Detroit—bands whose names never fail to impress when dropped. Actually, if Kip had a claim of his own, that would be it: he knows everybody. He understands the power of fame, and he's good at maneuvering close to it. That's the only reason he's here at Dooley's with Reese. It's all about getting Rick Leach on the list of people he knows.

The next pitcher comes. The bar gets more packed. Kip and Reese get squeezed further into the corner. By this time, Kip's worn down the defenses of one of the girls. "I'm pre-law," he shouts over the din.

She laughs. "Didn't you say you were a freshman?"

"Yeah."

"How does that make you pre-law?"

"I'm getting into law school," Kip insists with a crooked smile. "I'll bet you on that right now."

Reese fills Kip's mug. "I better go."

"No. Stay, man. One more. We'll get a round of shots. One, two…" Kip counts the girls. "Plus four: six Kamikazes."

Three guys wedge into the huddle of coeds. They're wearing Michigan letter jackets and they're huge. The girl who was so sure Reese wasn't on the team puts her arm around one of them and points to Reese. "So Mitch, this guy says he's on the team."

Mitch is a square-jawed linebacker type. He eyes Reese and breaks into a mischievous sneer. "Hey guys! Look who's here?"

"Wart!" the other two jocks shout together. As much as Reese tried to stop the name calling, he never anticipated his teammates would go after his last name, Ward.

"So he *is* on the team?" The girl's incredulous.

"Told you," Kip boasts.

"Just an ugly little wart," one of the players jokes.

The bartender lines up the Kamikazes in front of Kip. Mitch cordons off three with his meaty hand. "You don't mind, right?"

"Naw. It's cool. I'll just get more." Kip holds out his hand. "By the way. The name's Kip. Kip Knight."

Mitch ignores him. "Isn't this past your bedtime, Wart?"

"Screw you," Reese mutters.

"What did you say?" The burly player who called Reese an ugly wart steps around the girls.

"Come on," Kip says. "He's just kidding." The player keeps coming. Reese flings what's left of his beer into the player's face. Then he ducks past Kip and tries to slip into the crush of people. He isn't fast enough, though. The third player grabs his arm and jerks him around. Reese swings his mug and grazes the top of the guy's head.

The players descend on Reese. He swings his fists wildly. Kip stumbles going to Reese's aid and falls. Feet stomp all around him. He covers his head. Now he's getting yanked off the floor. A bouncer's pushing him toward the door. Up ahead, another bouncer has Reese. He's flashing a blood-stained smile at Mitch, who's straining against a buckling line of bartenders. He has a bloody nose. "You're dead, Wart! Tomorrow, you're a dead man!"

The last thing Kip sees in Dooley's as they shove him past the line to get in is Rick Leach laughing at him. Then they fling him out the door. He lands on the pavement next to Reese. Reese picks himself up and holds his hand out to Kip. "We gotta get outta here."

Kip gets up on his own. "What the hell, Reese?"

"I can't take it anymore." Reese spits out blood.

"Leach was right there when they kicked us out." Kip shakes his head and starts off down the road for South Quad where they live.

"You don't know what it's like."

They go a ways in silence, past Nickels Arcade and the McDonald's. Across East William, Kip plops down on the curb. "That was it. That was my chance to get in good with Leach. And we blew it."

Reese is looking back toward the bar. "We should keep going."

"They're not coming, Reese. They'll just get you tomorrow."

"Tomorrow…" Reese rakes his fingers through his beer-drenched hair. The action throws him off balance. He reaches for a nearby parking meter to steady himself.

Kip looks hard at Reese for the first time since the fight. "Don't worry. Nothing'll happen. Just talk to the coaches."

Reese huffs, releasing a spray of blood into the glow of a streetlight. He gives the meter a shake, then another. Now he's wrenching it back and forth with the same fury that he swung his fists in the bar. The meter wobbles.

"Is that loose?"

Reese stops his shaking and backs away. "Sorry."

Kip tests the meter, shaking it back and forth. "I'll be damned." He yanks the post right out of the cement. "Oh, man, we gotta take this! It's perfect!"

"For what?"

"We'll put it in our room. Show it off. A souvenir from the night we fought the football team."

"I don't know."

"Come on. It's a great story. And it's yours more than mine. Hell, we deserve to get something out of this shitty night."

The meter's one of those dual-headed types that look like Mickey Mouse ears. Kip cradles the two banks and points the stem of the meter at Reese. "Pick it up."

"If we get caught..."

That stops Kip. He tries to hide the meter head under his shirt. It's too big. "Gimme your coat." Reese takes off his jacket. Kip wraps it around the Mickey ears, then picks it back up. "There. This could be anything now."

Reese picks up the stem. Kip leads the way down Maynard. They cross into the plaza with the big black twirling cube that balances on one corner. Reese gives it an easy spin as they pass. Kip steers them away from State Street. They don't run into anyone until they get to the side of West Quad. A man's sitting there on the steps, hunkered down in a coat too heavy for September. His head pops out as Kip and Reese pass. "Our reward for the night," Kip feels compelled to say.

He and Reese continue for a few more steps. Then something behind them lets out an electric cough. The man on the steps mutters, "Madison and Thompson." Kip realizes the situation immediately. He drops his end of the meter and runs across Thompson, away from the dorms. For a second, Reese continues on, scraping the meter along like he's trying to plow the sidewalk. Then there's another radio squawk and he understands, too. He bolts toward South Quad just as a police car turns down Thompson. Sprinting up Madison in front of West Quad, Reese finds his stride. And now you can see why he's on the football team. When he cuts between the cars parked along the street, his body angles like a tilted blade.

The police car's headlights swing onto Reese and blind him. But they can't catch him now. He's nearly across the street, and no one's out chasing him yet. He'd be faster than them anyway, because he's always been faster than everyone—

Dooley's

There's an awful screeching. His left knee explodes in shards of pain. He crashes against the road. Lights cross above him. People shout. He's blocked between the car that hit him and the cop car. He tries to stand. His knee buckles. He careens into the dented car. He gets up on one knee—

Something else hits him. And now someone's forcing his face into the pavement. They're wrenching his arms behind him, handcuffing his wrists. He stops struggling. Still, the officer who tackled him keeps his knee driven into the small of Reese's back. Reese can only see cockeyed legs crowding into the fringes of the police strobe. Then suddenly a face breaks into view. A girl kneeling, cocking her head to look at him. Her eyes are big and soft, filled with worry.

"What is your *problem?*" She pushes at the policeman kneeling on Reese. "Get off him! He's hurt!"

Another policeman pushes her back. "Calm down, honey."

"Honey?" She twists away, but the cop grabs her around the waist and carries her out of view. Reese bucks the policeman off his back, rocks up on his shoulder, and gets to his knees. The girl's back by the crowd, still resisting the cop. Her eyes shift. And now she's looking at him. Reese knows in that instant that they're fighting together. He wants to rush to her defense, but he can't lift off his bad knee. Then they're on him again, two of them. This time, when he goes down, his head hits the street hard and there's a clap of light.

Later, in the white room inside the police station, when the officer asks who helped him steal the meter, Reese just gazes up where the camera is. And when the officer tells him the meters had $78 in them, three over the limit for a felony, Reese shrugs. Another officer comes in. He says they suspend students for crimes like this, but if he told them who the other guy was, they'd go easy on him. Reese folds his arms. "I'm not going to tell on a friend."

When they give him a chance to make a phone call, Reese thinks about calling his running back coach or calling home to Bad Axe.

But one would bring trouble, the other sorrow. Then he thinks about the girl in the street who came to him, who looked into his eyes and fought for him. That's who he'd call. But he doesn't know her name. Reese tells the officer he doesn't want to call anyone.

He spends the night in a holding cell with a hippie in a red cowboy hat who mutters to himself. He's scared at first, but they keep the lights on, and the guy falls asleep quickly. Reese can barely bend his knee. When he gets up to piss, he has to lean one hand against the wall and limp to the open commode. He sees his face in the mirror—the cut over his left eye, the scrapes down his cheek, the fat lip and chipped tooth. For a second, he doesn't know who he's looking at. Then the face grins at him, laughs, and turns away.

The next day, they bring Reese in front of a judge. His court-appointed lawyer, a guy named Kevin O'Shea, advises him to plead *nolo contendere*. He says it's more like throwing yourself on the mercy of the court than admitting guilt. It doesn't matter to Reese, so that's what he pleads. The two lawyers and the judge talk it over. Then the judge tells Reese that because it's his first offense, he's only getting 50 hours of community service. Later, outside the courtroom, his lawyer says they got a call from someone on the football team. At first, Reese feels bad that they found out. But then he decides he's quitting, and he thinks about the way they treated him. He deserves something for what he put up with; a free pass out of jail seems fair.

In the afternoon, when he knows the players are at practice, Reese hobbles into South Quad and up to his room. Kip isn't there. He fills a duffel bag full of the belongings he can't do without. As he's locking up to leave, Kip comes around the corner.

"Reese."

"I didn't tell them anything."

"What happened?"

"It's okay. I just have to go to this place and do dishes once a week. It's called Flood's. You heard of it?"

"I think it's a bar. Way downtown."

"Well…" Reese picks up the duffel bag.

"You going somewhere?"

"There's a guy I know from high school. I'm staying with him."

"I saw that Mitch dude this morning," Kip says, as if to confirm the wisdom of Reese's decision. "His nose was messed up."

Reese leans against the wall and flexes his knee. "Can you imagine that meter right here when you walk in?" Kip says. "Like hanging out with us is so cool, the time's worth charging for. You know?"

Reese nods. "I better go."

"Alright. Well… we'll see you around." Kip closes the door. Reese limps away, lugging his duffel bag. It's a struggle to get downstairs and out of the dorm. Reese stops to catch his breath once he's outside. It's a cool day for September. Leaves are swirling all around, yellow and gold and red ones. Reese doesn't rest for long. He flexes his knee to unstiffen it. Then he continues on, heading west, toward the older part of town.

He doesn't really have a friend from high school, and he doesn't know where he's going to stay. For some reason, though, he's happy. It's sunny and he's free and there's no one around he has to hide from. And maybe, somewhere on the street from here to where he ends up, he'll run into that girl with the big eyes and the heart to fight for him.

2. Extremes

Her name is Kate Evermore, and just an hour ago, she was engaged in—well, there's no polite way to put it; it was an orgy. She's in the passenger seat of a green Chevelle, passing the Business School on Tappan. It's late. The guy driving is older, just out of school and working at the Grad Library. He's dressed like he didn't have time to change between his information desk and the orgy. His name is Hal McCallum.

"So who was that guy with the curly hair—the tall one?" Kate asks, looking straight ahead as they pass Dominick's then the Law Quad.

"Alec something." Hal eyes Kate until she looks at him, then he focuses back on the road. They come to the stop sign at State Street.

"What's his story? He seemed so... so..."

"Cocky?" Hal says, and this time he holds his eyes on her.

Kate doesn't dignify the joke. "I was going to say distant. It didn't even seem like he wanted to be there." She adjusts in her seat and wipes the corners of her mouth to fix her lipstick.

Hal turns on State. He glances over again under the brighter lights. Kate's thin white dress hangs loosely off her breast. Her curly hair glows with a rusty haze. "So that's how to get your interest," he says. She's pretty in an innocent way, with big wide eyes, guileless yet penetrating.

"Who said I was interested?"

"He's a teaching assistant," Hal finally divulges. "Clem knows him."

They turn left for South Quad. "I just like to know," Kate explains herself. "It makes it seem more friendly."

"*Friendly.*" Hal smirks. "Why are you still living in the dorm?"

"What do you care?"

"I just don't know any juniors who do that."

"I'm a sophomore."

"Really? Wow. I thought you'd been around longer. You know everywhere to go and everyone when we get there…" Hal can't figure out how to go on. He's glad to find a space so he can focus on parallel parking.

"So this Alec. What does he teach?"

"I don't know." Hal swings his car into the spot. "English, philosophy, something like that. He's always spouting off crazy rhymes."

"So he's a poet."

"For someone who isn't interested, you sure talk about him a lot."

"It's just curiosity, Hal. Basic human curiosity."

Hal shuts off the car. "And I'm just making a basic human observation. You've been asking about him the whole ride."

"I should've walked home."

"Don't be mad." Hal puts a hand on Kate's knee. "I'm sorry. Okay?"

Kate pushes it away. "I don't like to be judged."

"I said I was sorry. Can we just drop it?"

Kate cracks open her door. "Fine."

"So are we going to see you around next week?"

"I don't know," Kate says. "Clem needs to find more girls. I like to be admired as much as the next person. But there *is* such a thing as too much attention."

"Even if there were more girls, you'd get the most attention, Kate. You just have too many… admirers. You know I'm one of them."

"We're not going to talk about this again, are we?"

Hal looks down Madison where the street slopes away from campus. "I suppose you'll want a boyfriend at some point."

"I don't know about that."

"Not every guy would be as understanding about… sharing you."

"That's not my problem."

"Maybe not. But I know who you are. And I'm okay with it."

"You know who I am."

"I think so."

"Then why would you think I'm looking for a boyfriend?"

"Don't call it a boyfriend then," Hal says, this time holding his eyes on her dark profile. "But you *are* looking for something. That's why you come to Forest."

"You've put a lot of thought into this, haven't you, Hal?"

"Yes. I have."

"Then why hasn't it occurred to you that I come for the simple reason that I like it?"

"There's more to it than that. It's like this Alec thing."

"This Alec thing?"

"Asking all the questions. Circling back to him over and over." Kate opens her door. "So what is it, Kate? What do you want?"

Kate turns to him now. "You know what I want? I'll tell you what I want." There's an edge of anger in her voice, contained but simmering. "I want to do what *I* want to do. I don't want to be tied down or questioned or judged. I want to be in charge of my life."

Just then, someone runs in front of them and breaks out into the street. Headlights swing into Kate's eyes. There's a screeching behind them. Red and blue and gold lights swirl. For a second, Kate thinks they're the ones in trouble. But when she looks back, she sees the runner lying in the middle of Madison under the front of a police car. The kid tries to get to his feet, but a cop grabs him by the neck and forces his face to the pavement. Now there are more cops huddling around him. One is wielding a club.

Kate springs out of the car and rushes toward the huddle. It happens so fast Hal doesn't have time to warn her against it. She's pushing at the cop who has the kid on the ground. And now she's kneeling next to him. Another cop tries to pull her away.

Hal opens his door. The lights go on. One of the cops turns to him. He shuts his door, puts the Chevelle in drive, and edges out of his spot. There's just enough room to get by the police car. Hal finds Kate in his rearview mirror, getting carried off by the police. He turns out of view.

I have to stop going to Clem's, Hal tells himself. *I can't see Kate anymore. Why would someone so into indulging her selfish desires stick her neck out in such a selfless way? Why hide behind the safety of numbers for your pleasure, then run all alone into danger for your principles? Who wants to be with a person like* that?

Hal slows to a stop at the red light on Packard. He hums at his thoughts. *Kate's right: I don't know who she is. But I do know this: she's a woman of extremes. Unfathomable extremes… maddening contradictions.*

How in the world am I going to quit seeing her?

Why would I even want to?

3. Fragels

About that orgy house on Forest. It's a rental in the student ghetto. The owner has no idea what's going on there. He's never stepped foot in the place. That's because he only became the owner three months ago, when his father died and he inherited the property, along with a few other rentals.

His name is Chase Tyson, and right now, he's sitting on a stool in the front window of Mister Tony's Sub Shop, looking out on South University Avenue. It's the Friday before homecoming and it's warmer than usual for October. The rain just stopped and the sun's out. Everything's shimmering. It makes Chase think of the spring, when he didn't have a thing to do with his father's rentals and he'd planned to drive cross-country to Wyoming. He laughs bitterly.

Dean Harper, the cook, sees Chase shaking his head. He comes up beside him. "You and me both. Those frat jerks make me sick."

"What about them?" Across the street, at the side entrance to Village Corner, a group of guys in rugby shirts are sorting out how to carry all the beer they bought. The empty-handed ones toss a football back and forth, looping it over the heads of passersby.

"Strutting around like they own the place. It'll be worse tomorrow when they have the Mud Bowl."

"I've never seen it," Chase says. Every homecoming, the fraternity on the corner fills its yard with mud, and they slog through some rivalry with another frat before the real Wolverines play in front of 100,000 people.

"You're not missing anything," Dean says. "Just a bunch of drunk knuckleheads. You here tomorrow?"

"Yeah."

"You'll see. They'll crowd in here and raise hell. Last year, one guy barfed in the bathroom. So you got that to look forward to."

"You saying I'll have to clean it?"

"We'll make the new guy do it. But I'll need you at the register."

"I can do that." Chase watches the rugby crew head past the Bagel Factory, laughing and jostling each other. It's nearly five. There hasn't been a single call yet. But it's early still. Plenty of good nights start this way. And it's Friday, so they'll get a late rush when the bars let out. Chase could use a good night. He needs the money. Even though his dad left him a bundle, it's all tied up in investments. Chase feels his first urge since getting in to have a smoke. He didn't bring a pack on purpose, thinking that might help. It hasn't. "Mind if I run over to V.C. for a sec?"

"Make it quick."

"Give me ten minutes. I gotta stop at the Bagel Factory."

"Don't tell me: Clem hasn't paid yet."

"He's just a couple days overdue." Chase is surprised to hear himself defending his chronically late-paying tenant.

"Told you. That guy'll take advantage of you every chance he gets."

"He always comes through. Eventually." Chase leaves the store. There are already more people on the street than usual, clusters of students waiting to get into the V-Bell, a stream of customers filing up the stairway to Bicycle Jim's. Chase ducks inside Village Corner, slips past the line waiting for liquor, and goes down a narrow aisle to the counter for household supplies. There aren't any cigarettes there, but no one's in line. He's been to the clerk enough to know he'll walk down and get him his smokes.

Back outside, he lights a cigarette. This is the part of taking over his dad's places he hates—confronting problem tenants. It isn't in his nature to be a hard-ass. Then again, when he doesn't, he feels like he's letting his dad down. He heads for the Bagel Factory. Everyone who passes him is about his age, have no worries, and belong to something. A hall in a dorm. A group of buddies. Greek brothers or sisters. Chase has more worries than he can sort out and doesn't belong to anything.

Before the entry to the Bagel Factory, there's a big window, fogged around the edges with sprayed-on powder. It looks in on the workers making bagels. Chase peeks around the fringe of the fog. Clem's back where they mix the dough. Chase can pick him out right away by his floppy afro. Near the other side of the window, a guy with a ponytail cuts a mound of dough into board-like slabs. He has a helper who takes the slabs, carries them like fat snakes across the window, and feeds them into a machine that runs the depth of the store.

Chase has seen this all before, but he cranes his neck anyway to watch a huge gear turn like a paddle wheel, grab the strip of dough, and pull it into the machine. It isn't the way the contraption gobbles the slab that interests Chase. It's the girl on the other end of the machine, where little dough balls drop onto the conveyor. She's small and thin, and she does her job with delicate speed. It's hard work, too, snatching those balls and placing them on four thin straps before the conveyor spits them over a ledge onto an overflow tray. Chase has never seen a single ball on that tray when the girl's working. And he's seen plenty on other shifts, even with two workers. Her intensity, her quickness and precision—she reminds Chase of a bird. And it amazes him that she's there, fluttering in the midst of everyone, escaping their wonder.

He's so busy watching the girl, he almost doesn't notice Clem slip out the back door. He flicks his cigarette away and goes inside. The line at the counter's half a dozen deep. When it's his turn, Chase asks the guy if he can talk to Clem. The guy's peeved to have to track Clem down, but he does it anyway. While he's gone, the bird-like girl crosses into the store.

"You're good at that," Chase calls out. She stops and eyes him. "The way you keep up with that machine."

"The habamfa," she says.

"The what?"

"That's what the machine's called."

"Well, you're good at it." She looks down at the floor but doesn't move. It's like she's waiting to be dismissed. "Anyway, I noticed."

The guy working the counter comes back, and the girl retreats. "Clem's in the freezer."

"Just tell him his landlord stopped by."

When Chase gets back to Tony's, Dean says, "That took a while."

"Sorry. Any calls?"

"Not yet."

"We should just tell Baskin not to come in." They always schedule two drivers on the weekends.

"Too late." Dean cocks his head. Baskin's back by the oven, making himself a pizza. Chase retreats to his stool, opens his backpack, and pulls out a study guide for his Eastern European history class.

"What're we reading?" Jeremy Baskin sits beside Chase with his pizza. People have told him he looks like Bob Dylan, and you can see why, what with his squinty eyes, wolfish grin, and curly hair.

"Hegel."

"Ah, more communist tripe."

"It's not communism," Chase corrects him.

"From each according to their abilities, to each according to their needs," Baskin recites.

"That's Marx."

"Same difference."

"Not really."

Dean blows out a mouthful of pent-up air. "I'm not going to have to listen to this all night, am I?"

"That's for Szporluk, isn't it?" Baskin ignores him. "I took that class. He's a card-carrying commie. You can tell."

"Oh yeah. How?"

"The way he quotes Marx. The adoring tone in his voice. He buys into that shit. Government dedicated to the management of things, helping everyone in a big happy utopia."

"You're wrong. He always talks about the dangers of communism."

"In practice. Not in theory."

"So what? Everything sounds good in theory."

"And you've just made my point."

Chase isn't sure he did, but he laughs to signal he's done debating.

"What Szporluk never says is that when they talk about the management of things, they include people." Baskin's shakes a finger at Chase. "People are things to communists, too. Ever thought of that?"

The phone rings. "Chase," Dean calls out. "It's for you."

Chase goes over and takes the phone from Dean. It's Clem. "Hey man, sorry I missed you. I was moving racks in the freezer."

"That's all right, Cole." That's Clem's real name, the name he signed on the rental agreement: Cole Emory.

"Ever been in our freezer? You could die in twenty minutes."

"O-kay..."

"Listen, man. I'm going to get your bread. There're just a couple guys who haven't come through is all."

"That's not my problem. You're two weeks overdue."

"I hear you," Clem says. "So how about this: we'll trade you a dozen fragels for a large pepperoni pizza."

"How does that get me my rent?"

"I told you, man. It's coming."

"When?"

"Tomorrow. Come over to the store around noon."

"All right." Chase starts to hang up.

"So fragels for pizza. Is it a deal?."

"Talk to Dean." Chase passes back the phone. He doesn't care one way or the other. Fragels are deep-fried bagels covered with cinnamon and sugar. They're tasty when they're hot, but they don't keep.

Plus, there's something about trading with Clem that seems like giving in. Chase slumps down on his stool feeling vaguely defeated.

"We're getting fragels!" Dean announces seconds later. "We have to take the pizza around back, down that alley by the bike shop."

"That's your delivery." Baskin points to Chase.

"That doesn't count."

"Those are the rules. We alternate calls. You were here first."

"It's not real business, though. Right, Dean?"

"That was the deal. You're the one who wanted it that way."

"Because Baskin was cherry-picking all the good orders!"

Dean shrugs and disappears into the kitchen. Minutes later, another call comes in, this time for a real delivery. After Baskin hangs up the phone, he waves the order tag at Chase and waggles his tongue. Chase goes outside for a smoke.

"How about you lay off Chase," Dean says.

"What? This is the way we interact. This is us getting along."

"You know his dad died a few months back."

That stops Baskin. "No, I didn't." He peers out the front window from behind the counter. Chase stands to the side, having his smoke. *Why didn't he tell me about his dad?* Baskin wonders. *We're friends.*

When Clem's pizza's done, Chase hustles it over to the alley between the bike shop and the Bagel Factory. Clem's sitting on a milk crate at the far end, sharing a joint with a few guys. He holds out his arms when he sees Chase, like he wants a hug. "There's my man."

"Where're the fragels?" Chase asks, all business.

"I figured you'd want them hot. They got a shelf life of a minute." He nudges the ponytail guy. "Go get my man six fragels." The guy gets up and disappears through the back door. Clem holds the joint out to Chase. He waves it off. "Man, you are dangerously serious."

"If you say so."

The door swings open. It's the wiry girl who runs the habamfa. Chase looks down at the ground. Clem notices. "You know Leah?"

"No," Chase answers. Then he thinks how that might sound to her. "I mean, I've seen her. She works that one machine."

"Yeah, she does. Better than anyone we've ever had." He passes the joint to her. She takes a hit, holding one arm tight around her stomach. Chase tries not to stare at her.

"Leah's hanging at the house for a while," Clem says. "That's cool, isn't it?"

The question flusters Chase. "As long as I get my money."

"Chase is our landlord," Clem tells Leah. "Can you believe that?"

Leah Vogel squints at Chase for a long moment. "Yeah."

Clem bursts out laughing. "She's got you pegged as some heartless ball-buster. That's not you. I know. I see through that."

The ponytail guy comes back and gives Chase the bag of fragels. Chase gives over the pizza. Clem laughs again. "I'd tip you, Chase. But I gotta pay my rent. Sure you won't take a hit?"

Chase glances at Leah. "All right."

"There's my man."

Chase takes a deep draw. It goes down easier than his cigarette, so easy he coughs. After one heave, though, he manages to hold it in, then lets the smoke seep out slowly. He shows Clem his best attempt at a smile.

"Yes, indeedy! Yes, indeedy!" Clem looks around at the crew, grinning. Then his sight settles back on Chase. "So we will see you tomorrow, Sir Chase."

"Tomorrow." Chase shakes the fragels. Sugar rustles in the crinkling bag. Leah cocks her head to the sound. *Just like a bird*, Chase thinks as he turns and walks back up the alley.

4. Halfass

It's been snowing all day, and the radio says it'll go on all night. The university has already cancelled classes for Friday. But even with the freedom of a snow day, hardly anyone has ventured outside.

Ben Hadley sits at a stool on the stage of the Halfway Inn, fixing a broken string on his acoustic guitar. He's been playing for over an hour, mostly to an empty room. The open guitar case at his feet has two dollars in it. If he were inclined to believe in luck, Ben has plenty of reasons to suspect that his has gone bad. Here, on his first night playing to a live audience, a blizzard swoops in. Not only has it kept outsiders away, but the storm's novelty has distracted East Quaders from heading to the basement of their own dorm, where the little student-run lounge they affectionately call "the Halfass" is located. Now, as the biggest group of people all night settles in at the far tables, Ben's still fiddling with his guitar string.

"Anyone know a good joke?" he says to remind them he's still there.

"You!" someone shouts. A couple others laugh.

"Come on, Newbold," one guy hushes them. "Be cool,"

"I'm just kidding, Grant." Newbold thinks twice and calls out, "Sorry, man!"

"No sweat," Ben says. "Maybe you're right."

"Had-ley! Had-ley!" the Grant guy starts chanting. The rest join in. Ben wonders how they know his name. Then it comes to him: the Halfass put placards with a list of musicians playing that month on the tables. He starts in on "Wild Night," a Van Morrison tune. He was going to sing a song of his own, but the chanting has increased the pressure to please. It isn't Ben's style. He plays the song slow, his voice halting. When he sings the *ooh-woo-ooh-wee* that comes before *the wild night is calling*, he breaks it into a series of groans. And when he has to warble the word *wild*, he goes so slow it's hard to tell what he's saying unless you know the song.

Ben sees Newbold whisper to his friend and laugh. He closes his eyes and strums harder. Next thing he knows, another voice is propping up his faltering wail. Grant's standing in the middle of the room, singing at Ben's same slow pace. He finds the tune again. From there on, with Grant's backing, the song is powerful and whole, still deliberate, but forceful.

When it's over, the group gets ready to go back into the storm. Grant holds his arms out, "Where're you going? We got Ben Hadley! On stage, right now!"

"Time to hit the Blue Frogge," someone says.

Grant slumps his shoulders, making a show of disappointment. He pulls out his wallet and extracts some bills. Then he circles his friends. "Come on, gentlemen. We're talking Ben Hadley here." They all fish out a few dollars, even Newbold. Grant walks the money up to the stage and drops it in Ben's guitar case.

"Thanks man."

"Thank *you*," Grant says. "Keep on keeping on, Ben Hadley."

Ben bows his head. Grant bows back, turns, and catches up with his friends. When he opens the door, a dusting of snow sweeps across the floor. Another person bustles in, bundled so tightly in his parka he looks like a deep-sea diver. He slips on the sheet of snow, lurches back, but doesn't fall. Still, Ben can tell he's drunk by the way he staggers to the counter and leans against it.

Ben starts to play the tune he was going to do before he resorted to something familiar. This time, he closes his eyes and imagines he's practicing in the quiet of his room on Lawrence.

"Got any coffee?" the drunk asks the girl at the counter.

"We have hot cocoa. But it's an hour old."

"Long as it's warm."

She goes to the canister, fills up a Styrofoam cup, and hands it to the guy. He's looking off toward the stage, bobbing to the music. He makes the girl smile. Yes, he's drunk, but he isn't dangerous. He's loose and happy. "Sixty cents," she says.

He digs his wallet out from underneath his coat and gets a dollar. "Want some advice?" He smiles a crooked smile. The last time we saw that smile, Kip Knight was sitting at the bar at Dooley's, bragging how he'd get into law school.

"I could always use good advice," the girl says.

Kip takes a sip of his cocoa. He shakes his finger. "Never get in a drinking game at a frat house in the middle of a snowstorm."

"I definitely won't do that. Thanks."

"You, m'dear, are more'n welcome." Kip pushes off the counter and sails across the room. He flops down on a couch just offstage. Ben's still playing with his eyes closed. Kip watches with stupefied wonder, holding the cocoa up to his mouth, not drinking. Ben repeats the chorus he's already sung twice, but he's louder now, working up to the end of the tune:

Are you any, any closer now to where you want to be?
Are you trying, trying anymore to let your mind go free?
Would you walk right out into the night to where you've never gone?
That's where the rapture is, my friend. It doesn't take that long.

Ben punctuates the final words with a quick flurry on his guitar. Then he stops and opens his eyes to the lone listener sitting across from him. Kip's head rocks back. "Wow. You're really good!"

"Thanks." Ben examines the tuners on the headstock.

"That's deep stuff. Trying to get free. Isn't that what we all want?"

"I guess so."

"Well, didn't you write it?"

"Yeah, that one's mine."

"Know what you should do?" Kip sets his cup down on the arm of the couch. "You should make a tape. Send it around."

"You're probably right."

"Damn right I'm right." Kip picks up the placard with the artist names. "Ben Hadley, eh? I'm Kip."

"Hey Kip."

"Ever heard of Grand Funk Railroad?"

"Sure."

"My dad signed those guys. He's a lawyer. He could help you."

"Is that so?"

"Point is, if you make a tape, I could get you a shot."

Ben pulls his guitar in tight and brings his pick hand to the strings.

Kip misses the cue. "It's all about who you know."

"I've heard that."

"He wants me to be a lawyer," Kip says. "I guess that's what I'll be then. Hell, he's the one paying. Know what I mean?"

"Mmm-hmm." Ben picks off a run of four notes. "Let's see if you know this one."

Sailing heart-ships through broken harbors
Out on the waves in the night.
Still the searcher must ride the dark horse,
Racing alone in his fright.

A couple comes in. They sit at a table by the door. The woman pulls off her cap and unwraps her scarf. It's Kate, who we last saw kneeling over Reese outside South Quad.

The man she's with is older. He sweeps his arm out at the room. "What did I say? No one's here. Let's just go. We're already late."

"One drink," Kate says. "Get a coke and an extra cup."

He shows her a twisted grin. "You are something else."

"What?" She acts annoyed, but she's smiling, too. "This is nice, Alec. This is what I wanted. We're out."

"Oh yeah. This beats the hell out of Clem's."

The girl behind the counter has been watching him since he came in. When Alec comes to order, she says, "You're my Shakespeare T.A."

He heaves a deep, dramatic breath. "I am indeed."

"Alec… Alec…"

"Bucksley," he says. "And you sit in the third row by the window."

"Yes!" She's pleased that he noticed her.

"Do you like the class?"

"Bauland's nice. I just don't understand what we're reading."

"I got a secret for you." Alec leans in. "Neither do I." He winks and holds out a dollar. "Can I get a coke and an extra cup?"

When he gets back to the table, Kate's shed her coat and taken off her boots. "Make yourself comfortable." Alec pours half the coke into the other cup, then takes a flask out from inside his coat.

"I see you made a friend."

"One of my students, believe it or not."

Kate catches the girl looking their way. "You should invite her to the party."

"She's a student, Kate."

"I'm a student."

"Not *my* student."

Kate turns to the stage. Ben's just finished the Neil Young tune. Kate catches his eye. He acknowledges her a with nod.

"Play something happy," Alec calls out.

"Play what you want," Kip counters.

"How about this?" Ben starts in on a slow dirge of low notes, staggered so far apart the melody struggles to hold together.

"Where did our love go?" I heard her say.
"Life goes too fast now with you this way."

Trust me, babe, all that glitters ain't gold.
Time goes too slow when you're all alone.

Alec and Kate can't hear the words. "Louder!" Alec shouts. Kate punches his shoulder. "Happier!" he shouts again, laughing. Kate gets up and starts dancing. It isn't the song for it, but she manages to find the slow groove, rocking her hips, reaching high with her arms, twisting them around. She moves across the floor. Kip stops listening to Ben. Alec sips his drink, looking from Kate to Ben to Kip and back. When the song's over, Kate keeps her arms up. Kip claps.

Kate holds out her hands to Ben, as if it was his performance that mattered. He hangs his head. "Who knew that song was a dance tune?"

Kip leans in. "Was that one of yours, too?"

"It was."

"I'm telling you. Make a tape."

"Play another one," Kate insists.

"Something faster," Alec adds. "And louder. We can't hear you."

"Fair enough. Here's got one I think you'll like."

He plays "Strawberry Fields Forever" by the Beatles, slower than the original and bluesier. For once, his halting, uncertain voice matches the song, makes it feel immediate, original. Kate winds into the same snaking dance as before—the reaching arms, the twisting hips, the open mouth. She gets up on the step below Ben, comes down again, then rises up onstage beside the singer.

Living is easy with eyes closed
Misunderstanding all you see
It's getting hard to be someone, but it all works out
It doesn't matter much to me

Alec slaps the table and sucks down his drink. He takes Kate's drink and finishes it, too. She keeps dancing. Ben keeps winding his guitar around the hypnotic melody. Alec gazes across the room with a far-off look. Then, like he's come to some sudden decision, he gets up, strides over, and bounds onto the stage. He clamps Kate's arm and tugs at it. She opens her eyes slowly and gives him a drowsy smirk. Then she resists. They stumble back and wind up sitting beside Ben. He stops playing.

"What the hell?" Kip stands up. "Leave her alone."

"Stay out of it," Alec says. Kate laughs and covers her face with her hands. He slings an arm around her shoulder. "Show's over."

Kip steps toward Alec, still unsteady from the drinking games. Alec shoots out a stiff arm. "You really want to do this?"

"I'm not afraid of you," Kip snaps but comes no closer.

Kate draws her knees up and makes a ball of herself. She starts giggling. "Is this funny to you?" Alec says.

"You're making an ass of yourself," Kate says. Kip comes forward now. Alec gets up and shoves him so hard he falls back onto the couch. Kate scrambles behind Ben, by the high windows where the snow swirls. Kip gets to his feet, but Alec pushes him back right down. He kicks at Alec to fend him off, but Alec catches his foot.

The girl comes out from behind the counter. "Come on, you guys. Don't make me call somebody."

"Alec," Kate says quietly. "Let's go to Clem's."

Alec stands there for a long moment, eyes darting around. Then he pushes Kip's foot away and heads back for his table, hands up like he's done with everything. "One drink. And this is what I get."

"It's alright," the girl from his class excuses him.

Alec turns to her, head hanging. "I'm embarrassed."

"Why don't you ask your student to the party?" Kate calls out from the stage. "You want to have some fun, honey?"

"Awright, Kate. It's over." Alec puts on his coat.

"Maybe I want to extend a few invitations. How about you?" She motions to Ben. "Wanna join us?"

"I'm going outside," Alec announces. "I'm waiting one minute. Then I'm gone. *Gone* gone."

"I'm heartbroken." Kate smooths out the tunic she's wearing.

"You love this." Alec smiles bitterly. "I don't know why, but you do." He finds the flask in his coat pocket, takes it out, and has a swig. Then he heads for the door. Before he opens it, he points at Ben. "A little advice, my friend. You're singing for people, remember. Not for yourself."

"Screw you," Kip snaps.

"One minute." Alec opens the door and walks into the storm.

"Don't listen to him," Kate tells Ben. "Make yourself happy." She goes back to her table and starts bundling up for the snow.

"I would've fought him," Kip says, putting on his coat, too.

"I don't doubt it," Ben replies.

The door swooshes open and Kate's gone. Kip flips up his parka hood. "Maybe you should wait a few minutes before you go out there," Ben suggests.

"I'm not afraid of him. I don't care if he's a teacher."

Ben strums at his guitar. "Well, just be careful."

"I'm serious about the tape. If you make it, I can pull strings."

"Okay."

"You think I'm full of shit, but you'll see."

"I don't think you're full of shit."

"Everyone needs a little help," Kip says, putting on his gloves. "Just five or six own songs ought to do."

"Alright."

Kip walks out of the Halfass. The girl working the counter gets up on a chair and pulls down the metal shutters to close off the kitchen. Ben starts in on his guitar again, wandering around a new melody.

"Can you believe my teacher came in here?" the girl says, shutting off the lights in the lounge. "On the only day I work this month. What are the chances?"

Ben stops playing and looks up at her, like he's trying to reckon those odds. She shrugs. "It's just strange, you know?"

Ben goes back to playing the guitar. And now, under his breath, he adds some words to the melody. "This whole miracle thing… gonna make you holler…"

The girl listens to him try out a few different lines, then she gets impatient. "I need to be somewhere," she calls out.

Ben doesn't seem to hear her. "Gonna bowl you over…"

"I can't lock up until you leave."

"Let me finish this one thing," Ben says. He weaves the song back to the beginning.

5. Blind Date

Remember the guy who sang with Ben at the Halfass? His name is Grant Markham, and he's one of those people who believes the best in everyone. He connects with all the guys on his hall in the Markley dorm—the engineering geeks, the frat wannabes, the over-studiers, the potheads. Nearly everyone who knows Grant considers him a good friend.

That's why his hallmate Clancy's attitude is so curious. It's the last day of classes, and there's a bunch of people celebrating in Clancy's room—his roommate Newbold who heckled the singer at the Halfass, his buddy Waz, Scorgie and Zack from down the hall. Grant just asked who the girl was in the picture frame Clancy has on his desk.

"Nobody," is all Clancy says. You wouldn't think twice if he was dismissive to anyone else. But with Grant, it comes off as mean.

Grant being Grant, though, he doesn't detect the annoyance in Clancy's tone. "An old girlfriend?"

"I don't know, Grant. Honestly."

"Well, she's pretty."

Newbold laughs. "That's one girl you have *no* chance with."

Newbold and Clancy and Waz all went to high school together in Grosse Pointe. Grant figures they know her from there. He picks up the picture. "What's wrong with her?"

Now Clancy laughs. "Fine. She's my sister. Okay, Grant? Can we stop talking about that picture now and start partying?"

"Alright." Grant sets the picture down. "Sorry."

"She's your sister?" Waz screws up his face at the photo.

"Really, Waz? You're asking me that?"

Newbold elbows Waz. "It's an old photo."

Newbold's girlfriend Jackie shows up then. She sits on the low bunk beside him and leans back against the wall. Everyone's used to having her around. They don't talk any differently than when she isn't there. Grant's quieter today, though. Nobody seems to notice except Jackie. From time to time, she glances over at him. One of those times, Grant catches her. She looks away. But she can't help herself—and glances again. He's watching her now. The talk goes on around them. When Newbold puts his hand on Jackie's knee, Grant looks away and picks up the picture again.

Later that week, Clancy catches up with Grant on the walkway between Stockwell and Mosher Jordan. "Hey, sorry for biting your head off the other day."

"What do you mean?"

"When you were asking about my sister. The girl in the picture. Sorry. I just—it's hard to talk about her."

"I understand."

They're on the walking bridge that crosses over Washtenaw, the road skirting the east side of campus. Clancy stops and leans against the railing. Grant joins him. Cars disappear beneath them. "She's two years older than me. She was going to come here on a music scholarship, but she got mixed up in drugs her senior year." He stares down at the streaming cars. "One weekend, when my parents were gone, she took some acid. They found her locked in a closet. She said she was hiding from the devil. She's never been right since." Clancy glances at Grant to gauge his reaction.

"Wow. She looked so confident in the picture."

"She'll get better." Clancy nods like he's convincing himself.

"I'm sure she will."

"I'm going to see her Friday." Clancy pushes off the railing. "She's coming up for the night."

"Friday? That's the party—"

"Yeah, I forgot all about that. I was thinking… nah, never mind."

Grant looks up. "What?"

"Maybe you could keep an eye on her. Make sure she doesn't get caught up in anything bad."

"Sure. If you think it's going to help."

Clancy musters a smile. "Thanks. It's no big deal. I'll be around too. It's just—she doesn't like me checking up on her."

"I get it."

Clancy pats Grant's shoulder. "I appreciate this, man."

They start off for the Diag. Both of them are quiet for a long time. "What's her name?" Grant finally asks.

"Oh, right. I never said. It's…um… it's Maggie."

"A good Irish name."

"Yeah." Clancy smiles but can't hold it. "Look, Grant. She's nothing like you see in picture. Maybe I should tell her not to come."

"It's okay, Clancy. Honestly. I *want* to do it."

One side of Clancy's mouth rises and sticks. "Alright."

On the day of the party, Waz and Newbold join Grant for lunch in the cafeteria.

"I hear you got roped into Maggie-sitting," Newbold says.

"I wouldn't put it that way," Grant says.

"I told him flat out, no way," Waz breaks in. "Not after last time."

"He told me about the drugs and what happened."

"So he knows already," Newbold says to Waz. "Leave it alone."

"Fine. I just think he should know what he's getting into."

"I'm just showing her around," Grant says.

"Did he mention to wear a cup?" Waz jokes.

"Geez Waz!" Newbold throws a French fry at him.

"See? He *didn't* tell him everything."

"What?" Grant looks from Newbold to Waz and back.

"Did he tell you about the Ren Cen?" Waz asks.

"No."

Waz holds out his hand, signaling for Newbold to tell the story. "Okay. You should know: Maggie's—what?—kinda wild with men."

"Last time I saw her," Waz says, "she tried to go down my pants—in front of a whole roomful of parents."

"It wasn't that bad," Newbold protests.

"It was pretty bad. And then she got nasty about it."

"What happened at the Ren Cen?" Grant asks.

"She went nuts one weekend," Newbold says. "Got a room at the Ren Cen downtown, ran up a huge bill, picked up a bunch of men. The cops busted her and called her parents. Can you imagine?"

Grant shakes his head like he's clearing cobwebs after a punch. "She's better now," Waz says. "She couldn't come here if she wasn't."

"Yeah…" Grant nods absently. "Anyway, I promised I'd help."

Two hours before Maggie's set to arrive, Clancy calls Grant to his room to play him a Van Morrison record he'd picked up at Wazoo. "This one doesn't hit you right away, like *Moondance*," he says. "It's called *Astral Weeks*. It's a story about a guy falling in and out of love." He gives Grant the album jacket as the bass line of the first song shambles over the shuffle of drum brushes.

> *If I ventured in the slipstream*
> *Between the viaducts of your dream*
> *Where immobile steel rims crack*
> *And the ditch in the back roads stop*
> *Could you find me?*
> *Would you kiss-a my eyes?*

The guitar jangles, a flute dances over the words. Everything's coming together and apart all at once. Grant's never heard anything like it. It's brilliant—sweet, yearning, otherworldly. He studies

Morrison's photo on the cover, lit up in a circle like he's sighted in a scope. "This is amazing."

"Wait for the next song," Clancy says. "I'm gonna go wash up." When he opens the door, Jackie's there. Grant smiles and waves. She waves back. Clancy pulls her away. She rolls her eyes like she's going along with something she doesn't understand. The door closes.

Clancy's right, Grant decides. *This new song is as stunning as the first.* Morrison's wailing reminds him of the singer at the Halfass. *And these lyrics: "to never never never wonder why it's gotta be, it has to be."*

The phone rings. Grant turns down the volume and answers it. "Clancy and Newbold's."

"Is Clancy there?" the caller asks in a thick, wounded voice. Something bad has happened; Grant knows it immediately.

"I'm sorry. He stepped out."

"I need to reach him. Can you find him?"

"Hang on. Let me see." The phone's on the wall beside the door. It has a long cord. Grant carries the receiver out into the hall.

"Hello? Is anyone there?" The caller's voice is panicky.

"Sorry. I was checking if he was coming back."

"This is important. This is… oh dear God."

The caller sounds like he's crying. "Can I take a message?"

"This is Clancy's father. There's been an accident. Clancy's sister, she—uh—she… Maggie's dead. Oh God, she's dead!"

Grant's chest seizes like he got the wind knocked out of him. There's an awful silence. Grant can't get his breath unstuck.

"I need him to call me," Clancy's father says. "Do you understand? Can you tell him that?"

"Okay," Grant answers. "Yes. Okay."

The phone clicks. Grant hangs up. His heart is thumping so hard he can feel pulsing in his temples. He knows he has to go find Clancy and tell him to call his father. But should he say why? How can he not, standing in front of his friend and knowing?

Grant eyes the photo of Maggie. She stares back at him with a knowing grin and penetrating eyes. Grant leaves to find Clancy. The hall seems to twist as he walks it. The door to Waz's room opens ahead. Out comes Clancy. Grant stops.

Clancy holds his hands out. "You didn't like it?"

"It not that. It's—" Grant looks at his friend with a kind of pleading sorrow.

"What?" Clancy says, smiling still, the pain in Grant's eyes lost on him. "What?"

Grant has to say it. "Your dad called. There was an accident. It was Maggie."

Clancy's face transforms instantly. He looks at Grant with a mask of dread. "And…"

"She's—" Grant can't say it. Clancy leans closer. "She's—" Grant tries again. Clancy's mouth twitches. "God, Clancy, she's—" And now Clancy stifles a laugh. Grant's bewildered. Waz and Newbold are peeking out from the room Clancy left. In an instant, Grant knows. They've fooled him.

Clancy backs away, hands up in surrender. He's never seen Grant so mad. Then he bolts down the hall. Grant chases him. Clancy bangs open the stairwell door and heads up the stairs. When he tries to pull open the door to the next floor, Grant tackles him on the landing. "What the hell, Clancy?" he shouts. "*What the hell?!*"

"It was Newbold's idea!"

"So she's okay. She's still coming."

"Who?"

"Your sister."

"I don't have a sister. We made her up."

Stunned, Grant rolls off Clancy and sits against the wall. "So who's the girl in the picture?"

"She's nobody," Clancy says. "She came with the frame."

Grant and Clancy return with arms slung around each other's shoulder. Everyone apologizes to Grant, admitting they went too far. Newbold says he was sure Grant would recognize his voice on the call. Clancy claims he had second thoughts right from the start. Grant says he's just glad nothing really happened. "I *am* a bit relieved not to have to contend with Clancy's nymphomaniac sister," he jokes. The whole room cracks up. They start partying.

Jackie stays with Newbold nearly all night. But even after the beer she drank and the pot she smoked, she can't shake the fact that her boyfriend could pull off such a cruel prank. After midnight, Jackie sneaks off to Newbold's room to get her purse so she won't have to come back in the morning. When she opens the door, Grant's sitting at Clancy's desk. "Sorry. I shouldn't be here."

Jackie shuts the door and links the chain lock. "Don't apologize. Hell, if you want to trash this room, go ahead. I'll even help you."

Grant waves her off. "It's alright. They were just having fun."

"That's not my idea of fun."

"They didn't know how gullible I can be," Grant laughs softly. He picks up the picture of the unknown model. "I came to get this. I don't know why. I had to have it."

"Take it."

"Just the photo." He slides the clips off the backing and turns over the frame. The picture falls out with the glass. "It's a stupid thing to want. I'll never know who she is. It's just that I had this image of her for days. I thought about her, you know?"

"I can see that."

"She was Clancy's sister. And I know they were telling me all these stories to scare me, but that just made me think about her more. I kept coming back to this face."

"I was there when they called. I didn't know—"

"It's okay." Grant sets the picture down and puts the frame back together. "Funny thing is, I thought maybe I could help her."

"It was a terrible thing they did."

"No. It was good in a way. There was this moment after they said she died. Something passed through me, like a ghost. It was overwhelming. I couldn't get on top of it. Just the thought of her, so fragile, haunted—then dying. This face." He taps on the photo. "These sharp, lively eyes. And she was dead. I'd never felt that close to death. The enormity of it. It felt like jolting out of some long dream."

"And nobody had to die," Jackie says, completing his logic.

"Exactly."

There's a clatter at the door—someone trying to get in.

"I can't be here," Grant says in hushed desperation.

"Go out the window," Jackie suggests.

The door jolts open then stops against the chain. "Who's there?" Newbold yells. Grant opens the sliding window, gets up on the ledge, and feels for the pins that hold in the screen. "Is that you, Jackie?"

"I don't want to see you," she calls out. Grant pulls the screen off and sets it to one side.

"I told you I was sorry," Newbold says.

"Leave me alone."

Grant slides the picture off the desk and curls it in his hand. "Don't be too hard on him." He gets up on the ledge, swings his legs around, and slips into the night.

"Jackie, open this now!" Newbold shoves the door over and over against the chain. Jackie looks at the open window.

When Newbold finally snaps the chain and the door bangs open, the curtains billow up and settle back. Even still, Newbold glances around a few times before it registers that his girlfriend has disappeared. The chill of the cold spring night runs through him.

6. Spring Love

Like everywhere else, spring is the season of love in Ann Arbor, but it's more intense than in most places. Students who decide to stay here instead of going home enjoy freedoms they've never known before—more time, less pressure, no parents, and others awakening to the same freedoms. This is the time when many students meet the loves of their lives. It's also when they make their worst mistakes. There's no reason that separates one fate from the other. But there *is* something common about those who face either fortune: they dare to take a chance.

Dean Harper's one of these people. You've met Dean. He's the cook at Mister Tony's. Now, he's sitting at one end of a couch in an apartment on State Street, staring down at his bloody hand.

A girl sits at the other end, head cocked, trying to catch Dean's eye. Her name is Carrie Asbury. "You should go to the hospital."

"It's not that bad." He picks a shard of glass out of his knuckle.

"I can see the bone."

"That's because it's right under the skin." He spreads open the cut and shows it to her.

Carrie winces. "You need stitches." She gets up, crosses the room, and pulls up the blind that shuts out the traffic and the grimy backside of Bell's Pizza across State. Gauzy light floods the room, exposing the dust that hangs over the decades-old furniture.

"We don't open that," Dean says.

"I live here, too."

"You're a sub-letter, Carrie."

"So I have to live in a cave for the next month?"

"I'm just telling you what everyone'll think."

"They can shut them when they're in the room." She fluffs up the cushion of a chair. A cloud of dust rises into the light.

"Are you cleaning up for him?"

Their eyes connect for the first time since they kissed 10 minutes ago. Seconds later, Carrie told Dean she was getting married. "I thought you knew. Really. The night I moved in, I told everyone I was getting married in August."

"I was working that night."

"I thought someone would've mentioned it."

"So why did you let me kiss you?"

"You just kissed me."

"You kissed me back. And remember what you said?"

"I'm confused," Carrie says. "I mean, I *was* confused."

He gets up and goes over to the dining room's double doors, where he put his fist through four glass panes. Wood bars dangle from the frames.

"Don't start fixing that now."

"I'm just getting this off the floor." He kicks some pieces of glass into a pile. "I'm not cleaning up for your friend."

"He's not a friend. He's my fiancée. You're my friend."

"He's not your friend?"

"You know what I mean."

"No, I don't."

"He's more than a friend."

"And I'm less than more than a friend."

"You're my friend. A good friend. Can't you just be that?"

Dean gives her a soft, defeated smile. He points at the pile of glass. "I'll sweep that up before I go."

"Don't go. Stay and meet him," Carrie says. "He won't be surprised to see you here. I already told him about you."

"You told him about me?"

"I told him about everyone here."

"I see. So *there's Chuck and he's getting his Master's in Econ, and Melanie's studying dance, and then there's Dean and he's a dropout who makes pizza.*"

"Nothing like that."

"Or, *here's Dean and we hang out every day and go to movies together and spend afternoons lying in the Arb. And he comes to my room at night, and he gets me laughing so hard I cry.*"

"Stop it."

"*And just today,*" he ignores her, "*when he was lying on the couch, I jumped on him and he pulled me down and I watched his eyes. All the way. And I knew he was going to kiss me. And I let him. And I kissed him back. And it wasn't a friends' kiss.*"

"Please. Don't."

"Why are you marrying this guy, Carrie? You're twenty-one."

"I've known him my whole life," she says. "And I love him."

"You've known him your whole life."

"And he's smart and he cares about me. And he has a plan."

"Ah, a plan."

Carrie's eyes get hard. "You think you know me, but you don't."

"So what's this plan?"

Carrie doesn't say anything. He asks again. Finally she snaps. "What does it matter? You're going to make fun of anything I say."

"Tell me this: does he love you?"

"He asked me to marry him, Dean."

"I know, but does he *love* you? Does he think about you all the time? Does he live to see the way you laugh, the way you throw your head back and your throat trembles? Does he love you like that?"

Carrie starts crying. "Maybe you *should* go."

"What's the answer?"

"He loves me for lots of reasons. They don't have to be your reasons, and I don't have to tell you what they are."

"Because we're not friends," Dean says. "Not really."

"Don't ruin this, Dean. Please, can't we just forget this?"

"*This.*" He laughs bitterly. "You know, maybe I will stay."

"Don't. Not now."

"I know. I'll answer the door, introduce myself, and I'll shake hands with him." He holds up his bloody hand.

"You're upset. You don't mean any of this."

"Then when he asks what happened, I'll say, *That's a funny story. You see, I kissed your fiancée and told her I loved her. She said she didn't know what love was. So I said I thought it was what we were feeling. Then she said she was going to marry you. So I put my fist through the door.*"

Tears roll down Carrie's cheeks.

"I'm sorry," Dean goes to her, arms open. She leans into them, making herself small in his embrace.

"Please don't be mad at me," she says. "Can't we just keep it like it was? We can forget this. Like I never said anything."

The doorbell rings. Carrie tenses in his arms. Dean lets her go. "He'll know I've been crying."

"It doesn't look that bad."

"Do you want to meet him?"

"No." The doorbell rings again. "I'll go out the back way." Dean brushes past her. She wipes her face.

"Dean," Carrie calls out. He turns in the shadows of the hallway. "I'll be back in two days. Will you be here?"

"You better get the door." Dean disappears into the kitchen. She hears him unlocking the deadbolt. She composes herself and goes to the front door.

7. Collection

Nine months after taking over his dad's rentals, Chase finally visits the house on Forest. When he knocks on the door, he figures it'll be a while before anyone answers. He told Clem three times he'd stop by on Saturday for the rent. But all Chase got by way of acknowledgement was a wobbling afro. Chase barely finishes knocking, though, and the door sweeps open. Clem's right there, staring with a crazed gawk. "Captain! What are you doing here?"

"Captain's" a new one. Clem's always calling him something—Chief, Star, Kemosabe. "I told you I was coming for the rent."

"Really? Oh man. I don't think we have it."

"We're two weeks into May. I can't keep doing this."

Clem pulls at the whiskers under his lip. "We always pay, right?"

"That's not the point." Chase is determined this month to hold a hard line. "It's the hassle. It's having to come here."

"You always *say* you're going to come, but you never do. I was starting to worry you were mad at me."

"I just want the rent on time."

"But here you are!" Clem gushes, slapping Chase's shoulder. "Paying a visit. And it's a good day, too. Come on in!"

Chase lets Clem guide him inside. They've darkened the place with sheets over the windows. There's a horseshoe of three beat-up couches, and a handful of guys slouch on them, watching *Bugs Bunny*. A sharp chemical odor hits Chase.

"Gentlemen," Clem says. "This is my main man, Commander Chase. The lord of this land. The overseer."

One of the slouchers flops his head back and eyes Chase. "Shoot me now! Shoot me now!" he says. The others giggle.

Clem grins. "They love their Bugs."

"What is that smell?"

"What smell?"

"I don't know. Like nail polish. Or gasoline."

"Oh man. You can smell that?"

"What is it?"

"Freak Dave doused the carpet with ether a few days back," Clem explains matter-of-factly. "It was a gas for a night, but it gets old after a while. Hey, *a gas*… get it?"

"He doused the carpet?" Chase eyes the rug under his feet.

"Not this one. Just a mat we found. Freak Dave wanted to douse the whole first floor. But I was looking out for you."

Chase is a step ahead of Clem when they go into the dining room. There's a pile of what looks like puzzle pieces on the table. By the time Chase realizes it's pot, a dark-eyed guy at the end of the table's staring him down. "Who are you?" he says. He seems out of place among the longhairs helping him clean the pot. Not only is he older, but he's clean-shaven and wearing a powder-blue Izod shirt.

"Whoa! Hang on Boz. Sir Chase is the owner of this domicile."

"Get out of here?" Boz laughs. "How'd you get a place like this?"

"It was my father's."

"Privilege," a stringy-haired guy beside Boz grumbles.

Clem flashes Chase a toothy smile like he just got complimented. Chase feels his chest tighten. On the wall, there's a mirror with swirls of some sort of gold shellac and spongy yellow chunks. On one side, a knife has been taped to the wall. On the other, there's a taped fork and a glass sticking straight out. It's a sideways place setting. "You like that?" Clem says. "Bucky had pancakes on the mirror one night and decided it was a masterpiece."

The guy weighing weed on the other side of Boz raises a fist.

"It's eight hundred dollars," Chase blurts out, voice shaking.

Everyone stops. "I'll take it," Bucky says.

"The rent for May. It was due two weeks ago."

Clem frowns. "Aw, man. Don't get your nose out of joint."

"Who's on the lease?" Chase eyes Boz. For a long moment the only sound is Bugs and a muffled jumble of music.

Then Boz stands up. "I can respect a man with a business to run." He takes out his wallet and counts out a packet of bills. "Clem, I know you've got four hundred. Here's four hundred more. I better get paid back soon or I'll be pissed." He holds out the bills. Chase steps forward and takes them. "Clem won't be late anymore. Will you, Clem?"

"I got that four hundred!" Clem has a wad of bills pinned under his scruffy chin, and he's fishing through his pockets.

"That's not an answer."

"Yeah. Sure, we'll be on time. I didn't know it was that big a deal."

Boz smirks. "It's a big deal." He sweeps his hand out to Chase, "For the landlord of one-two-two-one South Forest."

"Landlords," Bucky the pancake artist grouses. "Sucking the life out of regular people."

"Welcome to the real world," Boz says. "Nothing's free."

"I'm just saying, where's the bond? I never see him here. What's he have to do with our space?"

"I do own that mirror you ruined," Chase says.

Boz booms out a laugh. "Bucky, you may as well join the Buddhists in the Diag. You don't get the mechanics of the world."

"I get how the world works. I'm just saying it should be changed."

"Is this house bugged?" the stringy-haired guy pipes up.

Chase thinks he's talking about insects. "I don't think so."

"You think they're bugging us?" Bucky whispers.

"Think about what we do here. What we talk about. If you were in charge, wouldn't you bug us?"

Boz groans. "Have another joint, Freak Dave."

"I'm serious. We don't know half the people that come here. They could be spies. *You* could be a spy." He points at Chase.

"Nobody's a spy," Boz snaps. "We just take too many drugs."

"Guilty." Bucky raises his hand.

Freak Dave crosses his arms and stews. "I'm telling you, man."

Boz turns to Clem. "So is our guest partaking in the festivities?"

"Oh wow, man. I didn't even think of that. Sure. Why not?"

"I'm just here for the rent," Chase says.

Boz ignores him. "Take our landlord out on the porch."

"I really have to go. If I could just get—" Chase points to the bills in Clem's hand.

"Oh right! The money!" Clem thrusts the wad at Chase. Then he waves him deeper into the house. "Come on, man."

"Enjoy yourself," Boz calls out. When Chase looks back, Boz is eyeing him with something between a grin and a sneer.

Clem leads Chase past the kitchen to a door in the back corner of the house. When he opens it, smoke rolls out. It's a glassed-in porch. Lilacs press against the panes. There's a circle of people lounging on shabby couches and beanbag chairs. Nobody's talking. They all gaze into the smoke as a scratchy Doors record plays. The only connection between them is a circling bong. When it's passed to Chase, he sees that the woman offering it is only wearing panties. He glances around the room. Everyone is in some stage of undress.

Clem spins in the middle of his friends and sings along with the record. *"Listen to this, I'll tell you 'bout the heartache. I'll tell you about the heartache and... loss of God."* He points to each person as he wheels around. *"I'll tell you about the hopeless night, the meager food for souls forgot. I'll tell you about the maiden with wrought-iron soul!"*

"Is Kate here?" asks a kid who looks like he's 16 years old.

"No, man. But Chief Chase is! The absent father of our happy tribe." Clem snatches the bong and thrusts it at Chase. "Give my man a hit." Chase waves it off. Over Clem's shoulder, he catches sight of a girl pulling her knees up in front of her bare breasts. Even through the haze, there's no mistaking who it is. "Oh yeah! You know Leah. That's right!" He motions to the guy sitting beside Leah. "Move over, would you, Zack? Make room for the Big C."

"Who is he?" Zack asks.

"Who is he?" Clem snaps. "He's your mom. Okay?"

"Just asking."

"You don't get to ask. You're just a guest—a guest of a guest. My man Chase owns this place. So we're really all his guests. Got it?"

"I got it. Geez, mellow out."

"Don't gimme that. Just move your ass." Chase has never seen Clem so mad. It's one more reason to resist his pull. But when Zack vacates the seat beside Leah, Chase finds himself going there.

Clem tilts the bong toward Chase. He takes it, covers the carburetor hole, and sucks through the top. Water gurgles. Smoke fills the chamber. He takes his finger off the hole. The smoke leaps into him. He catches it in his lungs and holds on. It burns. Chase coughs. Someone laughs. He passes the bong to Zack in sheepish defeat. Zack points it Leah's way. She's still tucked into herself. Chase taps the bong on her calf. She reaches out and takes it. Her leg falls to one side. Chase sees her breast again, small and pointed. He looks up into the smoke.

Leah takes a hit, passes the bong, lets the smoke go, and arches her back. All at once, she turns and locks eyes on Chase, strangely serene. "Anything on your mind, Chase?" Clem's grinning in a way Chase suddenly sees as sinister. He sits up. Clem keeps grinning that grin, hands steepled, fingertips tapping. Chase tries to fend off Clem's gaze with any easy smile. But he can't do it. He springs off the couch, climbs over the tangle of legs, and staggers to the door.

"Whoa! Hang on, Chief. We haven't even started yet."

"I need to go."

Clem puts a hand on his shoulder. "Come on. Don't freak out. Everybody wants you here. *Leah* wants you here. Right, Leah?"

"It's not right," Chase says. Leah tucks her legs back up.

"Hey! Don't do that!" Clem jabs his finger at Chase's face. "Don't bring your bullshit hang-ups here!"

"I just want to go." Chase steps to the side. Clem blocks his way.

"This is *your* problem. No one else's."

"This is my house." Chase insists as he edges past.

In the dining room, a slick-haired guy swigs a pint of Jack. Chase tries to slip behind him, but he blocks the way. "We have a newcomer." He tips his bottle. "Here's to you, whoever the hell you are."

"Mind your manners, Alec," Boz warns from the end of the table.

"What? I'm toasting." It's Alec, from of the Halfass.

"Chase is our landlord." A big-eyed woman with champagne lipstick and a flowing white dress shows up in the archway. Kate.

"Landlord, eh?" Alec drops his jaw in mock admiration. "Well, all I can say to that is..." He makes a show of pondering his words.

A bookish guy appears beside Kate. Last time we saw him, he was driving away from Kate at South Quad. "Are you going to do this every time someone new comes around?" Hal McCallum grumbles.

Alec unleashes a torrent of gibberish: *"Next to of course God Chase I love you landlord of us pilgrims and so forth oh say can you see by the dawn's early my country 'tis of centuries come and go and are no more—"*

"Oh, Alec. You're so wise," Hal interrupts. Kate nudges him.

Chase looks to the kitchen. That may be the easier way out.

"—What of it we should worry in every language even deafanddumb thy sons acclaim your glorious name by gory by jingo by gee by gosh by gum."

"How about something original?" Hal raises his voice.

"Why talk of beauty. What could be more beautiful than these heroic happy dead who rushed like lions to the roaring slaughter they did not stop to think they died instead then shall the voice of liberty be mute?"

"I can't believe you're still amused by this," Hal says to Kate.

Alec stops. Chase turns to go—and there's Leah. In her bra and panties now, she's sneaking around the crowd to the basement.

"*He spoke. And drank rapidly a pint of whiskey.*" Alec polishes off his bottle. Boz pounds the table and howls. There's laughter all around.

Hal starts a slow, loud clap. "Thank you, E.E. Cummings."

Alec stares him down. "Are you enjoying yourself, Hal?"

"Yeah, I am."

"Good. For a minute there, you sounded like a miserable prick."

"Alec. Don't," Kate says.

"And for a minute, you sounded like a pathetic windbag."

"We're not doing this again," Boz grumbles. "Somebody get Clem."

A kid beside Chase heads for the porch, clearing the way through the kitchen. Chase sees Leah peeking out from the basement stairwell.

"Why are you here, Hal?" Alec says. "Kate's done with you."

Kate stomps off for the front door. Chase makes his move to the kitchen—just as Clem breezes by. "What's going on?" He's back to his spacey persona. "This is not cool. Not cool at all."

Hal ignores him. "I think the important question for you, Alec, is why does *she* keep wanting to come around? Aren't you enough?"

Alec shoves Hal. The pint of Jack crashes on the floor.

Chase rushes to Leah. "I want to go, but my clothes are upstairs."

He motions her into the basement. It's crowded with old household junk. Chase finds a white sheet splotched with red paint and brings it to Leah. "Put this around your waist." She makes a skirt of the drop cloth. Chase takes off his jean jacket. "And you can have this."

"I don't have any shoes."

Chase finds a pair of muddy red boots. They're so big, Leah looks like a little girl playing dress-up. "Good enough," Chase says.

"Where are we going?"

"I've got a place across town." Chase leads her up the stairs. They go out the back door and across the yard, toward a high stand of junipers enclosing the property. Chase heads to the corner of the yard by an old shed. Beside it, there's a stack of firewood high enough to climb over the spiky brush.

"Are you ditching me?" Kate's standing inside the shed, smoking.

Leah hangs her head. "She's leaving," Chase says.

Kate flicks away her cigarette. "You can't go looking like that."

"My clothes are upstairs. I don't want to go past everyone."

Kate kicks off her sandals. Then she pulls off her white dress. Underneath, all she has on is pink panties.

Leah drops the sheet, puts on the dress, and slips into the sandals. "You can have my clothes," she says. "I think they'll fit."

"I better get back," Kate says. She picks up the sheet, wraps it around her shoulders, and heads for the house. To Chase, the splattered paint on the sheet looks like blood.

They cut through a parking lot and head up Church Street. It's the sort of day townies wait for all year—warm for spring with the students gone. Chase and Leah walk in silence. Beyond the Halfass, there's a moving truck in front of the Blue Frogge. The disco's sign is propped against the loading ramp. All down South U, Chase sees more closed stores, and he thinks about the rumor that Mister Tony's may go under. But he puts the thought out of his mind. All he cares about now is protecting this fragile girl beside him.

They enter the Diag. On the far side, standing on a bench, the Diag preacher—Pastor Jim—is plying his trade. "We like to think we're different," he cries out across the square, "that we're in control of our fates. But deep down, we know it isn't true." Chase quickens his pace. "The endless march of death shows us that our ambitions, desires, and dreams—all these worldly efforts to assert our individuality—they're futile in the grand scheme of things."

It isn't until Chase is past Jim that he realizes Leah stopped. He turns back. Jim's crouching down, talking directly to her. "God can save us from ourselves," he says as if imparting a secret. "All you have to do is believe." Chase returns to Leah. She finally continues on with him, but she keeps looking back.

8. Pass/Fail

It's September 1978. A year has come and gone. So it begins again. An influx of freshmen replaces the graduates leaving in the spring. The balance of idealism and disillusionment is restored. A fever of innocence spreads across the university.

It's rare for a freshman to break out of the confines of campus in these early days. But Tom Whelan isn't your typical freshman. See him there, in that stream of students heading toward the Diag? Now watch. No, he's not the only one to skirt the heart of campus. But the others are all older, and they stride the walkways like they know where they're going.

Tom doesn't. And that's how he wants it. He wants to explore. He wants to be different. He wants to be a writer. He's made it into a select composition class of promising freshmen. And he has his first assignment. "No pressure," said the professor, a block-headed snoot named Barlow. "This is a pass/fail exercise." They have to sit somewhere for 15 minutes and just record what happens. Tom wants to display his talent right from the start. Sitting in the safety of campus is no way to stand out. Barlow's probably given the same assignment for years—and suffered through the same forgettable stories. Tom will get his attention. He'll go somewhere no one else would dare to go. He'll find something extraordinary.

Tom plans to get as far from campus as he can get before sundown. He comes up on State Street. He's been to the left to get books at the Michigan Union. He's gone through Nickels Arcade in front of him, shopping with his parents when they dropped him off. He hasn't gone right, where a big red "STATE" sign rises vertically over the buildings. The sign perches atop a movie marquee announcing *Animal House* and *Eraserhead*. A street called Liberty runs straight away from the theater, into the sun setting over a distant ridge of trees. The whole block on his side of the street is a department store called Jacobson's. It seems out of place with the patchwork of run-down storefronts he sees across Liberty. There's Schoolkids'. Someone told him it's the best place in town to get new records.

The store's closed, but there's another record store called Aura Sounde just ahead with a poster in the window of four punky geeks called Talking Heads. The band stands awkwardly in front of a red wall, their image fractured into hundreds of off-kilter tiles. *These guys can't be serious*, Tom thinks. Nothing about the poster, even the name of the album—*More Songs About Buildings and Food*—is cool; in fact, it's flagrantly uncool. A subversion of the rock-and-roll aesthetic. *What will the cover of my first book look like?* Tom wonders. *What kind of pose will I strike for my photo?* All his favorite writers look like they're about to tell you the harshest truth they know.

Tom passes a little food stand called Le Dog and stops at the intersection of a one-way road with cars rushing left to right. It's Division Street, and it seems to mark the boundary between the safety of campus and the mystery of the greater town. He waits to cross with the walk sign even as others amble through gaps in the traffic. There's a cement park on the other side of the street, sunken below the sidewalk. It's a square the size of a baseball diamond, guarded by low walls and lines of small trees turning yellow. Their minnow-like leaves flip over and over in a swirling breeze. A few people are sitting on the benches scattered around the park—a couple facing each other cross-legged, a bum fidgeting with something. They're all on the far side of the park, though.

This is the place. Tom sits on a bench near the steps, pulls out his pocket notebook, and unclips the pen. It's hard to get started, to decide what to write and what to leave out. The way the leaves jitter in the wind seems important. And he jots down a few notes about the couple on the far bench, how their foreheads touch each other as they talk. But he doesn't write anything about the bum who's older than the hippies on the Diag and whose clothes are more ragged. His eyes keep wandering over there, though, catching him once muttering to himself.

Tom turns to face the sidewalk. Farther down Liberty, he sees a man in a long overcoat, a hulking shadow in the dying sun, dragging something that clatters on the cement. He looks like he has horns. But when he gets closer, Tom sees that it's a red cowboy hat. The guy's pulling a toy wagon. A woman ahead of him slows down to wait for the light at Division. The cowboy speeds up, scuffling his boots right behind her. "Hup to, hup to," he barks. "Who's in charge? Not me. Not you. I'm crazy! And you're crazy, too!"

The woman faces him. "Who's crazy?"

The cowboy jerks his head back. "You answered yer own question!" He cackles, stomps his boots, and wheels the red wagon away, back to the park, now clunking down the steps. He goes to a bench across from Tom, slumps down, and leans back, gazing at the sky. He tilts his hat down and yawns. Then, smacking his lips together, he rolls his eyes over at Tom. Tom looks away. The cowboy lets out a raspy giggle. "Hup to, hup to," he says. Then he repeats it softer and slower, like he's confiding his logic to Tom. "Agent Orange comes after you. Déjà vu. Déjà vu. Oh, you double Déjà vu. Will you die with me at the count of two?"

Tom can feel the madman looking at him. He wants to see what those eyes are like under the brim of the cowboy hat—whether they're vacant or as focused and imploring as the words are. But he's too scared. He gets up abruptly and hurries to the other side of the park, where a big arrow sign points down saying, "NEWS CENTER."

"One!" the cowboy calls out. Tom walks faster. "Two!" he roars. Tom tenses, like some calamity's actually going to strike. Nothing happens. And he doesn't hear the wagon clattering. Still, Tom doesn't look back until he's well down the street. The cowboy's covered his face with his hat and he looks to be sleeping.

Tom crosses another one-way street—this one running right to left. For a while, he just walks and doesn't try to put words to what he sees. Then he comes to an intersection where the buildings are older and taller. It's Main Street. The light at the crosswalk changes. Liberty starts angling down a hill to a wasteland of warehouses and railroad tracks. He's reached the edge of town. On the other side of the tracks, Liberty rises again and disappears between a gauntlet of golden trees and little houses. Tom's standing beside a diner called "Fleetwood." He crosses the street and starts back up the other side. There's a bar called Mr. Flood's Party with a guitarist playing in the window.

Tom goes inside. The place is stodgier than he expected, cluttered with statues, stained glass, Tiffany lamps, and assorted Americana. All the tables are empty. Just a handful of people are at the long bar. Tom takes a stool at the near end, with his back to the guitarist. A young couple sits around the corner from him, three stools away. They're exchanging whispers while the guitar gently winds around a melody. The bartender comes over and asks what Tom will have.

"Do you have Stroh's?"

"Got some I.D.?" Tom shows him his driver's license. The bottle of Stroh's comes just as the singer finishes up.

The couple start talking louder. "We should do this every month," the woman says. She's dressed to impress. The man looks like he just got out of work—sleeves rolled up on his button-down, tie tugged loose. They're an attractive pair.

"Every month?" The man scoffs.

When the woman looks at the man, Tom can see her face. "It's good to have a reason to get out of the apartment," she says.

"I don't mind going out, Carrie. I just don't need the pressure of remembering a date every month."

Carrie's about to argue. (Remember Carrie Asbury? The one who kissed Dean Harper?) Her eyes shift to Tom. He looks into his beer. "Don't worry, Joe. It's not a test." She gets up and heads for the bathroom. Tom eyes her, hiding behind his Stroh's. Joe watches, too. When he turns away, he lets a long sigh escape and shakes his head.

I ought to write this down, Tom thinks. But he's afraid Joe will see him scribbling in his notebook.

Two girls come in. They're dressed for a night on the town. "Can we sit at that front table?" one asks the bartender. He says it's fine. Joe watches them walk away. He catches Tom eyeing him, grins, and cocks his head toward the girls, like *how about them?* Tom looks down and digs for his wallet. The bartender's talking to a guy who's come from the back to deliver a rack of steaming glasses.

"You outta here, Grease?"

"Pretty soon." The guy eyes Joe then heads back to the kitchen. Tom doesn't notice his limp. It's so slight, you'd have to be looking for it. And why would Tom do that? He didn't see the accident that wrenched the guy's knee. He doesn't know Grease's name is really Reese, short for Maurice. But *we* do. We saw the accident. We saw him hobbling away from South Quad. This is where he ended up.

Carrie comes back from the restroom. Joe pretends he's surprised when she sits down beside him. He turns to Carrie, eyes her up and down, and says, "Hey there, gorgeous. Where have you been all my life?" Carrie rolls her eyes. Joe laughs. "Can you pay? I'll be back in a minute." He goes to the restroom. Carrie notices Tom glancing away from her.

"He was just joking," she feels the need to explain. "He's really my husband. We've been married one month today."

"Ah." Tom takes a five out of his wallet.

"We've known each other since grade school."

Tom feels pressured to say something. "You must know each other really well."

"We do…" Carrie whispers. She sounds sad.

The bartender comes over. "That enough?" Tom points to the five.

"I'll get your change."

"Keep it." Tom hurries out of Flood's. He doesn't know where he's going; he just wants to get away. *Was she* really *sad?* Tom wonders. *What was I saying when she got that way? Something about her knowing her husband? She said she did, but she wasn't happy about it.*

Tom starts heading back to campus. He passes an alley. Sunlight angles high against the back of the buildings there, up by the rusty landings of fire escape ladders. The rest of the alley's filled with shadows. Tom ducks in and walks past a row of dumpsters. A smaller alley breaks off and goes behind Flood's. There's an air conditioning unit there. He sits down, leans against it, and takes out his notebook. The shadows are so heavy he worries he won't have time to see enough happening. He starts jotting down observations. A bronze line of sunlight climbs the brick wall. A high window wrenches open. A woman's hand reaches out and empties an ashtray. Flies circle around a dumpster. Inky liquid sneaks along cracks in the cement. *To where?* Tom wonders. But wondering gets in the way. He imagines a trickling drain but can't hear it. He thinks about the way the world turns away from the light but can't feel the sensation. Time lurches ahead on him. It's darker. *Stop thinking. Just watch.*

Tom gives himself over to recording the alley's rhythms. He doesn't stop writing even when the last line of light disappears over the top of the walls. Whether this is or isn't what Barlow wants, Tom doesn't care. It's enough. It's all he can gather here in this alley at this moment when the night's overcoming the day. He feels complete, in possession finally of something real, even though there's nothing of himself imposed on the perfect pace of these darkening moments.

Somewhere down the alley, a streetlight crackles and flutters on. *Enough*, Tom decides. Right then, the back door of Flood's creaks open. Two men come out. It's Joe and Reese. Reese props the door open with a milk crate. Tom folds his legs in behind the A/C unit and ducks down.

"I don't know if I want a whole ounce," Joe says.

"It's just forty bucks." Reese lifts up a boombox, flips it over on top of a garbage can, and takes off the battery panel. He pulls out a bag of pot.

"See, that's too much. How about half of that?"

"I'm not measuring it out."

"Fine."

Reese takes an empty bag out of the boombox. "I'll split it the best I can, but I'm going to pick which bag you get," Reese says. "And I gotta have twenty-five bucks."

"That's fair."

Reese works to even out the bags. He holds each up in the light and shakes them before handing one to Joe. "Close enough." Joe puts the bag in his pocket, then hands over the money. Reese pulls out a roll of bills and wraps the new ones around the outside.

Joe heads back inside. Reese snaps the panel back on his boombox, swings it onto his shoulder, and starts up the alley. Tom curls up tighter behind the A/C unit, pretending he's passed out. But he doesn't get his feet tucked all the way in. Reese clips one and nearly trips. "What the hell?"

Tom stirs like he just woke up. "What?" he mutters, making a show of shaking off cobwebs before looking up.

"Don't look at me!" Reese barks. Tom turns his face against the wall. He waits. He hears the clatter and scrape of shoes. He makes sure they fade all the way out before he peeks around the A/C unit. There's no one in the alley as far as he can see. He gets up and hurries out to Liberty. All the way from there to his dorm, he never slows down. He keeps his eye out for that dishwasher the whole time and never notices anything new.

It takes him until three a.m. to finish the paper. He starts right off in the alley, recording the rise of the shadows up that brick wall. But when he gets to the moment before Joe and Reese come out Flood's, he changes what happened. The drug deal never gets made. The dishwasher never scares Tom into turning away. There *is* a stranger who comes down the alley—a menacing bum with a long overcoat and red cowboy hat; he *does* carry a hollowed-out boombox full of weed and *does* confront Tom. But Tom refuses to buy a bag and starts walking away. The bum grabs his arm and swings him around. That's when Tom sees the knife shimmering under the glow of the streetlight. He brings his hand up fast and knocks the boombox out of the bum's grasp. Bags fly everywhere. The box smashes on the cement. But Tom only hears this because now he's running away. And he hears the bum's last words, too: "I know you. I know your face! You better keep your eyes open."

He gets the paper back two days later. There are just two comments on it. Barlow's drawn a line between the part where Tom's alone in the alley and when the stranger shows up. Above the line, he writes, "This is real"; below, "This is a story." Tom debates going in and talking to the old man. Does Barlow like one part over the other? *None of it's completely real,* Tom argues with himself. *You can't record the truth; it's too big—and it moves too fast. You're always deciding what moments matter. You're always telling a story. Then people walk into your life and they pull you into* their *story.*

Tom wonders then why he didn't explain what really happened with the cowboy, and why he chose not to mention the young wife at the bar and the way her husband acted. *What does that say about me?* he asks himself, eyes running back and forth along Barlow's red line. He tosses the paper aside. *Who cares? It's not like I failed.*

Graduates

Most people leave town when they're done with school. Those who stay are trying to make something of themselves here, find themselves still, or pick themselves up and move on. Some would tell you they've found their chosen path. Others would say they're taking a little detour. And if you listen to the fallen ones, you might hear them complain that they're stuck in a rut, or they keep going down blind alleys.

Anyway, there are fewer of them. And life being what it is, they settle into routine, traveling in fewer circles. But they do it for longer than their college years. All of this has them more prone to run into familiar people. If they know the person, they might say to them, "Small world." But after so many intersections, they may greet them with nothing more than a nod. If it's someone they merely recognize, they might wonder, How do I know them? until they think enough to figure it out or they pass them so often they remember.

Soon, the world seems as small seeing a familiar stranger as it does an old friend. And if you cross two or three of these paths within a day, the world gets even smaller. "What are the odds?" you may ask. And when more paths cross, you might declare, "That's unbelievable." Someone may even suggest it was meant to be. And you might dimly wonder if it was.

Let's go back up into the belfry of Burton Tower. Fast forward a decade to 1987. Light up the trails of the people we've met. Notice anything? They're firing around the fringes of campus now, in the surrounding neighborhoods, in stores and bars and theaters downtown. The space they travel in has gotten compressed. They look like pinballs ricocheting around a shrinking machine, coming closer and closer.

Something else is happening, too. See how some paths curve? Remember: these are people; not projectiles. They're charged with the magnetism of free will. So sometimes, they're attracted to—or repelled by—each other. They go out of their way to meet or avoid someone. Think of it as the quantum physics of human nature. See that path bend toward that one? Or that path veer away from this one? And what about those two, joining together and becoming a third, producing a new path? Birth!

Then there are the collisions. Not just the passings and the meetings, or the accidental bumps, but full-on crashes. When they happen, they send everyone around them careening off in new directions. Some of those affected will get hurt, others will be changed forever, and a few lucky souls might say, "How in the world did I survive that?" Then, maybe for the first time, they'll decide, "That couldn't have just been by chance."

9. Baptism

For Chase, it isn't about the movies. It's about the money. As he sits behind the register, peering out the window of Takeout Movies, the town's first video rental store and the first business he's owned apart from his father's properties, Chase thinks about how lucky he is that passion doesn't rule his decisions.

At least a dozen times a day, people suggest videos to get—obscure silent films, art-house titles, cult classics. Chase writes down each request, but he never invests in a video until he gets the same request five times. By his way of thinking, there are two viable business strategies: stock everything you can, or get what most customers want; the few popular movies on video—*Casablanca, The Godfather, Cuckoo's Nest, Annie Hall*, that sort of stuff. Chase doesn't have the cash for a big inventory, so he's taken the second approach.

It's 1987, late in the afternoon of a rainy March day. Hardly anyone's been in the store. Chase has ample time to think. It's taking longer to get the business into the black than he planned. Most of his rental profits are going into the store. And that's putting pressure on him to make sure every unit is filled. Right now, four apartments are still open for the fall. He's hoping to get three signed before the students leave. The remaining unit is an attic apartment where he and Leah live.

Ever since Chase rescued her, Leah's stayed with him in the attic on Lawrence. It's going on 10 years now. At first, Chase treated Leah like a weekend guest. She needed refuge, and he offered it. But he didn't realize how wounded she truly was. Weeks became months, then years. She rarely left the attic for anything other than her job, making sandwiches at Zingerman's. Now and then, he'd coax her out for a walk at night, but they always went away from town, along the river or through the sleepy streets around Kerrytown. Once in a while, she'd surprise him by making a simple dinner—a tuna sandwich, soup, eggs and toast.

One night, around Christmas, he came home to a barely lit apartment. There was a lone candle in the kitchen and a glow coming from Leah's room. Normally, Chase wouldn't presume to check in on her. But Leah hardly ever left her door open, and it was never flickering like fire. "Is that you?" she called out, as if it could be anyone else.

"Yes." He stopped short of her door.

"Chase?" Finally, he looked in. There were candles all over the tiny wedge of a room—along the windowsill, on her nightstand, on the floor around her mattress. She was sitting there, wrapped in a blanket. "Are you cold?"

"It wouldn't be so bad without the wind." he replied. That's when Leah pushed the blanket off her shoulders. She was naked, like that time in the smoky room of the Forest house. Only now, there was no mask for her vulnerability.

"Come get warm." They'd made love a few times in their early days together, and he'd always been the one to initiate. But it made him feel like one of those Forest wolves. So he'd given up pursuing her. This was the first time Leah invited him into her bed. He went. Two nights later, she did it again. Then several times after that. It was always the same: Chase waited for Leah to call him before going to her. By now, he could've assumed an open invitation. But he didn't.

Chases watches raindrops weave down the store window. These last few days, he's come home to an empty attic. It's surprising enough that Leah would leave without him, but what's more bewildering is she won't say where she's gone. The first night she was missing, he was sure some crime had happened. Maybe the Forest cult had abducted her. He thought about calling the police. But just before 11, she showed up, cheeks flush, eyes bright and flickering. When he asked where she'd been, she said it didn't matter. And when he told her he was worried, she broke into an otherworldly smile. "Don't be." That hardly comforted Chase. Was she leaving him?

Still, they kept sleeping together. Last night, after they made love, Chase wondered why they shouldn't get married. He thought of telling her just that, professing his love in the dark. But he was afraid. Then the morning came and he left, still tormented by her disappearances. Now, in the cold reflection of day, Chase thinks that the only way to avoid a broken heart is to break up.

The bell above the door jangles. A man hurries in and heads for the back of the store. Chase can see in the security mirror that he's wearing a trench coat and his hair's dripping wet. His shoulders heave like he's catching his breath. The phone rings. Chase reaches for it with his eyes still on the mirror. There's something about the man that's familiar. "Takeout Movies."

"That's a crap name."

"Okay." Chase keeps his cool. "Can I help you with anything?"

"You've mellowed, Chase. I was sure that would wind you up."

"Baskin?"

"You remembered. I'm touched."

Chase smiles. "I don't know any other wiseasses but you."

"Seriously, the store name has to go."

"What do you mean? It's like takeout food. People take their movie home instead of going somewhere to watch it."

"But it isn't food. They have to bring it back."

The man in the trench coat's groaning now and rubbing his temples. "Is there something you want?"

"I'm just pulling your chain. There's a reason for this call."

"Don't tell me," Chase teases back. "Now that you flunked out of law school, you need a job."

"I didn't flunk out. I dropped out."

Chase realizes he's cut too deep. "So what do you need?"

"I'm helping sell an album by a local singer. You know Ben Hadley?"

"I don't sell records. I rent videos."

"It's not a record. It's a CD. You could put a stack by the register."

"You should be talking to Schoolkids'."

"Bergman took some. But I need a place downtown." For Baskin, it isn't really about helping the musician. It's about escaping town. Ever since he dropped out of law school—never mind if it *was* a step ahead of failing—he'd been stuck here. A B.A. in philosophy and three years of waiting tables at the Whiffletree was all he had to show for the money his parents shelled out. So when his friend Kip told him he got a local singer a record contract and could use help promoting him in New York, Baskin jumped at the chance. He could tell his dad he was a music promoter. And he could finally leave Ann Arbor, distance himself from his failings. "It's consignment," he tells Chase. "You don't have to pay if it doesn't sell."

"I know what consignment is."

"It's a very Socialist concept."

"As usual, you're butchering the principles of Socialism." Baskin lets the silence hang. "Alright. I'll take five copies. If they don't sell in two months, they're gone"

"I'm easy."

"Right." Chase hangs up. He can't see the man in the trench coat anymore. He leaves the register and goes to the far aisle. There he is, hands on knees like he's going to be sick. "Are you okay?"

"I'm fine." The man straightens up and musters a quivering grin. In that instant, Chase knows who it is.

"Clem?"

He gives Chase a long look. "Oh. Hey. I go by Cole now."

Chase's first thought is that Clem—Cole—has come there to rob him. But the hollow eyes and bloated face suggest something more pitiful. "What are you doing here?"

"Just killing time."

Chase nods like he understands. But he doesn't. Cole's so different from the drug-addled tenant he remembers that he hardly knows what to say. "Well, you look—you look good," he lies.

"Yeah?" Cole runs his fingers through his wet hair. "I've got an interview in ten minutes. Just upstairs."

"Well, that's... that's great." Chase knows there's an office above him, but he has no idea what their business is.

Cole's eyes get wide. He wobbles his head in bewildered disbelief. For the first time Chase sees the old Clem. "I've never done this before. I have to keep telling myself it's just a job."

For Cole, though, it isn't about getting a job. It's about saving himself, making a stand against the forces that have been dragging him down for so long. It took Cole six years to squeak out of Michigan with a General Studies degree, an education that started in engineering, then meandered through philosophy, history, and psychology. When he graduated, Cole joked that he had a degree in the Path of Least Resistance. He quickly went about putting that education to use. He signed a lease for a room in Toronto before learning that Americans needed special papers to work in Canada. Then he went to Paris, tagging along with a rootless group of writers who never found time to actually write. And just before his money ran out, Cole flew to San Francisco and freeloaded with a pack of punk rockers who had a broken-down house in the Tenderloin district. Forest all over again, only bigger and wilder, drifters coming and going by the dozens.

And through it all, there were the drugs. At first, it was just pot and cocaine. But by the time he got back stateside, it was heroin—and every day was a desperate quest to get his hands on more stuff. When they got evicted, Cole hitched a ride back to Ann Arbor. Boz, his old partner from Forest, took Cole into his place at Circle North Apartments, closer to Eastern Michigan than the U of M. The place had none of the funky vibe that energized Cole in his college days.

But there was a bed and food, and there were drugs. Boz said it was a perfect location for dealing. They could use the bus system to get to both college campuses.

Cole had left Boz two weeks back. His long-absent dad sent him $500 of guilt money in a birthday card, and it had given Cole the courage to make a break. He knew he'd been an addict for a while. But it was only in those last months that Cole felt he was teetering over a truly dangerous abyss. They'd always stolen from people, taken bikes off porches, grabbed unattended backpacks. Cole justified it as a Darwinian consequence—the hungry and clever besting the bloated and ignorant. But in the fall, they'd started breaking into houses, jumping people at night. Boz had taken to carrying a gun. He told Cole, "You never know what you'll have to do." The night Cole realized he'd fallen into the abyss, he beat a man unconscious outside the bus station when he couldn't rip the watch off his wrist.

Now here he is, standing in front of his old soft-hearted landlord, minutes before the first real interview of his life. And whether it's nerves or cold turkey, he can't help but feel that this feverish gasping is some sort of cosmic judgment against him.

"Do you want to freshen up before you go?" Chase asks.

"No, I'm over it now. But thanks."

"Maybe just dry off your face. Comb your hair. Fix the tie."

Cole checks his watch. "I guess there's time."

Two floors above Takeout Movies, Grant Markham glances at his watch. *I've got some time.* He picks up the phone, dials his wife Jackie, and swivels his desk chair so he's looking down on Liberty. "Sorry I couldn't talk earlier. What's up?"

"Oh, just another bang-up day at Circle North." Jackie and Grant have been managing the Ypsilanti apartment for two years in exchange for free rent. With their three-year-old son, Brandon, and another child due in the summer, it's an ideal way for Jackie to stay home while helping with expenses. What they never counted on was how much they'd have to deal with tenant problems. There was Marvin, the blind tenant who kept taking people's laundry because he wouldn't stay in the room until his load was done and couldn't tell that it had been set on top of the machine. And Han, who was so convinced his young Vietnamese bride was suicidal he worked himself up into a nervous breakdown of his own. And Jack, the old drunk who thought the girls above him were running a whorehouse. And the guy who sold drugs up and down the halls.

Then there was Hal McCallum. A U of M law school grad, he focused his boundless capacity for moral outrage on the daily workings of Circle North. He called it "Nazi North" after Grant had broken up a few late-night parties. McCallum liked to play his music loud at all hours of the day. One morning, when three different tenants called about the noise and no one would answer McCallum's door, Jackie keyed in and turned down the stereo herself. McCallum found out and threatened a lawsuit.

The latest McCallum flap started with a complaint from his roommate, the hallway drug dealer. Edgar Boswell was his name—Boz—and he took exception to McCallum's insistence on keeping his motorcycle in their apartment. Grant would've never dreamed a guy as menacing as Boz would appeal to them to solve a domestic squabble. But just that morning, he'd called Jackie and asked for help.

"Tell me you didn't go down and talk to McCallum," Grant says.

"Oh no. I'm leaving that to you."

"Just what I want to do tonight. How's the little man?"

"Brandon's in his Batman outfit, beating up pillow villains."

"That's my superhero."

There's a pause. "You're not going to be late again, are you?"

"I'll be home by six. I've got one interview and then I'm done."

"Can we do something tonight? I'm going stir crazy here."

Grant closes his eyes. It's a familiar complaint. "It's Friday night, Jay. We gotta stick around. How about we go to the Arb tomorrow?"

"The Arb's enough. I'll hang my hopes on that."

There's a knock on Grant's door. He swings his chair around, expecting the job candidate. But it's his partner, Joe Teegan. "It's a deal. No weekend work," Grant says, as much for Joe as Jackie. "Gotta run. Love you." He hangs up and checks his watch. It's five past four, not a good first impression for a candidate to set.

"You got a technical writer hired yet?" Joe asks.

"One more interview."

"That last girl seemed sharp."

Grant squints at Joe. "Did you see her resume—or just her legs?"

"It's technical writing. We need someone to string a few sentences together. She's got a Masters in English."

"When I explained to her what CAD was, her eyes glazed over."

Joe shrugs. "Your call." He passes Grant a stapled packet of papers. "But this business plan isn't getting any easier to read."

"I'll have a writer hired by five."

"I want this plan ready before our MDSI meeting on Tuesday."

"I thought you said Thursday."

"They moved it up."

"You know the software won't be ready to show."

"It'll be good enough to cast a vision."

"It's hard to give a warm and fuzzy when it keeps crashing."

"I can't change the meeting again," Joe says. "I don't want to come off like a couple bozos playing with computers in their basement."

"I'll have the plan on Monday," Grant promises, in spite of himself.

Joe reaches into his shirt pocket and pulls out a folded check. "Here's the March money. Just a week late."

"Progress," Grant smirks, taking the check.

"And only a couple hundred bucks light."

"Oh?"

"I'd like to pay this writer on time at least once."

Grant pockets the check. "Got it."

"I cut my pay, too. Hopefully after Tuesday, it won't happen again."

"They're not gonna make a decision that soon," Grant says.

"You'd be surprised. These software companies move fast. Just watch. We'll have our first million before you know it."

Grant lets the argument go. It isn't so much about making a killing to him as making a difference, changing the way inventors work, making their dreams easier to attain. That's why he's been writing this program since engineering school. That's why he's been working late nights for as long as he can remember—well before marrying Jackie—trying to devise a way to make it as easy to create an object on a computer as it is to mold clay in your hands. The business was Joe's idea. He'd worked at GM right out of school. He saw how designers struggled to get concepts into a computer. It was so hard to do they still relied on wooden models to get their ideas across. So when Joe saw Grant's work at the senior show, he knew there'd be a market for it, not just with automakers, but with any manufacturer.

Then Grant's son Brandon was born, and he started having doubts. It wasn't that he questioned whether his software would make money. He knew someone would invest in it. And he was certain it would change the lives of countless engineers. He just wasn't sure anymore that those were the lives he should be striving to change. He missed Jackie, the closeness they had when they first met, and he didn't want to be sitting here, five years from now, wondering if he was making a difference to his family.

There's a knock on the door. A man in a trench coat with a pink bloated face peeks around the corner. "Am I in the right place?"

"It is if you're a technical writer," Joe says.

Cole's confused. "I said in my letter I didn't have experience."

"And so the interview begins." Joe smiles at Grant.

"Never mind him," Grant says. "He can't help being annoying."

Joe steps back and motions Cole into the room. Then, behind his back, he apes an expression of mock horror that only Grant can see. Grant's eyes shift to the candidate. "Come on in."

Within minutes, Grant can tell there's something off about Cole Emory. He speaks in jarring bursts. Others might've already dismissed him as a bad risk, but Cole's pitiful attempts to carry on a conversation have an unlikely effect on Grant. He finds himself pulling for the guy. "So you said you started out in engineering—"

"Yeah, it really wasn't where my head was at. Not then, at least. I'm coming around to it now. I've got that mindset, you know. I think spatially." Cole coughs, suddenly short of breath.

"You alright?"

"I'm just—I don't know. I got dizzy all of a sudden."

"Can I get you anything? You want some water?"

Cole waves him off. "Nah. I'm just nervous. I've never really done this before. This interviewing thing."

Grant twirls his pen between his fingers. "So you must've been pretty good at something to get into engineering school."

"I like math," Cole recovers. "It comes natural."

Grant drums his pen on the desk. He spins around in his chair and snatches up the business plan Joe gave him. "Read the summary on the second page. See if it makes any sense to you."

Cole takes the paper. He reads the page then thumbs through the rest of the plan. "Cool," he says, handing it back.

"You get it?"

"It's like you're taking computer modeling from building designs with toothpicks to some super flexible, super smart…" Cole twists his hands as he strains for the word. "Silly Putty geometry."

Grant laughs. "Sort of. Yeah. I mean, variational geometry isn't quite as malleable as putty—"

"Well, you wouldn't want it to be," Cole breaks in. "You need those rules you're talking about so the design hangs together."

"The constraints."

"Right. The constraints. That's what I meant."

Grant holds up the business plan. "You think you can make this read better without losing the gist of what we're saying?"

"There were some things I might change."

"We can't be talking toothpicks and Silly Putty."

"Oh yeah, I get that. That's just my way of understanding it."

Grant pulls out his wallet. "Here's sixty bucks. Rewrite this over the weekend and if it's better on Monday, the job's yours."

"No way!" Cole blurts out.

"Way."

Cole holds his mouth tight and blinks his eyes. Grant thinks he might cry. "This is going to sing, man. I guarantee it."

"I believe you."

Cole puts the papers in his briefcase and stands up. "I'll have it first thing Monday morning."

"I won't be in until nine." Grant stands up with him.

"I'll be waiting at the door." A big, relieved grin spreads across Cole's face. "Thank you, man. Seriously." He thrusts out his hand.

Grant shakes it. "Don't forget your money." He points at the twenties on the desk.

"Right!" Cole laughs, scooping up the bills. "Right."

He charges out of the room, turns the wrong way, wheels around, points the right way, and disappears. Grant hears footsteps bound down the stairway. He goes to the window and watches Cole hurry across Liberty. His breath catches in his throat. It's the best feeling that he's had all day.

Chase hasn't had a customer in an hour, but he's used to slow weeknights. This isn't a great location for foot traffic. The only open places nearby are the rundown diner on the corner and the sketchy massage parlors down Fourth. If he were pinching pennies, he'd close at six. The few rentals he gets in the last hour don't justify the cost to light the place—let alone the risk of getting robbed. It's advertising more than anything. He wants to draw the attention of dinner-goers passing on their way to the restaurants on Main. It's the right thing to do for a new concept like movie rentals. Chase just never counted on feeling so alone.

The bells over the front door clatter. Chase flinches like they were gunshots. The man who enters is someone he's seen a few times now, hurrying past the store. He greets Chase with a little bow and surveys the aisles. "How does this work?"

Chase is used to the question. "I take it you don't have a VCR."

"What's that?"

"It's what you play these tapes on. You hook it up to your TV."

"I've always wondered what you were doing down here."

"It's movies coming to you any time you want," Chase explains. "Not you having to go to the movies."

"Well, we're stuck in our apartment most weekends, so we can't catch the campus movies anymore."

"Then this is perfect for you."

"I see *Casablanca* in the window. Can I get that?"

"Absolutely. We've got all the classics."

"Grant Markham." The man points to the ceiling. "I'm upstairs."

"Oh yeah?" Chase thinks of Cole. The bells jangle again. It's Leah. She's shivering and dripping wet. "What's going on?" Chase asks, forgetting Grant in his alarm.

"I wasn't going to stop." Leah squeezes water from her long cord of hair. "It's just so cold."

Grant eyes Leah then Chase. "I'll come back."

"That's okay. It won't take long to set you up."

"Next week." Grant gives Leah a quick smile, slips around her, and hurries out of the store.

"I'm sorry," Leah says.

"Why are you wet?"

"I went to church."

"Is that where you go all the time?" Chase finally asks what he's wanted to for weeks.

"Mostly."

"*Mostly*. Where else? Where do you go and get so wet? It's not even raining anymore."

Leah blushes, timid and radiant. "I finally committed." She smiles and reaches out for his hand. "I'm reborn."

Chase doesn't know what she means. But she's so happy, so uplifted that he's afraid to ask. So he smiles back, and when he does Leah steps in fast for his embrace.

10. Voices

Ben doesn't realize they cut the mic. He's still singing, head thrown back, eyes closed. Kip goes up on the stage in the back of Ty's Sunspot and nudges him. Ben opens his eyes slowly and beams at Kip. Then he leans into the dead mic. "Thank you."

"Ben Hadley, everyone!" Kip starts clapping. No one joins in. Ben puts his guitar in its case, and the crew starts setting up for the next act. Kip keeps clapping as he follows Ben down the hall to the musicians' waiting room. The four members of Daisy Mae and the Maynards are sitting around a card table covered with beer cups, pitchers, and ashtrays. If you follow Ann Arbor music, you know everyone here. There's Nick Regal, a local beatnik troubadour type, flipping through a notebook. Daisy Mae sits beside him rocking and mouthing some song. Bill Richmond has his drumsticks out and he's tapping out a beat on his chair. Gord Bernard, the rockabilly guitarist with horned-rim glasses and Buddy Holly hair, looks up at Ben. "Short set."

"More time for you guys," Kip answers before Ben can.

Bernard fills an empty beer mug and holds it out to Ben. "Ty gets nervous with new people." He's talking about Ty Santoni, owner of the Sunspot. "All he hears is the strangeness."

Ben waves off the beer. Kip steps in to take it. "Thanks, man."

"*The strangeness*," Richmond intones with the delivery of a radio announcer. He beats out a stuttering rhythm on the chair. Daisy Mae and Bernard laugh. Regal taps on his notebook and waits.

"It's tough for a soft voice to carry such a long room," Kip feels compelled to say. "We did fine." He squeezes Ben's shoulder.

"Let's go 'Angelo's,' 'Borrowed Time,' then 'Fleecie,'" Regal says.

"I've never done 'Angelo's'" Richmond says.

Tracy Lee bites her nail. "Why would we do one of your solos?"

"I'm just trying to get all our voices out there right up front."

Ben's laugh comes as a surprise to everyone. They all turn his way. "Too many voices," he says. Kip is incredulous.

"Do you mind?" Regal asks.

"How do you tell one story?" Ben wants to know.

"Give us a couple minutes," Bernard says.

"No sweat." Kip practically pushes Ben out of the room. "What was that all about?"

"I have enough trouble just singing alone."

Kip pulls a pack of cigarettes out of his shirt pocket. "Never mind." He lights one, takes a draw, and blows it out slowly. "So that went almost like we planned it. Almost."

"I didn't get to do the last couple songs."

"No, you didn't. That's because you added that new one."

"That wasn't new. That's 'Beautiful Mask.' With a new end."

"That five-minute… thing… that was still 'Beautiful Mask?'"

"Yeah. I finally got completely out of the song."

"You definitely got lost in it."

Ben shakes his head. "No." And he's still shaking it when Ty Santoni bustles down the hallway.

"I need to talk to you." He points to Kip, ignoring Ben. Then he opens the musicians' door. "Can you be on in five?"

"I thought we were on at nine," Regal says.

"We had to speed things up."

"Don't worry about the set list," Kip hears Bernard say. "We'll make it up as we go along."

"God, don't say *that*," Santoni groans. "We already tried that tonight." He glances at Ben and glares at Kip. Then he motions for him to follow and lumbers away.

"Wait here," Kip tells Ben.

Alone now, Ben sits down, takes out his guitar, and starts grazing the strings. He whispers fragments of the revelations he had on stage. Nick Regal comes out of the room, then Daisy Mae and Richmond. Ben doesn't notice them. But then he senses that he's being watched. He stops and looks up. Bernard has a hand cupped to his ear. Ben strums a little harder. Bernard nods his approval before hurrying off.

Kip's friend Baskin shows up then. He's with this other guy Ben's seen somewhere before. "They didn't give you a room?" Baskin asks.

"No, that's ours." Ben points to the open door. Baskin and his friend go in. Kip comes around the corner. His face is red. "What's wrong?"

"We'll talk inside."

"Baskin's in there. With a friend."

"Great," Kip mutters. "Let's hear what *everyone* thinks."

Baskin holds up an empty pitcher. "Can we get a refill?"

"Ty isn't in the mood," Kip says.

"I bet he's pissed off, is what he is."

"Baskin—"

"What was *that*, Ben?" Baskin ignores Kip.

"What was what?"

"That—that… droning mantra."

"He got off track," Kip says. "The first few songs were good."

"I couldn't make out shit—and I *know* the songs. But don't believe me. Ask my friend Tom."

"And I suppose he's a music expert," Kip says.

Tom's busy watching Ben pat himself down. "You okay?"

"I lost my pick."

"You've got a whole bagful," Kip reminds him.

"You heard it, Tom," Baskin says. "Tell Kip what you thought."

"It was hard to hear where we were." Tom eyes Ben. He doesn't seem to care what anyone thinks. But Tom's a writer himself; he's sure that can't be true. "I don't think the acoustics are very good."

"Yeah, that's why Sonic Youth and R.E.M play here all the time," Baskin scoffs. "They love when their music sounds crappy."

"He tried something new, and it didn't work," Kip says.

"No." Ben is quiet but firm. "It was perfect. It was the song singing."

Baskin laughs. "What the hell's that even mean?"

"I get what you mean," Tom tries to help. "When I write—"

"There's nothing wrong with experimenting," Kip cuts in. "But not in the middle of a show. It's like that record guy said. You've got to establish your identity. People need to have an expectation of what they're going to hear." Ben widens his eyes. Kip tries to keep calm. "I have to talk to Baskin. Maybe Tom can help you find your pick."

Tom follows Ben into the hall. Ben gets on his knees and feels around on the carpet. Tom crouches beside him. "What color is it?"

"It's a leopard print," Ben says.

"What's so special about it?"

Ben sits back. "What do you think they're talking about?"

Tom sits beside him. "Baskin said you had to be ready for New York."

"There's too much *have to* going on these days."

"I hear you," Tom says. "But it isn't their music."

Ben thinks about it. "You know those songs," he finally says, "the ones on the tape? I wrote them years ago."

"They're good."

"But they aren't *now*. Everything needs to be now."

Tom doesn't say anything. He doesn't want to argue.

I'm serious," Baskin says. "I think he's lost it. He used to sing with soul. Now it's—I don't know what it is."

"He hasn't lost it," Kip says. "And keep it down."

Baskin lowers his voice. "It's bad enough that he jangles out some crazy solo and doesn't come up for air for five minutes. But did you hear what he was singing? I did. I got up close. It made no sense!"

"We have to reel him in. I get it."

"Polish the act. That's what your guy said. Get in front of crowds and get the songs on the album down. That's what he wanted."

"I know."

"And is that what's happening?"

Kip rubs his jaw. "So what do you want me to do? Chew him out?"

"I think we ought to be straight with him. Tell him if he pulls this shit in New York, they'll eat him alive."

"I don't know… maybe they'll love it."

"*This?* No."

Tom sees a glint blink on the carpet. He stretches out and pinches the guitar pick. "Lookie there."

A smile spreads across Ben's face. "You found it." He puts the pick in his shirt pocket. "Alright. Now don't forget, Ben: It's right here."

"You really think you'll forget that now?"

"When I'm working this hard on songs, sure. With all the voices in my head, all the ghosts vying for my attention."

"Voices?"

"People act like that's bad. But everyone hears voices."

Tom's eyes trace the crack of light under the musicians' door. Kip and Baskin are still arguing.

"Didn't you say you were a writer?" Ben asks.

"Trying to be."

"Then you know what I mean."

Tom looks at Ben. There's an unnerving innocence in his eyes. "Stop trying to talk over them and listen. They'll tell you."

"I'll give it a try," Tom says, but only to make Ben stop.

In the back room, Kip's finally coming around. "Alright, I'll be straight with him."

"He's got five more gigs," Baskin says. "Then he's in New York, and A&M's going to book him thinking he's got the album down."

"Three more gigs," Kip says. "Santoni cancelled his other two."

"He heard what I heard."

"Ben has a contract for two records," Kip reminds him.

"Yeah, and I have a one-year lease in the Village."

"What does that have to do with it?"

"If I knew how this was going to turn out last spring, I might've thought twice about committing to New York."

"Come on, Baskin. I'm the one taking the risk."

"And getting the rewards."

"I asked if you wanted to kick in," Kip says. "And you said no. *I'll just come along. It'll be fun.* That's what you said."

"Well, so far, it isn't exactly a hoot."

Kip shoulders through the throng toward the door. Ben follows. Baskin has fallen behind, watching the band as he goes. Tom leans in close to him. "I don't know about Ben," he says.

"Why didn't you say anything back there?" Baskin shouts back.

"Not the music. I mean mentally. You should've heard him. Something's off."

"I've gotta get out of this." Baskin knifes through the crowd.

It's a muggy night, even for July. Hardly anyone's walking the street. They're on what some would say is the seedy side of Ann Arbor. Kip waits for everyone beyond the Sunspot.

"I know you." A voice comes from the dark side of the building. A street person is sitting by the corner.

"I don't think so," Kip says.

"Yeah I do." The bum struggles to his feet, propping himself against the building. Then he hobbles out into the light. Kip's eyes go wide. "You remember me." Reese sounds almost relieved.

Ben comes up between them.

"Sorry, man," Kip says. "You have me confused."

"You remember me," Reese repeats with accusing certainty. Ben watches him limp closer and peer at his manager.

"What do you want, pal? You want a dollar?"

"I want you to say you know me."

"You're mixed up." Kip hurries away.

"Say you know me, Kip!" Reese shouts. "Just say you know me."

Baskin and Tom come up beside Ben. He's holding out a dollar. "Don't give him anything," Baskin says. "He'll just get drunk with it." He heads off to join Kip. Tom keeps staring at the bum.

"What the hell are you looking at?" Reese pushes away Ben's money. "I didn't ask for this."

"I know."

"Tell that to your friends"

Ben looks over to the intersection of Main and Huron. Kip and Baskin are waiting for him there. "Them?"

The bum laughs. He waggles his finger at Ben. "That's a good one."

11. Masquerade

The last place Reese had his own room was on Hamilton, two years ago. He and a few guys went in on an apartment at the far end near Jefferson. He hasn't gone down the street since moving out—and for good reason: showing his face there might get him a beating. When his roommates kicked him out for coming up short on rent, Reese lost his cool. It wasn't his fault he got sick and Flood's fired him. He needed some time to get back on his feet. Nobody else saw it that way. They moved a TV into Reese's room a week before kicking him out, and they'd watched it while he tried to sleep, like he wasn't there. So on the day Reese left, when everyone was gone, he opened the window, picked up the TV, and heaved it as far as he could. The quirky thing about Hamilton is that the houses don't have front yards. They hover over the road. If there was anything on the curb below, a well-aimed toss would've hit it. As it happened, that was where the guy who owned the TV parked his car. Reese's throw was dead on.

Reese still looks back on Hamilton wistfully, though. It was the last place where his dreams were grounded, where he felt like he belonged. Now, as he roams town, his dreams swirl through thousands of nameless faces, never settling in his head. All he has is the grim habit of living, the hopeless compulsion of routine that takes him down alleys, through dumpsters, and under any cover he can find.

On this golden October day in 1987, Reese turns down Hamilton—not for nostalgia, but because this is the fastest way to Blimpy Burgers. As soon as he enters the street, a strange calm comes over him. Reese lengthens his stride so his limp isn't so pronounced. He widens his eyes, remembering his reflection in the mirror of the library restroom. The muscles on one side of his face had gone slack. It made that eye droop and the other squint to compensate. Oddly, that didn't alarm him as much as his hair. Once sandy and flowing, it was grey, matted down, and already receding.

As he nears the house where he used to live, a woman comes out on her porch across the street, cradling two pumpkins. Reese veers over toward his old house. For an instant, he thinks he overshot it. But then he realizes the house is gone. In its place, there's the skeletal frame of a new structure, surrounded by scaffolding and covered with tattered blue tarps. He stops to take it in.

"Isn't it hideous?"

Reese turns around. The woman is leaning over her porch railing. A surge of fire leaps in Reese's chest. He knows that face. "I used to live here," he manages to say.

"That must've been a while ago." She sets a pumpkin on the railing. There are already a handful lined up there. "They've been building that monstrosity for two years. We don't even know who—"

"I know you."

The woman cocks her head, taking in the grubby stranger. "Oh?"

"You were there when I got hit by the car. You kneeled next me."

She squints at him. "Outside of South Quad…"

"I'm okay now," Reese says, like the accident was yesterday. "The limp looks worse than it is. And something happened a few years back." He slaps his cheek. "This side of my face barely moves."

"I recognize you now." She smiles for his sake.

"I'm not very good with faces." Reese looks down, kicking at the gravel. "But I couldn't forget yours."

"That's nice of you to say."

"My name's Reese, short for Maurice. But no one calls me that."

"And I'm Kate. So what do you do, Reese?"

"I'm going to Blimpy Burger."

"Are you a cook?"

"Oh no. I don't work there. I—I haven't worked since I got sick."

Kate places the last pumpkin. "Can you tell what these are?"

"They're monkeys. All sorts. Happy and sad. Scared. Mad…"

"That's right!" Kate says.

"You ought to put 'em in a barrel."

Kate laughs. "Now, why didn't I think of that?"

"I could work if I got a chance," Reese circles back. "It's just that when people see me, they get their mind made up."

Kate sets her elbows on the railing. "Could you lift fifty pounds?"

"I could lift a hundred. Easy."

"This party we're having," Kate says, "it's mostly for Halloween, but it's also to celebrate a bookstore I'm opening."

"Yeah, well, I'm not much of a reader."

"I just need someone to help move boxes. It's a week's worth of work. Say, two hundred bucks?"

"Two hundred? Sure, I could move boxes."

"Then it's settled." Kate slaps the railing. "Monday morning. Meet me at Liberty Plaza. You know where that is?"

"Yeah. It's a rough place. A lot of crazy people there."

"My store's right off the park, under the Pan Tree restaurant."

"Oh. Well. It's not as bad as it seems," Reese backpedals.

"It's as bad as it seems." Kate grins. Reese lets out a rare snicker.

The door opens behind her. A man steps onto the porch. He's wearing furry pants tucked into cowboy boots. His eyes shift from Kate to Reese. "*I thought* I heard you talking."

Kate holds her arm out as if displaying an exhibit. "Remember me telling you I saw a guy get hit by a car in college? This is him."

"Small world."

"Reese, this is Alec. My husband." Reese and Alec nod at each other. "Reese is going to help me move books."

"Is that right?" Alec smirks at Reese. "This must be your lucky day."

"It is."

"Can we talk inside?" Alec asks Kate.

"Wear whatever you want," Kate says with a hushed voice.

"I can find something else. If it's that important."

"It's not a big deal." Kate moves a pumpkin to even up the spacing.

"You're still going to have those monkeys on the railing?"

"At least they fit with the animal theme."

Alec snorts. "Tell me, Reese. Is a man turning into an animal a man or an animal?"

Reese frowns. "How do you know he isn't an animal turning into a man?"

Kate laughs. "I guess what I don't like about the monkeys," Alec hits back. "Is that they're just so obvious."

"So you're worried people will think you did this."

"People will *know* I didn't do it."

"Then what's the problem? Reese likes them."

"Oh," Alec says and stops. "Well." Another stop. "Then... shit."

Kate shows Reese a brittle smile. "So... Monday at nine?"

"Monday at nine." Reese hobbles away. Alec huffs and goes back inside. Kate watches Reese until he turns on Jefferson.

The caterers make the mistake of bringing the supplies in through the front door. Dean Harper is the crew leader. He tries to angle a table through the doorway and knocks a pumpkin off the railing. Its grin caves in, but he's able to bend it back into shape.

The first guests to arrive are Alec's friends, the youngbloods of the department, hungry for tenure and waiting for the old guard to retire. A few of them show up, too—Hirschbeck, Barlow, and Fallon. None are in costume. Kate points out a box of masks by the door. Hirschbeck picks a Batman mask. Barlow takes a Frankenstein mask and tilts it up on his head. Fallon still doesn't bother.

"How long you think they'll stay?" a guy dressed as a wolf asks Alec, as they wait for the bartender to mix their drinks.

"An hour, max." Alec has added clip-on goat horns to his costume.

"I'm surprised you invited them."

"You gotta play the game, Lanier," says a woman in a leopard costume. "That's how you get a sabbatical before you have tenure."

"I didn't have to play any games for that, Deb," Alec bristles. "They're the ones insisting I do my research in England."

Kate snickers, walking by. "Satyrs can be so touchy." She steps between the three and grabs her glass of wine.

There's an awkward silence. "Did you do those pumpkins, Kate?" Deb asks. "I love all the faces."

"Alec did. I think they're tacky myself." Her eyes dance to Alec.

"Well, I love the costume. A raven. For the Raven's Call bookstore."

"Quoth the raven," Lanier says, "nevermore, Kate Evermore."

The doorbell rings. Kate passes Dean on her way to answer it. "Could you walk around the shrimp plate? Oh, and feel free to throw on a mask if the spirit moves you." She points out the box of masks then opens the door. "Welcome to the animal masquerade!"

The man in front of her is Barry Ellard, the hippie politician who's been representing Ann Arbor in the state legislature since Vietnam. With his mop-top hair and granny glasses, he could be a John Lennon impersonator. "Barry!" Kate gushes. "You made it!"

"I am a man of my word." Ellard's dressed in black, but he has a white stripe of felt pinned down the front of his shirt.

"Now what are you?" Kate asks.

"I'm Pepe Le Pew. And this is the love of my life." He turns to a woman dressed like a cat. Dean gets one look at her and rushes off.

"He's kidding," she says. "I just work with him. I'm Carrie. We're friends of Barry's." There's a man behind her wearing a hawk mask.

"We aren't friends, we're lawyers. I'm Bill Newbold." He points at the bartender. "There's my true friend." Carrie turns toward the bar and catches a glimpse of Dean hurrying into the kitchen.

Before Kate can rejoin the party, she hears tromping on the porch. She opens the door so fast it startles the young man there. He jerks back like he's been shocked. The group behind him laughs. "Now we're in trouble," Kate says. "You must be Alec's protégés."

"We're notorious," says a girl in the back.

"Good thing we're in disguise." The man Kate surprised pulls a cow mask down over his face. He's wearing a black-and-white suit with pink udders. As he passes Kate, he gives her a deadpan "Moo."

The rest of the students file past, sliding their masks on one at a time. "I like this bunch." Kate shuts the door behind the last student, a kid with a pig's snout. "Now which one is Whelan?" The kid points over at Alec, who's grabbing the udders of the guy in the cow suit.

"Why buy the cow when you can get the milk for free?" Alec jokes to his cronies.

"Sure you're getting milk there, Alec?" Lanier says.

"Whelan's my radical thinker. His critiques are very ambitious. I do wonder, though, how much he reads the books he writes about."

"Good for you!" Deb tips her wine glass to Tom. "Reading is a highly overrated element of literary theory."

"I read the books," Tom says. "I just don't read the critics."

"Careful. You'll be one of them someday," Lanier says.

Tom gets a beer. Alec watches him, a sneer forming. "The problem with applying modern sensibilities to older works is that you find meaning the author never intended."

"Does it matter what the author intended?" Deb wonders.

Alec ignores her. "Whelan here has submitted quite a provocative thesis on *The House of the Seven Gables*."

"Uh-oh, treading on your territory," Lanier says.

"His contention—correct me if I misstate this—is that Hawthorne has taken the conceit of narrative intrusion to the extreme."

"Something like that." Tom sips his beer.

"He's arguing that the character Holgrave is the secret narrator. *And* the murderer of Pyncheon. I can't wait to read your argument."

"I'm sure you can't," Deb says.

Tom turns and scans the room. Across the way, Professor Barlow's staring at him. Tom saunters over. "Are you spying on me?"

"Protecting you," Barlow counters, with his usual formal tone.

"I didn't know I needed it." Tom nods to the other two profs.

"They're a rather hungry bunch," Barlow says.

"A bunch of assholes," Fallon mutters. Hirschbeck laughs.

Barlow changes subjects. "I'm still waiting to see one of these stories you're supposed to be writing."

"I'm not quite ready yet."

"No pressure. I just recall you saying you wanted to finish your doctorate this year. How long has it been now? Five, six years?"

Fallon nudges Barlow. "It's a party, Harvey. Give the guy a break."

"I do have one finished," Tom says. "It's more of a sketch, though."

"Then you're writing. That's the more important thing," Barlow softens. "Is it fiction?"

"Some of it's fiction. Some of it's real."

"But is it all true?"

The living room is crowded with dozens of people, so it's easy for Dean to avoid Carrie. But now Ellard's motioning him over. Dean's seen Carrie from afar a couple times since he punched that glass door, but they haven't talked. He takes a Woody Woodpecker mask out of the box, slides it on, and goes over with the shrimp.

Carrie spears one, smiling. "You remind me of an old friend."

"No, I'm just a pecker."

Dean walks away so fast, Ellard drops his shrimp. "That was rude."

"Let it go, Barry," Newbold says. "That's your ideal supporter. A lowly, over-educated waiter. They're this town's Noisy Majority."

"I'll get you your shrimp." Carrie turns to follow Dean. Tom Whelan crosses in front of her on his way to the kitchen. She bumps into him. Ice cubes launch out of the glass.

"Sorry," Tom says.

"No, it's my fault." Carrie bends down to recover the cubes.

Tom joins her. "No harm." Carrie gives him a quick smile. Then she rises and heads off, cat tail bobbing behind her. Tom watches her weave through the crowd. He doesn't recall that they've met before.

Tom finds a place to himself in a nook off the kitchen. Cow mask pushed off his face, he stares out the window at the waning moon, looking for Burton Tower in the silhouetted skyline. He can't find it. But over the house next door, a dark monolith looms in the autumn night. *Which building is that?* Tom can't believe he hasn't noticed something so big before. He taps his pocket under the cow suit for the notebook where he jots down thoughts. But he's forgotten it.

"Are you gonna jump?" The voice startles him. He turns. Kate's staring out the other side of the same bay window.

"Excuse me?"

"A cow, contemplating the moon..."

"Ah."

"We didn't meet. I'm Kate." She extends her hand.

Tom takes it. "Sorry. I thought we had. I'm Tom Whelan."

"I know who you are."

"And I know who you are."

"So why are we doing this, Tom?"

"I don't—I don't—"

Kate laughs. "I've tongued-tied the Boy Wonder."

"Boy Wonder?"

"When you have professors passing your papers around, debating your ideas, you aren't just any old grad student. It must be gratifying to be the talk of so many great minds."

"I hardly think that's what's going on."

"I know for a fact it is. You forget. I sleep with one of them."

"Which one?" Tom deadpans—and immediately regrets it. "Sorry."

Kate toasts him with her empty glass. "I underestimated you."

"Honestly, I'm sorry. That's not like me."

"Well, that's a shame. I thought you were going to be fun."

"I should get back." Tom steps away from the window.

"Be careful. Really. Get your work copywritten."

"Are you suggesting your husband would steal my ideas?"

"Original ideas are hard to come by." She holds her glass between them. "What are you drinking?"

"I'm done."

"Another shame."

"I'm curious. Why would you warn me about your husband?"

"Ooh. He's curious." Kate bites her thumbnail.

"It seems like a betrayal."

"Ambition can't help itself," Kate says. "Anyway, by April he'll be in London, and you'll be left alone."

"And you, too."

Her eyes dance. "How do you know I'm not going with him?"

"I just imagined, what with the Raven's Call opening."

"You were imagining me. I'm flattered."

"You're putting word's in my mouth."

"I wouldn't put anything in your mouth," Kate counters. "Unless you asked me nicely."

Right then, Dean hurries across the kitchen to the back door. He only notices Kate and Tom after he flings the Woody Woodpecker mask on the counter. "I left something in the van," he says.

"Is everyone happy?" Kate asks.

"Probably not. But at least they have drinks."

Kate and Tom wait until Dean's outside before they laugh. "Leave it to the waiter to see this party for what it is," Kate says.

"I better get back." Tom reaches for his glass.

Kate moves quickly to put her hand on his. "It was nice to meet you. I'm sure we'll see more of each other… as the seasons wear on."

"Maybe so." Tom pulls his hand away and heads back for the party. Kate waits until he's gone before taking in that same looming monolith Tom pondered.

Dean gets into the catering van in the driveway. He finds the pack of Camel Lights he crushed on the way over to force his resolve to quit and manages to bend a cigarette reasonably straight. He gets out and lights it. Carrie got after him for smoking that summer… Well, he doesn't have to think about that now. She's too busy chasing power—like she'd been doing since the day he left her. *Who was that guy she was going to marry? He didn't seem to be in the picture anymore.*

Dean sucks in the crooked smoke. *What a miserable prick you've become. You don't know Carrie. You never did, even back then, when you had that one kiss. What's wrong with her making the best of her life? The difference between then and now isn't Carrie. She's the same. Even looks the same. Better really. The difference is you. It isn't her fault you're still working a job any student could get.*

Footsteps scrape in the gravel. Dean looks to the back door, expecting to see Kate, out to berate him. "Who're you?" the voice comes from the street. Dean turns to stocky guy in a parka. He's in shadow, so the fur fringe of his hood looks like the woolly head of a bear.

"I'm just the caterer." The guy huffs and lumbers away.

Someone passes by the window. Kate remembers the caterer storming out. *I should see what's bothering him.* She swings open the door. A furry head is pressed against the screen. "Happy Halloween, Kate."

She deflates. "I don't remember inviting you, Boz."

"Darn. And I had this costume all picked out." Boz thrusts his arms over his head. "Look at me. I'm the big bad bear."

"What are you doing here?"

"Your husband invited me."

"He wouldn't do that."

"People are funny."

"Get out." Kate starts to close the door.

"Fine. If you'd rather I come to the front door."

"You're a shit. You know that?"

"I'm an acquired taste."

"You're a drug dealer."

"Are you going to get Alec?"

Alec is already striding across the kitchen. Kate blocks his way. "Isn't this a heartwarming reunion?"

"Relax, Kate. It's not for me."

"Right. That's why your old dealer snuck up to our back door."

"Someone else wanted some, so I said I'd make a call."

"I see. Someone asked out of the blue, *Wouldn't it be great if we had some coke?* And you said, *What a coincidence! I used to be big into that! I don't want any myself, of course, but if you do, it's only right to help.*"

"I'm not here to watch your little spat," Boz cuts in.

"It's a party, Kate," Alec says. "This is what happens at parties."

Kate throws her arms out. "Well, shit, Alec. I didn't know this was the kind of party we were having. Maybe I should call up some old friends and have them work the room."

"Maybe you should," Alec says. Boz laughs.

Kate storms out of the kitchen. She nearly runs into Carrie. "Sorry," Kate says. "Are you looking for something?"

"Actually, I was looking for one of the waiters. Tall, wavy hair."

"He went outside." Carrie nods her thanks. "You're a lawyer, right?" Kate asks as she passes.

"I am."

"You didn't see what you're about to see. Or maybe you did."

Alec holds a baggie of cocaine up to the porch light. Carrie opens the door then freezes. Now she knows what Kate meant.

"Getting some fresh air?" Boz asks like it's an accusation.

"There's a bench on the front porch," Alec says. "And pumpkins." He can't help but snicker. "Fucking monkey pumpkins."

"I'm looking for someone," she says.

Boz ignores her. "Fucking monkey pumpkins?"

"Yeah. Fucky monkin—funking muck—" Alec stops. He giggles. "Fuck. Try saying that five times fast."

"Fuck-fuck-fuck-fuck-fuck." Boz counts off with his fingers.

"Your wife told me—"

"My wife? She's the one who carved the damned things."

"She said he came out here."

Boz turns his woolly head flush toward Carrie. Then he points behind her. "Out there."

When Dean sees Carrie, he drops his smoke and starts walking away. "Dean! Come on. I just want to talk."

He stops. "Speaking to the help. How noble of you."

She's across from him now, her face clear in the moonlight. "I came out to say... I was sorry."

"What for?"

"I'm sorry I wasn't very nice," Carrie says. "I'm sorry, after all these years, I can't just say... *it's good to see you.*"

"Whatever happened to the engineer?"

"We got married too young."

"So much for the big plan."

"Are you really this bitter? Still?"

Somewhere down the street, there's a rumbling, like a metal wheel rolling toward them. "I guess I must be."

"Then I'm sorry for *you.*" Carrie retreats to the back door.

"Wait," Dean calls out, but the rumbling's too loud. Dean looks out to the road. There on the sidewalk, a shabby figure crouches beside a metal drum turned on its side. He grunts as he lifts the drum off the pavement and stands it up.

"You've got it wrong way up." Dean points at the stenciled upside-down letters of "Blimpy's."

"I know."

"What's it for?"

"It's for the owner." Reese hobbles up the porch steps and picks up the first pumpkin in the row.

"Do they know you're doing this?"

Reese comes down and sets the pumpkin on top of the drum. "They have to look like they're inside the barrel." He goes to get the next pumpkin. Dean decides to help. Two more trips, and all the pumpkins are by the barrel. Reese tries a few formations, Dean suggests some adjustments, and within a minute, it's done. They step back together and assess their handiwork. It actually does look like there's a barrel of pumpkin monkeys staring up at the house.

"I wish I could see her face," Reese says.

Dean looks over and sees Reese's bad eye flickering. He lays a hand on his shoulder. "She's going to love it." He thinks then of Carrie. And he wishes he could get a second chance with her.

Kate doesn't wake up until noon. She comes downstairs to find a mess on the dining room table, a mess that was made after the caterers cleaned up. Beer bottles and ash trays. A hand mirror with smudges of white dust. Kate calls out for Alec, not loud, not like she wants a response. She picks up the mirror and wipes it clean with the corner of her nightshirt. The blinds in the front window are still slanted to thwart the daylight. Kate opens them. That's when she sees furry legs propped up on the porch railing. She goes outside.

"So you never went to bed."

"Nope." Alec takes a swig of a near-empty pint of Bacardi.

"Who did you expect to clean up the dining room?"

"I don't know, Kate. Who's going to get rid of your idiotic art project?" He hurls the pint over the railing. It smashes onto the road, spraying shards all the way under the scaffolding of the unfinished house across from them. Kate sees the barrel and the stack of pumpkins on top of it. Their eyes and mouths are black, and their faces have caved in on themselves. You can't tell anymore what they were meant to be. She laughs.

"It's important to hurt me, isn't it?" Alec glares back at her.

"I didn't do that. Honestly."

He takes his furry legs off the railing, leans up in the chair, and pulls himself unsteadily to his feet. "Yeah," he says, wobbling down the steps, "but you know who did."

She flushes. The upside-down Blimpy's sign is a dead giveaway.

"I saw that Maude's guy sneaking back inside."

Kate smiles at his ignorance. "He has nothing to do with this."

Alec stumbles over to the barrel. He lifts one leg, stares up at Kate, then kicks the drum over. Some of the pumpkins crack on impact. Others wobble into the street.

"Then I guess it's a mystery," he grumbles, staggering away.

Kate watches him head up the narrow road. When he's out of view, she goes down into the street, stands up the drum, and starts filling it with pumpkins. The biggest one's rolled all the way across the street. She picks it up and turns the face so it's staring at her. One side of it has collapsed and the eye is twisted nearly closed. The black mouth has caved in on itself, too, like a secret smile. Kate smiles back. She carries the misshapen pumpkin to her porch, sets it in the middle of the top step, and disappears inside.

12. Revolutionary

Chase watches himself sway in the bathroom mirror at Ashley's. He's drunk. *This beard is ridiculous,* he thinks. *I look like Lenin. Baskin would have a field day. And what was I thinking with this hat?* Chase bought the pork pie hat at Rebop Vintage Clothing after seeing the singer of SLK, a local ska band, wearing one at Rick's. He thought it made him look the part of "cinema revolutionary." That's what the *Ann Arbor Observer* called him in their "Around Town" piece. Chase takes off the hat. *God, my hair looks worse.* He puts it back on. "Face it, Tyson. You're a ska rude boy," he accuses his reflection. "And a communist. A *ska-munist!*" He giggles and staggers out.

When he gets upstairs, he scans the bar for anyone he knows. The place is packed. *How long have we been here?* Chase wonders, as he sneaks to the booth in the back corner. He and Sheryl, the real estate agent from Olympia Properties, met at five when the bar was empty. *Now what time is it? I should've stuck with beer. What was that paint thinner Sheryl ordered? I gotta get home. Throw a couple twenties on the table, say goodbye, and leave. That guy at the bar; this is the third time he's looked my way. Where have I seen him?*

Another glass of paint thinner waits at the table. "Oh, no!" Chase shakes his head. The sharp blonde woman in the pinstriped business suit grins. "Sheryl, I can't."

"One more."

Chase slides into the booth. She raises her glass. "To the future."

"The future." He downs his drink. The alcohol simmers all the way to his stomach. *It does feel good.*

"To Tally Hall!" she says.

"Tally ho!"

Sheryl throws back her head and laughs. Chase smiles to see his effect on her. "I'm telling you. Someone's going to make a killing there."

"I know—"

"I just don't want it to be some other video store."

Now it's Chase who tips his glass. "You're looking out for me."

"I don't think you're taking me seriously."

"Sure I am."

"I'm not pushing because it's what Olympia wants. They get their money whether you go to Tally Hall or stay put. I'm pushing because this is your chance to do something great—and I don't want you to miss it. I'm pushing because maybe you're more than a client to me." She looks at Chase, eyes gleaming.

The moment sticks, drifts, then clicks in again. He feels pressured to respond. "And you're more to me," he hears himself say.

"I don't think you really realize how people view you."

He laughs. "Nobody views me any way."

"What about everyone running the cinema guilds?"

"Oh. Well, they hate me."

"And how about the theater owners?"

"So you're saying everyone thinks I'm a prick—"

"No." She leans in like they're conspiring. "I'm saying they're afraid of you—the change you're bringing. They know the power you have, and they're worried you're going to use it. So... *are* you going to use it?" There's mischief in her eyes.

Chase adjusts his pork pie hat. "I think I need to see the space."

"I think I need to show you." Sheryl downs the rest of her drink.

Through his alcoholic haze, Chase senses something's just happened. "Did we get the check yet?"

"You want to go now?"

"I really gotta get home."

"Oh." Sheryl tugs at one of her earrings.

"I still want to see the space. I just—not tonight. I can't."

Sheryl leans in close. "You don't get it, do you?" Chase shrugs. "You can have whatever you want."

Chase stands in the Maynard parking structure, listening to Sheryl's car wind down the spiraling floors. Whose idea was it for him to walk her to the car? He wipes his lips, inspects his fingers for lipstick. He has to get this straight. He said he needed to get home. They left the bar. Then what? How did he find himself walking her through Nickels Arcade? He remembers saying he was just being a gentleman. Did they both know it would end like it did? Her touching his face, them finding each other's mouths?

It isn't until another car's lights fix on him that Chase shambles away. When he gets out onto Maynard, he's near the end of the line for Dooley's. For a second, Chase isn't sure where he's going. Then he remembers: home, through all these rowdy kids. He pushes his hat down and hurries to the other side of the street.

"I know you." A figure steps out of an alley on the other side of the crosswalk. "The house on Forest. You were the landlord, right?"

Chase freezes. "So?"

"So, nothing." It's the guy who was looking at him in the bar.

Chase takes his hands out of his coat, gets ready. "Do I know you?"

The man laughs. "You must've seen a lot of crazy shit in that house. You don't remember me starting a fight?"

"I guess not." Chase turns to get away.

"They were pissed off. Clem said he was going to kill you for sneaking that girl away."

Chase's head snaps around. He gives the stranger a long stare. "I remember now. You got mad at that poet guy. Alec. It was a fight over Kate, right? The girl with the lipstick."

"You still see her?"

"No."

"What about the other girl? The one you took away?"

Chase tenses. "What is it you want?"

"Sorry, man. None of my business. I just thought..." He glances up and down Maynard. "If you still saw Clem, you could warn him."

"Warn him?"

"Just tell him Boz is after him."

"Boz..." Chase recalls the guy cleaning pot in his dining room.

"If he ever finds Clem, it's going to be bad."

"Well, I don't know where he is."

"He'll kill him. I mean it. I live with the guy. He's nuts."

"If he hasn't found him by now, then he probably left town," Chase tries. "You can't hide in Ann Arbor."

"I'm Hal, by the way. And you are... what was it again?"

"What does that matter?"

Hal laughs softly. "I'm trying to do a good thing here." He turns away and disappears back into the alley. Chase hurries off for Liberty. Behind him, there's an echoing rumble. Then Hal thunders by on a motorcycle. Chase watches the bike roar out of sight.

Maybe Hal was *trying to do a good thing,* he thinks. *But maybe not. He still lived with Boz. If Boz was so dangerous, why not get away from him? And why ask for my name? Was he going to look me up?* If Hal found out where Chase worked, Hal would've found Clem. Chase saw him all the time, heading off for lunch, leaving for the day, popping in occasionally to rent a video. Of course, he didn't call himself Clem anymore. He was Cole. And he didn't look like the old spaced-out Clem. He was clean cut, heavier, more subdued. Maybe Hal wouldn't even recognize Clem if he saw him. But it was right not to take the chance.

He didn't owe Clem anything. After all, this was a man, if Hal was to be believed, who once wanted Chase dead, a man from whom he still shielded Leah. She knew he'd bumped into Clem, but Chase never told her that he worked above the store. Leah visited so rarely Chase figured the odds were slim that they'd run into each other. If they did, they did. But he didn't want to encourage a meeting. He still didn't trust Clem. Then again, he wasn't ready to sentence him either. People could change.

Chase crosses Liberty in front of Schoolkid's. The music store took up three storefronts. When Chase started school in '74, they sold three-dollar records out of orange crates in a space no bigger than a living room. Now look at them. Borders was the same: small beginnings, huge success. It happened with music and books. Why not movies? *Sheryl's right: this* is *my time.* He realizes then that he's approaching Tally Hall. He stops in front of the towering new mall. There's a light on in one of the back stores. It casts a dim outline on the circular structure of the building. The open space in front of him is where Sheryl wanted him to be, where she would've taken him tonight.

Sheryl. So it hadn't been just business. This was the fifth after-work meeting to "talk about the future," as Sheryl always put it. At first, Chase figured he was getting sold. Then he started looking forward to their meetings. And tonight he let himself think maybe it wasn't just him who was interested. Now, he's sure. Right from the start, Sheryl understood him—not just what he said, but what he left unsaid. Time after time, she'd finish his thoughts. And they'd smile at each other, silently exhilarated to be on the same wavelength. Sheryl believed in him—more than he ever believed in himself.

Does Leah believe in me? She did once, back when I saved her—believed in me, followed me, needed me. But she believes in God now. And that belief's so all-consuming, there isn't anything left for me. I can't reach her. She *did* marry him, but only after he agreed to weekly meetings with Pastor Jim. She needed to know he'd at least try to join her in faith. And Chase all but promised he would.

He comes up to the Ann Arbor News building, the pillared edifice that guards the quiet north side of town. He hears the muffled rumble of machinery deep inside and feels it shaking the pavement.

Of course, he'd disappointed her. After the pastor meetings, he went to church once, then never again. She didn't say anything. And he never brought it up. But the question was always there. God had become the silence between them. And nothing short of his coming to faith or her straying in doubt would break it. What if Leah knew Clem was close to her again, or that Boz might resurface? Would that change her attitude? She may have found eternal peace in God, but God couldn't protect her from worldly threats.

Chase starts running home. He cuts across the lawn of the Episcopal Church, hurries down Lawrence, goes around to the back of his house, and takes the steps of the private staircase two at a time. The door opens above him. Light tumbles out. Leah's silhouette is framed in the doorway. "I didn't think you'd be so late."

"Well I am." Chase tromps slowly up the last steps.

Leah moves aside as he enters. "You smell like beer."

"Yep." Chase sails through the kitchen and into the tent-like living room. Leah follows at a safe distance. "I can have a beer, can't I?"

"I just didn't know where you were."

"I told you. I had a meeting. With that real estate guy."

"You told me that? I don't remember."

"Yeah, I did." Chase takes his hat off and drops it on the couch.

"It doesn't matter," she says.

"No, it doesn't."

Leah switches on a floor lamp. The light catches Chase staring at the floor, swaying slightly. "Are you okay?"

Chase regards Leah for the first time since he got home. "Why do you love me?" he asks, arms lurching up.

"Why do I love you?"

"You can't think of anything. Can you?"

"Let me tell you something—"

He ignores her. "I don't believe what you believe. We don't like the same things. We don't even spend much time together. All we do is hide up here in this... this playhouse... and pretend."

"What's wrong? What happened?"

"Nothing happened," Chase lies. "Maybe I'm just waking up."

Leah comes closer. "Chase. Will you stop and listen for a minute?"

He looks up at the ceiling and sighs. "What's the point?"

"You remember when I went to the doctor's office last Friday?"

"You went to the doctor's?"

"I told you about this—"

"You're sick..."

"No. Don't you remember? I got my IUD out. Because the woman at church told me the way it works is by aborting the baby."

"Oh yeah."

"And remember I told you what the nurse said? That if I took it out, there was a small chance a fertilized egg could survive?" Leah smiles a small, trembling smile.

"I don't remember that."

"Well. That's what happened."

"What?" Chase doesn't get what she's saying. And now a tear slides down her cheek. "What happened?"

"Imagine if I'd waited one more day." She chokes back a sob.

"Waited for what?"

"Don't you see? God worked in me to save a life! I followed his will, and he blessed us with a miracle. A baby, Chase. A baby!"

Suddenly, with a shuddering flush, Chase understands. He stares into Leah's eyes, but it's a troubled, far-off gaze. "Wait..."

So Leah waits. But Chase only seems to get more confounded. "Do you see the miracle of it?" she whispers.

He nods slowly, like he's come to a decision. "I'm sorry," he mutters, without looking up at her, without listening. Leah cups her hand over her mouth. She rushes away. Chase realizes what he's done. He goes after her. The door to her room closes. Chase stands there for a long time. How can he tell her he wasn't sorry about the baby without confessing what he *was* sorry about?

In the morning, Chase leaves before Leah wakes up. When he gets to the store, it's still dark and hours before he's supposed to open. As he's fishing for the key to the store, he hears the sound of a guitar in the alley around the corner. As early as it is, he expects to find a street person—maybe Shakey Jake thrashing away on his toy guitar. But it's a young guy. He plays his guitar in sweet meandering flurries, mumbling out cryptic snatches of words. Chase is transfixed. When he stops playing, the singer looks up at Chase. "Sorry. I don't have that one down yet."

"No, it was good," Chase replies. There's something about the musician. Has he seen him before? How would he know him?

"You might be the only one who hears it," the singer says.

Chase reaches in his pocket and finds a few stray bills. He looks for somewhere to put the money. There's no open case, no hat, no cup. And now the singer's absorbed with a new song. Chase sets the bills by his feet and leaves.

There's only one dim light on in the store. It takes some time for Chase's eyes to adjust to the dark aisles. Usually, he'd sit by the register and fill out paperwork for the bank deposit. But he can't afford to make an error in the dark and doesn't want to turn the lights on this early. So Chase decides to tackle a job he's been meaning to do for months. He's always just alphabetized the tapes he rents, no matter what genre. It's time to fix that.

Chase starts taking tapes off the first shelf. He fills up an armload, sits on the floor, and sorts the movies into stacks of sections he figures make sense. With another armful, he realizes there are sections he hasn't considered, so he goes back through the tapes he already sorted. Soon, there are stacks all around his feet, and he can't keep them straight. He's gotten hardly any sleep. And his head hurts. He shoves a pile of tapes aside. "Here he is everyone," Chase says, lying back. "Your friendly neighborhood revolutionary."

When his assistant arrives to open the store, she sees the mess of tapes in the aisle and the body splayed on the floor. Her first thought is that she's caught some witless burglar. Then she notices the pork pie hat. Chase jolts awake at her touch.

The phone rings. The assistant answers it. "It's Sheryl."

Chase comes to the register and takes the phone from her. "Sheryl."

"Chase…"

"I'm going to stay where I am."

"What? I thought last night—"

"I thought about it, and that's what I want."

"But Chase. This is your chance."

"Just send the contract over for this space."

"Look, I don't care about the business—"

"Goodbye Sheryl."

Chase hangs up. He turns his back on the store and peers out the window. "So we're staying *here*?" his assistant asks.

"Yep." His assistant stomps away. Just then, Clem passes in front of Chase on his way to work. He doesn't notice Chase at first. But as close as they are, he must have sensed him, because he stops now, and looks through the glass. Chase waves. Clem waves back then continues on.

Chase picks up the phone again and punches in a number. Leah answers with a drowsy voice. "Why did you leave so early?"

"You've got church tonight, right?"

"I don't have to go."

Chase turns from the window to see where his assistant went. There on the counter are the CDs Baskin begged him to sell more than a year ago. "I was thinking maybe I could meet you there."

"Really?"

"Somebody's blessed us." Chase holds the phone in the crook of his neck and picks up one of the CDs. There on the cover is a photo of the singer he met in the alley. "It's time to find out who it is."

13. $720,000

Something's wrong with this car, Grant thinks. *It's worse than this morning.* The '69 GTO rumbles so loudly that people are gawking all along fraternity row. Grant slumps in his seat. *It's the muffler. Or engine. Or something.* As often as he talks to car engineers, you'd think Grant would know how a car actually worked. But beyond filling it with gas, getting oil changes, and fixing one flat, Grant doesn't know a thing. *Why did I buy this rust bucket?*

He eases to a stop at Hill, just across from The Rock. Kids are out painting it even now, a good hour before sunset. Grant always assumed The Rock got painted in the dead of night, that it was fundamentally a rogue act. But once he started driving from Circle North Apartments to his office, he saw that people painted The Rock at all hours. That disappoints him. Over time, he's paid less attention to the messages brushed onto the stone.

Tonight, Grant doesn't notice the painters at first. The kids have stopped their work, turned toward the GTO, and are roaring at it, pumping their brush-clenched fists. *Kids. They're—what?—ten years younger than me? How have I gotten so old so fast?* He shoots them a stony nod—the kind of look they'd expect from a guy with a vintage GTO. The light goes green. Grant punches it. The engine clunks and thunders. The car leaps. In his rearview mirror, Grant sees one kid still watching, brush raised high, a blue streak running down his arm.

Seven hundred and twenty thousand dollars. Unreal. If you told someone you'd gotten a check for 720 grand, they'd think you were rich. It's not enough to do nothing for the rest of my life, but enough to do something with it. Something that makes a difference. That's what his partner Joe didn't understand. Grant isn't dumb. He knows his software will be worth way more in 10 years. The Boston analysts put it at five million; Grant figures it'll be more like 10. So if he hung on until he was 38, he'd be looking at millions. But Grant would've lost another decade sitting in front of a computer, leaving on business trips, begging venture capitalists for money. He used to be able to convince himself he was already making a difference: his software would change the way manufacturers made products. But the more meetings he sat in at Ford and GM, the more draftsmen he met whose jobs would be lost to his software. Was business progress always necessarily good?

Grant eases off the gas as he sails into the gauntlet of stately homes that border Burns Park, the town's wealthiest neighborhood. The GTO grumbles as it slows to 25. Grant has been caught twice in this speed trap; he isn't about to fall for it again.

That's one thing $720,000 will do. It'll get us out of Circle North. I'll never have to hear another complaint about Hal McCallum, never have to worry about him harassing Jackie when I'm away. If he wanted to, Grant could buy one of these Burns Park houses free and clear. His boys could walk to school and play in the park—and they'd never have to fear some coke-addled punk accosting them in broad daylight. That isn't exactly true. Grant has seen enough in town to know that trouble can show up anywhere. Anyway, moving to Burns Park would use up too much of his buyout. *Still, some money has to go to escaping Circle North. Say it takes a 100 grand to get that condo along the river near the hospital. That'll leave $620,000.*

It could've been more, Grant catches himself thinking again as he cruises past the big Arby's hat sign that starts the run of strip malls along Washtenaw. He told himself as he was signing the papers that he'd never look back on the deal and wouldn't regret giving Cole Emory 10 percent of his share. That would've been another 80 grand, nearly the cost of the condo. But how would he feel if he cut Cole out after all the hard work he put in, all he went through with his breakdown and the rehab? The guy deserved a break. He earned the right to be part of their dream. Grant couldn't live with ignoring Cole's devotion.

Grant waits for the light at Huron Parkway. *Is that baseball card shop still open? The Upper Deck. That's what it was called, and that's where it felt like you were after climbing all those steps to the second floor. The owner—what was his name?—Marley. Jeff Marley. He came into big money too, bought a shoebox of cards for a $100 and found a Babe Ruth in it. Some collector told Grant that Marley got a million for it at auction.*

Grant slows as he's passing a strip mall and cranes his neck. The Upper Deck sign is gone. Brown paper covers the window. *So Marley lucked into a big card, made a killing, and quit. What was he doing now? He seemed like a nice guy, a straight shooter who genuinely liked people. What had he done with that money? Was he making a difference?*

The traffic stops near Arborland. *What about the poor guy who sold the Ruth card? Did Marley ever think about him? The guy must've felt awful, knowing he let so much money slip through his fingers. See? I couldn't live with that. I'd have to give the guy something. Maybe Marley did. He was a good guy. A clean conscience: when it's all said and done, you at least have to have that.*

Grant has to break quick behind a car that doesn't run the yellow light at Golfside. He finds himself staring up at the towering neon Ypsi-Arbor Bowling sign, with its stack of zigzagging red pins, yellow sunburst, and blue divided name. This isn't really the border of the two towns, but the sign makes it feel that way. Grant changes lanes on green and hits the gas. The old muscle car hurtles past a run of dawdling traffic. *The most anyone can hope for in this world is to control their own fate. Some can't do it because of money. But plenty of people have money—and still don't do any good with it. They either never had any intention of doing good, or they're putting it off for some day when they can afford to take a chance. Or they just can't see how their lives will spin out from where they are at the moment.*

Grant has always been lucky that way. He can see the end from the beginning sooner than most. He knew Applitex had no intention of investing in his software minutes into the first meeting. But Joe never saw it. For six months, he kept hoping. Then again, Grant knew weeks into turning his college research into a business that it wouldn't take him where he wanted to go. Yet he stuck with it for 10 years. *Until today. Until this,* Grant thinks, patting the shirt pocket where the check is. He knew at the beginning he wouldn't like the end. *So if you can see that far ahead, why not imagine the end you want, then look back to a beginning that gets you there?*

The Wayside parking lot is less than half full, here on a Friday night. And it isn't because of the film either. *Jaws* is the biggest movie all summer, and Christopher Potter gave it four stars in the *Ann Arbor News*. Can't the owners see that movie houses are dying? If it were him, Grant would gut the place and turn it into something else. Like that Nerf ball stadium idea that keeps rolling around in his head—miniature replicas of famous parks like Fenway and Wrigley and Tiger Stadium. *Wouldn't it be cool to hit one off the Green Monster or make a catch against the ivy wall? Is that it—the beginning of my end?*

Grant comes up to Circle North and his left turn at Courtland Avenue. The Dairy Queen across the street is still open. If they move fast, he and Jackie can take Brandon for a cone, a little celebration for the first day of the family's future.

So you get the Nerf ball stadiums up and running. Then what? So many people have bigger needs than that: the poor, the sick, the disadvantaged. Grant guns the GTO in front of traffic and coasts onto Courtland. *Maybe something that helps the homeless. Like that guy with the limp who hangs out in the alley by the office.* Yesterday, Grant saw him sitting by the dumpster at lunchtime, struggling to stuff books into his backpack. Grant just got back from Le Dog with a bowl of lobster bisque and something came over him. He went into the alley and set the soup down in front of the poor guy. His mouth fell open in stunned

$720,000

amazement. The look on his face… it was the only thing Grant remembered when Jackie asked him how his day was.

Grant eases the GTO into the Circle North parking lot. He looks up at his apartment on the top floor of the split-level building. The shades are drawn across the sliding glass door, but he can see a faint flickering light; Brandon watching TV. He comes inside to find Jackie on the phone, pleading with somebody to calm down. When she sees him, she rolls her eyes, covers the phone, and says, "More trouble in two-two-four."

That's Edgar Boswell and Hal McCallum's place. The drug dealer and the guy with the motorcycle who calls him a Nazi. "Let me take it."

"Hang on," Jackie tells the caller. "Grant'll help you." She hands him the phone. "It's Marvin," she whispers. He's the blind tenant.

Grant asks Marvin to repeat what happened. "It's a big fight," he says. "The biggest ever. Shouting, screaming, banging. It's too loud. I can't take it anymore."

"Alright," Grant softens his voice. "I'll come see what's going on. We'll straighten it out." When he gets off the phone, Jackie's eyeing him with arms crossed. "What?"

"We should just call the police. I'm tired of getting in the middle of this shit."

Grant sighs. "We can't call them every time they argue."

Jackie turns away. "I can't wait to move out of here."

Grant catches her eye. He pats his shirt pocket. "You won't have to wait much longer," he says. "I got the check today."

"Really?" She smiles at him.

"We could get that place by the river now," Grants says.

"Should we call them? I don't want it to be gone."

"Let's talk after I take care of this." Grant heads for the door. Brandon is standing on the stairs with his Batman mask on.

"Can I come, Daddy?"

"Sorry, Buddy. I got go solo on this mission."

Boz and Hal's apartment is out near Washtenaw, second from the end of one of the spokes of the H-shaped building. The halls are dead quiet as he walks down there. When he stops in front of 224, he hears muffled talking. Whatever argument there was seems to be over. He knocks. The talking stops. No one comes to the door. He knocks again, and then he here's a cry: "Help me!"

Now Grant hears a thump. Before he can decide what to do, the door cracks open. Boz is looking out from behind it. "Everything's fine," he says. "We had an argument, but it's okay now."

Just over his head, Grant sees a splatter of red on the wall. He looks at Boz—and that's when he notices the flecks of red on his face.

"You okay, Hal?" he calls out.

"He's fine," Boz says. And he starts to shut the door.

Grant wedges his foot into the gap. "I need to hear Hal say that."

"Oh? Yeah?" Boz is suddenly angry. "Well, who the fuck are you?"

Grant realizes the situation is more dangerous than he assumed. He holds up his hands and backs away. "Okay, okay. Fine."

Boz opens the door wide now. "You're going to call the cops, aren't you?"

"No." Grant turns to get away.

The hallway thunders. His chest thumps. He misses a step and falls to his knees. *What is this?* A red blossom opens in the pocket of his shirt. He remembers the check and pulls it out. There's a hole through it. And now the floor swings up and smashes into him. Lying sideways in the hall, Grant sees Brandon, way down by the turn to their apartment. He's far enough away that he can't see the boy's eyes in the Batman mask, but close enough to see his mouth hanging open. *Run! RUN!* Grant tries to wave his son away, but his body is getting tugged back, now out of the hall, now behind Boz's door.

I didn't see this one coming, Grant thinks. And then he doesn't think again.

14. Luminaries

"Don't say it," Alec mutters without turning toward Kate.

She can't help herself. "He crossed the street to avoid you."

They're waiting to get into the Michigan Theater. The line comes from two blocks away, bunches up under the glittering marquee, and hooks into the grand entryway. It isn't your usual line of moviegoers. Everyone here has a special invitation to the night's event, and under their coats, they're wearing formal attire. These are the patrons who've come to celebrate the reopening of the historic movie house after a multi-year effort to restore it to its former glory.

Kate shifts on her high heels. "He saw you, spun around, then actually crossed the street to get behind us."

"I told you. Not everyone's going to be happy."

"I know. But Lanier? He's your friend."

Alec looks up at the towering "MICHIGAN" sign and the marquee that highlights *It's a Wonderful Life*. "When they make you department head, nobody's a friend. They're either mad they didn't get it, suspicious of how you did, or worried about what you'll do."

"Well, I'm glad you're so happy about it."

Alec scowls at her. She grins. He leans in and kisses her cheek. "How could I not be happy? Look around us."

So she does. They're under the bright lights of the outdoor alcove now. Everyone's face is flush from the winter chill. And Kate recognizes so many. There's the pizza mogul. There, the famous actor who never moved away. Kate points out the ex-racecar driver who orders books from her. And Alec waves to a man insiders say will be the university's next president. As they approach the doorman, though, Alec and Kate look in opposite directions. Alec peers into the foyer.

Kate glances over her shoulder, where the movie poster cases angle out to the sidewalk. They give the doorman their invitation. "I'll get in line for drinks," Alec says. "You get the popcorn." Kate is still looking back outside. "Kate?"

She turns, sees Alec eyeing her, then gazes up at the bright swirling carvings on the preserved ceiling. "Isn't it beautiful?"

"Did you hear me? I get drinks; you get popcorn. Okay?"

"Sure. Go ahead." Kate watches Alec until he's out of sight then goes back into the alcove, over by the posters on the sidewalk. There, leaning against the one closest to the street, Reese watches her approach, his good eye blazing at her. Kate pretends to read the poster beside him. "What are you doing here?"

"We got more than we thought," he says, his voice as low as hers.

Kate stares at Reese's reflection in the glass case. "Okay. If they're titles I asked for, I'll pay for the extras."

"They're all *Far Side*s. That *Day in the Life* one was too bulky—"

"We talked about this, Reese. You can't be following me around."

"But I had to tell you. We got so many books I couldn't carry them all. So I hid a bag by that dumpster behind the store."

Kate turns to Reese. "When?"

"After you closed. Nobody saw."

Kate opens her wallet. "Okay. I'll get them in the morning."

"See why I had to come?"

Kate holds out a five-dollar bill. "I understand." She forces a smile.

Reese takes the money like a beggar would. "You're better than all of them."

"Find somewhere warm," she says and hurries inside.

Alec edges through the crowd under the glittering chandeliers and the gilded ceiling. He charges up the marble steps that split off into two facing balcony stairways. On the landing between the staircases, Tom Whelan scans the lobby. When he sees Alec bounding his way, he gazes past him. It's only after Alec stops in front of Tom that his eyes focus on his former advisor.

"I know why your theory's wrong." Alec wags a finger.

"My theory?"

"*The House of the Seven Gables*."

Tom laughs. "You thought that was wrong a year ago."

"But I figured it out," Alec says with a triumphant smirk. "You see, there were two doors into the shop. Not one. Two."

Tom's baffled. "I know. That's the whole point."

Alec shakes his head like he's trying to convince a stubborn child. "No, you see. There were two—" He stops. He glances around like he's lost something. Then he stomps back down the marble steps.

"He seemed rather keen to find you." Tom turns. It's Professor Barlow, his old mentor and the only reason Tom's here among this exclusive crowd. He's coming down the stairs from the balcony.

"The things he worries about. I don't know what to make of him."

Barlow peers over his horned-rim glasses. "I do."

Tom's about to press for an explanation, but then he spots Kate finally, laughing and waving as she weaves through the luminaries.

"Where are the drinks?" Kate asks when she gets to their seats. Alec is standing alone in the near-empty theater, listening to the organist play the old Barton pipe organ at the foot of the stage.

"I got to talking and forgot."

"There's still time," Kate says, scanning the empty seats.

"I suppose. So what do you think?" He taps the back of the chair.

Kate has to squint to see the lettering etched on the gold nameplates. *Alec and Kate Bucksley*. "Oh. Yes. There they are. Very nice."

"Monaghan's two rows behind us. Look."

Kate makes a show of peering at the nameplate. "I'll be."

"I'll bet these seats were more than those."

"Maybe so."

Alec takes off his coat and folds it over the seat. Kate brushes a fleck off his tuxedo's lapel. He sits down. She takes off her coat, smooths her dress, and sits down beside him.

"Where's the popcorn?"

"The line was too long," Kate says. They fall silent.

As soon as *It's a Wonderful Life* is over, Alec nudges Kate to go. But she fell asleep and is only just waking up. By the time they file into the main aisle, they're stuck in the shuffling mass. Alec tries to steer her toward a side exit, but an older man squeezes beside her and cuts them off. "I'm told that you're Kate Bucksley."

"Yes," Kate answers, delighted to be someone that somebody might ask about and others would know.

"You left a message on my phone the other day."

"Mister Leonard! Yes, I did—"

"Please, it's Elmore." He smiles and adjusts his glasses. "Anyway, I'd love to do a signing. I've heard great things about your store."

Kate blushes. "Well, thank you. That means a lot."

"I'll call you on Monday and we'll figure out a time." Leonard turns to Alec. "I understand you've distinguished yourself as well."

Alec isn't sure what he means at first. But he recovers quickly enough. "The same could be said of thieves."

Leonard grimaces. "We're all thieves in our own way, aren't we? I, for one, steal words. And people. And their lives."

Alec laughs. "Take my life," he jokes, grinning at Kate. "Please."

Leonard eyes the two. "I'm sure there's a story *there*." He moves off with the crowd. Kate and Alec gape at each other, starstruck.

As they're leaving the lobby, Kate says, "I better go to the ladies room." She slips through the crowd and climbs the staircase to the loft. Tom leans over the railing there. Kate comes up beside him.

"Are you spying on me?"

"If I was, you wouldn't have caught me."

"So you admit to wanting me to see you."

"I was hoping you would. Yes. I wanted to—"

"It's not exactly the safest place—"

"—to find out what Alec said," Tom finishes.

Kate straightens up and pulls her gloves out of her coat pockets. "And here I thought this would be pleasant."

"Did you tell him?"

Kate gazes up at the ceiling. "I think I'm changing my mind."

Tom scans the thinning crowd. "Look, Kate. You said it yourself. He could be the father, too. You have to tell him."

"Or he never has to know." Kate tugs on her second glove.

Tom turns to her, stunned. "Don't do that. You'll regret it."

Across the loft, Barlow's walking away from a circle of professors. He peers over his thick glasses at Tom and Kate.

"We can talk about it next week," Kate says.

"No." Tom watches Barlow lean over the railing and pretend not to notice the two. "I don't want you coming. I've been thinking—"

"I'm coming to San Francisco," Kate cuts him off. "I have to for the book convention."

"We need to end to this, Kate. It's the best thing. For everyone."

"We'll see," Kate says, cheerfully dismissive. As she passes behind him, she brushes her hand across his back. Then she looks over at Barlow, smiles, and waves.

Alec steps out from under the marquee and lights a cigarette. As he takes his first draw, he notices the beggar on the sidewalk across the street. He's got his knees pulled up to his chest and his arms propped on them. Most of his face is hidden in his hood. But Alec can see that one eye, lit by the theater lights, peeking out on the scene. He drops his cigarette and hurries across Liberty. When the beggar sees him coming, he hangs his head. Alec glares down on the back of his grimy hood. "You think you're fooling me? You think I didn't see you ogling my wife by the ticket booth? Or last week, when we were waiting outside Gratzi?"

He kicks Reese's foot, hard enough that his elbows slip off his knee. Reese peers up at Alec. "She gives me money."

Alec laughs. "Lots of people give you money." He reaches under his coat and pulls out his wallet. He counts out five twenties and drops them at Reese's feet. "Is that enough to keep you away?"

Reese doesn't reach for the bills.

"I see you around her anymore, I won't be as generous." Alec turns, crosses Liberty, and mixes back in with the luminaries.

By the time Kate comes out, Alec has eased back against the poster cases as though he'd been waiting there all along. The two fall into step without a word. They're two blocks away from the theater, across from Kate's bookstore, before Alec speaks up. "You know, we're better than we give ourselves credit for. We're some of the luckiest people in town."

Kate finds his hand and squeezes it. "Yes," she agrees. "Yes, we are."

15. Justice

"This is driving me crazy," Baskin says as Kip starts to explain the details of the contract.

"What?"

"That waiter. Where the hell do I know him from?"

They're sitting in the big room at Maude's, back against the mirror that runs the length of the room. "I don't know, Jeremy."

"It just bothers me."

"Can we focus for a minute?"

"Sorry. You were just getting to who gets what, right?"

Kip leans back in to run through the numbers. Baskin's eyes follow the waiter past their table into a side room, where a private party has just quieted down to a lone voice.

Dean times it so his return to the party coincides with the toast. He moves quietly among the dozen or so people standing at their roundtops, holding out his platter to offer each a champagne flute. When he gets to Carrie, whose hair is as dark and long as the day he met her, and whose eyes still have that startled intensity, Dean bows so his face is level with hers. She smiles softly, takes her flute, then shifts attention to the man in front of everyone. Dean hurries out into the big room of regular diners.

"I'll keep this short and sweet," the toastmaker says. Tie unloosened, shirt untucked, swaying from an hour's worth of scotches, he looks the part of a man cutting loose after a long week. But his hair, those boyish bangs, is still perfectly in place. And even in this unguarded moment of celebration, his elation can't entirely wipe off the sober mask he's spent a career carving into his face. This is Kevin O'Shea,

Ann Arbor's top prosecutor, and the man whom Detroit's morning newspapers will herald as the lawyer who brought Edgar Boswell to justice in the Circle North murder case. (As you may recall, he was also the lawyer in Reese Ward's parking meter case over a decade ago.)

"I don't have to tell you how hard we worked these last months," he says. "And we all know the odds we were up against. I must've had ten colleagues tell me not to push for second-degree. Markham keys into Boswell's apartment, allegedly starts a fight, then gets shot. Arguably self-defense. Manslaughter? Maybe. But second degree? Malice? Intent? That was a risk none of them would've taken.

"Every one of you went above and beyond to get this verdict today. But there's one person who deserves credit for pushing me to take such a big risk." He looks at Carrie, eyes blinking like he might cry. "Truth is, I was going to go with manslaughter. The longer your career, the more jaded you get. You won't take a chance because you don't want to lose." O'Shea stops talking. He looks at the floor. People glance at each other. Finally, he rallies. "Carrie Asbury." Now his voice is as strong as it was hours before in the courtroom. "Thank you for not letting me settle. Thank you for convincing me of the truth of what happened at Circle North. And thank you all for making that truth such a compelling story. I wish…"

O'Shea decides not to go on. He nods at Carrie. She nods back. They tilt their flutes to one another like it's a private toast.

Outside the celebration, Kip struggles to keep Baskin focused on the contract. "Cheer up a little, would you? I can write you a check for ten grand right now. Or if you want to roll the dice for ten percent of the royalties on every song we sell, you can do that."

Baskin screws up his face. "While you get fifty, the musician you sell it to gets forty—and the guy who wrote it gets nothing."

"Five hundred bucks a song isn't nothing."

"And you get a hundred times that much—"

"I'm doing the work!"

Baskin catches the waiter's eye as he's bustling into the private party. "Hey Baskin. Long time."

Baskin throws his napkin on the table. "Shit. It's like we saw each other yesterday."

"Ben?"

"No. The waiter. You heard him. *He* knows *me*."

"Screw the waiter! We need to get this done."

"Fine."

"It's not like we're doing this behind Ben's back. He doesn't want anything. He just wants someone to have his songs."

"Because Ben's crazy," Baskin reminds him.

"He's not crazy. He's just wired different. Money isn't his thing."

Baskin taps on the contract. "I know why I'm in here. Don't B.S. me. You don't want me suing you down the road."

Kip hangs his mouth open in his best impression of incredulity. "You're my best friend."

Baskin laughs. "All right, Kip. I give. Show me were to sign."

Kip flips through the contract. Baskin looks back at the waiter. He's standing over the guy who gave the toast, staring off stone-faced. The guy is chewing him out. Now a woman comes between the two and says something. The toast guy throws up his hands. The waiter rushes away, seething.

After Dean storms off, Carrie says, "Let's make this your last drink tonight, okay Kevin?"

Kevin gropes for Carrie's hand. "Why? You got another plan?" He rolls his head to one side and leers at her.

"Didn't you say you had a TV interview in the morning?"

"I'm kicking back a little, awright?"

"Fine. Just go easy on the staff, okay?"

"What? Mister Maude?" Kevin cackles.

"He's just trying to do his job."

Kevin squints up at Carrie and wags his finger. "You see what I mean? That's exactly what I was saying. You're a born defender."

"Maybe so. But it's you I want to keep out of trouble."

"Aw, don't bullshit a bullshitter," he says, loud enough that a few people turn. "I saw you getting friendly with Mister Maude."

"I wouldn't call him that again."

Kevin pulls himself up in his chair. He motions for Carrie to come closer. "I got a surprise for you."

She pats his hand. "Not here. Okay?"

"You're right." He grins. "When we're alone."

"Kevin, I told you I didn't—"

"I told Jen I'd be late," he slurs out. "We could get a room."

Carrie gives him a brittle grin. Then she moves off slowly and takes a seat among her colleagues.

"Where'd you see him last?" Kip swirls his goblet of cognac. "Why? He won't be there now," Baskin says. Kip ordered him the same drink to celebrate the deal, but he hasn't touched it.

"I've got three days to find Ben and get this signed. I tried the Diag. Checked Nickels Arcade. Looked in Graffiti Alley."

"I saw him a couple days ago in the Engineering Arch."

"And you talked to him?"

"I wanted to. I stood and listened through a song. He even looked up. But it's dark in there. And after the song ended, he just started into the next. So I left." Baskin's eyes drift back to the private room. The waiter is coming over to the drunk guy everyone abandoned. As he leans down in profile and holds out his platter with the single drink on it, Baskin gasps. "I know where I know him!"

"Who?"

"Mister Tony's. He was the cook. Dean!"

Kip looks back at the waiter. "Mystery solved."

"He was always in the kitchen, looking out a little strip of window. I rarely saw his whole face. Isn't that funny?"

"Yeah, funny," Kip says. "Look. You're the one who's so concerned about getting Ben his money. I got a check for those two songs. You gonna help me get it to him or not?"

Dean has barely stepped foot in the room, and that jerk is already starting in on him. "Come on, Maude! Get over here, you ugly old hag." Dean thought about asking another waiter to take this last round to the party. He didn't want to lose his cool in front of Carrie. But he wanted to show her that a guy like this couldn't get to him. Just because he was a bigshot lawyer, it didn't make him a bigger man.

"Let's go, li'l lady," barks the blowhard. "Chop, chop."

It's only as Dean's extending the platter that the impulse hits him. He tips the tray forward slightly. The drink slides down, hits the lip, and topples into the lawyer's lap. Kevin gapes at his wet crotch.

Dean smirks. "Oops."

"You son of a bitch." Kevin grabs the glass and backhands it at Dean. It hits him just above the right eye. He staggers back. Kevin lunges at him.

Carrie's already between the two when Dean goes down. She stiff-arms Kevin back, but he's close enough to kick Dean in the ribs. She begs him to stop. He sweeps his arm and knocks her out of the way. She reels back and trips over a chair into the public dining room.

Kip doesn't notice what's happening until Baskin springs to his feet. He sees a woman on the floor, rubbing blood from her mouth. The guy who gave the toast is trying to pry his leg away from the waiter. He's bent over, driving his head into the stomach of the hopping man. They slam against the wall. Pottery falls off shelving and crashes. Diners gasp. Others in the room swarm to the combatants. One starts kneeing the doubled-over waiter.

Baskin charges into the room. Kip downs his cognac. Then he grabs Baskin's drink and downs that, too. He sighs. Finally, he folds his napkin on the table and gets up from his seat.

Baskin rushes into the fray. The fight escalates into a fist-flailing brawl. Dean gets free, knocks Kevin down with one punch, and starts after the guy who kneed him. More co-workers come to Kevin's defense. Baskin swings wildly at everyone. A chair gets thrown. Waiters and managers sweep into the room.

Carrie crawls away from the melee. She's wrenched her ankle and needs a chair to pull herself up. As she reaches for it, a hand's there to meet hers. Carrie takes it and comes face to face with a composed, soft-eyed businessman about her age. "You alright?"

"I don't know." Carrie runs her thumb across her mouth and comes up with blood.

Kip gives her a handkerchief. "There's a cut on your cheek, too."

"That's what I get," she mumbles, looking back at the brawl.

"Nobody deserves to get hit."

Carrie marvels at his calm, earnest demeanor. "No, they don't." She hands back his handkerchief, thinking, *what sort of man carries one of these?*

"Keep it," Kip says.

The fight stops minutes after the Maude's staff steps in. A manager puts Dean in a bear hug and marches him out of the restaurant. The gash on his forehead and the scratches on his neck are his only visible injuries, though with the knee to the stomach, he has trouble standing up straight. Kevin doesn't come away with many battle scars either. He has a ripening welt under his left eye, his shirt is torn—and there's that stain on the pants. Baskin's the one who got the worst of things. He turned just at the wrong time to catch a roundhouse punch flush on the nose. Hand covering his crooked bridge, fingers spread like a mask around his eyes, Baskin follows the hostess to the office.

Carrie watches him pass. "That doesn't look good."

"That's my friend. He knew the waiter, so he decided to jump in."

"He knew the waiter?"

"I guess so." Kip gets to his feet. "Well… I better go help him out." He points at Carrie's cheek. "You should ask for some ice."

She blushes at the man's calm attention. "Thank you."

"I don't know that I did that much." Kip nods to her and leaves.

Carrie dabs her cheek, checking for new blood. "We're going to sue that lousy punk," her boss bawls out from the private room. "And we're going to sue this crummy restaurant. And someone's paying to clean these pants!"

Carrie gets up and goes back in the room to pacify the man whose advances she should've shut down from the start. She would've walked away from him, but she has her own reasons for convincing O'Shea not to get the police involved.

Kip talks his way into the manager's office. Baskin's there, holding an ice pack to his nose. The manager is searching through a file cabinet. "Let me see," Kip says. Baskin removes the pack. The knob between his eyes is as big as a golf ball, and there are purple bruises branching out beneath it. The rest of his nose is like soft pink putty someone pushed aside with a thumb. "Holy shit."

"I turned right into it," Baskin mumbles.

"Keep the ice on," Kip advises, as much for Baskin's well-being as to hide the monstrosity.

"They want me to fill out an incident report."

"It's just a routine thing we do." The manager hands over a sheet.

"To protect yourself," Kip says.

"And Mister Baskin."

"From what?"

The manager stares Kip down. "In case there's a complaint or someone calls the police or different stories get told."

Kip stares right back. "So you're going to get one of these reports from the lawyer that started all this, right?"

"I—uh—I don't—I would think so," the manager stammers.

"Right. Because asshole lawyers are always agreeable to documenting their own wrongdoing." He nudges Baskin. "Come on. You don't have to fill that out. These guys are just covering their asses."

The manager crosses his arms. Baskin wavers. "I don't know, Kip."

"I do. They got a waiter who gets in a fight with a customer—and another customer who gets his face rearranged."

"He didn't have to step in," the manager says.

"See what I mean? Let's get outta here."

It doesn't take much convincing for a lawyer as practiced as Kevin O'Shea to see that making a stink about a bar fight isn't in his best interest. Carrie just reminds him how it started. After that, she tracks down a bartender and asks what happened to the waiter who got attacked. The bartender says he's outside. Carrie doesn't see Dean anywhere on the street, but she hears arguing at the side of the building. Just as she rounds the corner, a waiter stomps past her. Dean's leaning back against the wall, looking out of the shadows.

"I should've never taken your party."

"It wasn't your fault." Carrie steps into the same shadow he's in.

"I wanted to show you I didn't have a problem with it."

"You don't have to prove anything to me."

Dean studies her face. "I see you and the next thing I know I'm getting in fights and quitting my job."

"Why would you quit over this?"

"I know. Stupid, right?"

"Dean..." She reaches for him, but they aren't close enough to touch. She pulls her hand back.

Dean takes the step between them and puts his hands on her shoulders. "What am I going to do?"

Her eyes swim away from his. "Just ask for your job back—"

"Not about the job."

Carrie finally meets his gaze.

That's when Baskin notices the two. He's leaving the restaurant with an icepack pressed against his face and his friend Kip by his side. "Sorry Dean!" he yells out, apologizing as much for not recognizing the old Tony's cook as for making such a poor savior.

"I would've gotten my ass kicked if you didn't step in."

"And thank *you*," Carrie breaks in.

"It was nothing," Kip replies, the slits of his eyes glinting in the streetlight. "Really."

Dean glances from Kip to Carrie. She allows herself an audible sigh and turns back to Dean. He's dropped his hands from her shoulder. Exactly when, she hadn't noticed.

At the corner of Fourth and Liberty, across from Takeout Video, Baskin figures they're out of earshot. "So you rescued a damsel in distress, eh? I missed that. What exactly did you do?"

"Beats me," Kip says. "I guess I was just there."

"Figures," Baskin mutters.

16. Top of the Park

Sitting at the top of the steps that lead into the Rackham Building, Ben Hadley strums his guitar and sings in a whisper down to the mall that extends across campus to the Diag. If you wanted to get noticed, this is a good place to play. But Ben isn't here to be heard; otherwise, he wouldn't have hid behind one of the sandstone blocks that bookend the stairway.

It's the last night for Top of the Park, the free music series the city puts on in June. The festival gives locals a chance to come together every evening for two weeks and celebrate the town. It's held beside the Power Center on top of an underground parking structure; hence the name. A vast platform of concrete slants down to where a stage is set up. Hundreds of folding chairs line the tilted floor, and on the high end behind them, there's a roped-off beer court.

People start showing up well before Gord Bernard and the Gutter Balls are set to go on. They come from all directions. From the neighborhoods near the hospital and across the Broadway Bridge. From the fraternities and the student ghetto. From the homes on the Old West Side. They're long-time residents and newcomers; teachers and students, graduates and dropouts; doctors and techies; minimum-wagers and hangers-on. They're babies and children and teens and adults, young and aging and old. Many would call themselves a townie—but few would agree on what that means.

Baskin has never been to Top of the Park and has no intention of going tonight. He's headed for the university hospital to work the night shift he's covered since becoming a nursing assistant. As soon as he comes into view, Ben notices him. He switches to a tune Kip sold and sings louder. Baskin stops, looks one way then the other, and finally spots Ben. He marches up the steps. "What are you doing up here?" He inspects the guitar case at his feet. "What a surprise. No one's climbed the mountain to honor you."

"I'm not playing for money right now." Ben smiles at his friend.

"Not playing for money, my ass." Baskin gives the case a kick. "You've got this open. What are people supposed to think?"

"That I took out my guitar?"

Baskin rolls his eyes. "You're still getting the checks, right?"

"Kip sold more songs?"

Baskin masks his dismay with a blank stare. "I was asking you. I haven't seen Kip in a while."

"Hey, I've got these new songs I've been writing. Maybe you could get them to him." Ben rummages through some crumpled papers in the case.

"Don't—" Baskin stops. "I mean, I don't know where Kip is. He travels a lot."

"I wonder if he got the last ones I mailed. Can you find out?"

Baskin's shoulders slump ever so slightly. "Yeah, sure."

"Thanks." Ben puts the pages back in his case. He points to Baskin's scrubs. "So you're working at the hospital now."

"I'm not a doctor," Baskin says straightaway. He's still sensitive about how his career has turned out—dropping out of law school, failing at the music business, and now not even a nurse. "I could've been, but it would've taken too long."

"So you did what you wanted."

"I did."

"Then… good." Ben thinks for a moment. "Right?"

"I guess."

Ben strums an idle chord, the matter settled. Baskin looks off at the gathering crowd. "Anyway…" He turns back. "It's nice to see you, Ben." He leaves the singer, taking the steps two at a time.

Someone bumps Cole and apologizes. Cole recognizes him: that driver from Tony's who loved fragels. Baskin. Cole follows him. He sees so few friends from his school days anymore. It would be good to show someone from back then that he'd gone straight. They're under the canopy of trees in front of the Power Center, the only two people leaving the festival. Cole is about to call out, but then stops. Baskin's in a hurry and dressed for the hospital—probably some big-shot doctor. Why would he want to stop to reminisce with an ex-stoner he barely knew? Cole turns and heads back to Top of the Park.

All week, ever since the big news at work, Cole's been feeling the weight of his loneliness. When he learned that Joe Teegan sold the company, and Cole had become a millionaire, he felt the same giddy high he chased with drugs. But after the office celebration, Cole found himself alone in his dingy apartment down by the lumberyard. He'd just become rich. And there was no one he was close enough with to share the news.

Cole buys a beer and finds a table on the edge of the rim overlooking the stage. He nurses the beer like he has for years and tries to imagine how a conversation with Baskin might've gone, but the woman at the next table keeps distracting him. It's the cadence of her voice, the swagger. She has her back to him, but he knows who it is. Cole leans up for a better angle. Sure enough: Kate. "I love the Pan Tree." She casts out that inviting laugh of hers. "They're the gift that keeps giving. Whenever their kitchen floods—"

"Kate," a man tries to stop the story. Cole takes a glance. Alec is next to her among a handful of people. He'd heard the two got married.

"It's not like it's a secret," Kate says. "The water comes through our ceiling and leaks on my books. The first time it happened, I took the damaged books upstairs and said, *we've got a problem*. The manager asked what they cost and wrote me a check on the spot. Two weeks later, same thing. Now, the Pan Tree's my best customer!"

A chair scrapes on the concrete. Cole can feel Alec looming over him. "Who wants another beer?"

"So I got smart," Kate carries on. "I moved my pricey art books under the leak. My last check was six hundred bucks!"

Cole watches Alec head off to the beer court. Then he stands up. Time to go. These are two old friends he'd rather not meet.

"Maggie!" Cole turns to see a little girl with one leg over the half wall that guards against a drop to the level below. Cole lunges, grabs the girl, and pulls her off the ledge. Kate's at his side by then. He hands her the child. "Maggie! What in the world?" She rolls her eyes for Cole's benefit. "This one climbs on everything."

Cole flashes a smile and hurries away. Alec returns with the beers. "How'd she sneak away?" he asks, barely disguising the accusation.

Kate holds Maggie out to Alec. "She's too clever for me."

"I haven't seen Clem since Forest," he says, taking the baby.

"Where was he?"

"Weren't you talking to him?"

"Who?"

"The guy who helped Maggie." Alec scans the crowd. "There." He points out Cole, passing behind the sound man at the mixing board.

"That's not Clem."

"The hell it isn't. Give him an afro and a shit-eating grin."

Kate watches as Cole walks to the far rim and stations himself along that railing. "I'll be damned. Our jester's all grown up."

"He seems so serious," Alec observes. "So… sad."

"That makes two."

"I'm not that sad."

"What I mean is, that's two Forest people I've seen. Remember Leah?" Alec looks where Kate's pointing. To the left of the stage, about 10 rows up, Leah's bouncing a baby boy on her knee.

"I don't know…" Alec is having trouble matching the self-possessed woman he sees with the waifish stray at Forest.

"And I'll lay odds the guy next to her is Chase Tyson."

"Him I don't remember."

"Wouldn't that be a surprise to bump into them?" Kate says.

Chase does his best to listen to Leah, but as close as they are to the band and as preoccupied as he is checking the crowd, he isn't getting the gist. "So if you do this, who's watching Max?"

Leah lifts the toddler off her knee, sets him on his feet, and points to a group of kids running around on the empty dance space beside the stage. "Look at all those boys, Max. You wanna go play?" Max watches a while then buries his head in her lap. "It's once a week," Leah says. "I'll work around your schedule."

"There are a lot of other causes you could volunteer for."

"This is the only one that matters to me."

"Counseling women not to get abortions…"

"Helping women who can't see any other way out."

"You could say the same thing about Planned Parenthood."

"We don't have to agree on this. But I *am* going to do it."

She faces the band, freeing him to study the crowd. Bernard launches into a deep rockabilly groove. Everyone turns to the stage. It's easier now to read faces. Chase sweeps across the rows. No Sheryl, thank God. He follows the line of the railing that looms over him. Then he stops with a jolt. There, at the end of the balcony, Kate's leaning over, watching the band. He's seen her a few times over the years; their stores are two blocks away. But he's pretty sure Leah hasn't seen her since the day she helped them escape Forest.

"Monday or Tuesday," he says over the music. "Either day's fine."

Leah puts a hand on his knee. "Thank you." She turns to watch the dancers beside the stage. "Look, Max. There's a mom dancing with her boys." She gets up and leads Max down that way.

Chase looks up to the balcony. Kate's gone. He checks the far aisle that feeds down to the dance space. She isn't coming. His eyes drift over to the street side of the park. That's when he sees Clem—Cole, as he knows him now. He's coming down the aisle under that side's railing, looking toward the dancers. Cole's a different person from those wild Forest days. But he's the one who corrupted Leah. Chase moves to the end of the row. *Never hurts to be ready.*

When Cole sees Leah guiding her boy to the dancers, he takes it as an omen. Now there are two women there he needs to talk to—one to beg forgiveness, the other to thank. He heads down the aisle. It's only after he crosses below the stage that Cole realizes he doesn't know where to start with either woman. He slides into a chair in the second row. From here, he can see how much Leah's changed. During the time he's worked downtown, Cole has seen his old—*she wasn't a friend, really; she was a follower, a runaway who latched onto me when I was at my worst*—he's seen her only once, looking out his office window. But here she is now, completely transformed. Where before, she held herself in a permanent cringe, now Leah stands tall, shoulders back, chin up. And her eyes have a calm, fearless quality. *Good for Leah. She made it out.* So many people he knew from those days didn't. Had he stayed with Boz, he'd be one of them. *What do I say to her? I'm sorry? I was as lost and scared as you?*

And what made him think he could approach the other woman, a woman he never met but who held such a strong link to his fortune? He recognized her instantly from the photo Grant had on his desk. Jackie Markham. He hoped one day this moment would come, but he never expected it to happen here. If he were in her shoes, dancing would be the last thing he'd do. Everyone whirls around her like she isn't there. Yet in that purple dress, with that big smile and her hands twisting to the sky, how can they not notice her? She's like a dream Cole conjured up, blooming in secret, vividly fragile. *I've got to talk to her tonight. No matter what.*

About this time, Kate is making up her mind, too. She holds out her hands. Maggie shifts in Alec's arms and reaches for her. "I'm going to go say hi." Kate sets the girl on her hip. "You should come."

"I'll see how it goes." Alec swirls his beer.

"You'll miss the surprise."

Chase watches Cole watch Leah. If she comes back the way she left, she'll go right past him. What could he possibly say to her after all these years? Maybe it's a simple apology. Still, why let Leah go through that? Chase gets up, wheels the stroller around, and hurries up the center aisle. If he can make it to Leah before the music stops, she'll never cross paths with Cole. He's almost up to the top of his aisle when he sees Kate striding down the far aisle, her little girl bouncing on her hip. There's no way to catch up.

Kate squeezes through the crush of dancers until she's right behind Leah. After Bernard spins out the song, Kate taps Leah's shoulder. "Well, I'll be. I barely recognized you."

"Kate," Leah says without surprise.

"Look at us." The music kicks in again. Maggie squirms in Kate's arms. She sets her down.

"It's been a long time."

"And this little man." Kate tousles Max' hair. "He's a mini-Chase." The two women regard each other's toddlers as if it's their burden to interact. Max and Maggie stare shyly at one another. "How old is he?"

"Two. And your daughter?"

"Maggie's fifteen months. You remember Alec; he's the—" Kate stops. Then she recovers with a brittle grin. "He's my husband."

Leah nods. Max pokes at a flower in Maggie's hair. "Be gentle, Max."

"Look at her." Kate cocks her head toward the woman in the violet dress. She's still stretching for the sky. "You know who that is, don't you?"

Leah can't see the woman's face through her tumbled hair. "No."

"You remember Boz, right? The guy he killed… that's his wife."

The women fall into a long silence as they watch the dancing widow. Finally, Kate says, "Can you imagine wanting to dance—after something like?"

The widow's hands flutter now like tethered birds. Leah finds herself fighting off tears. "I pray for you sometimes," she admits over the music.

Kate turns to Leah, stunned. She sees that Leah's about to cry. "Aw, honey, you don't have to do that."

Cole feels a slap on his shoulder. Alec is sitting behind him, grinning. "Small world." Cole tenses. Alec motions toward the dancers. "Did you see Kate and Leah?"

"No, I didn't." Cole notices Kate for the first time. He hasn't looked Leah's way since the crowd cleared around Grant's widow.

"I saw you here and I thought, *you should go say hi to old Clem.* It's good to see you landed on your feet."

"I guess—"

"Good to see we *all* landed on our feet. Well… except Boz." Alec leans in to talk over the music. "I never figured him for a psychopath."

"He was a drug dealer."

Alec laughs. "Lots of people do that. They don't gun down people. Hell, you didn't."

"What do you want?"

Alec puts up his hands. "Sorry man. That came out wrong. I was just making a point. The whole Boz thing was a surprise. That's all."

"You didn't live with him."

"I mean, he was doing pretty damned good business. Just from who I knew." Alec raises his eyebrows.

"Are you asking me to get you drugs?"

"No. I'm just saying, Boz left a bit of a hole…"

Cole laughs through a trembling sneer. "Get away from me."

Whatever Alec sees in Cole's eyes makes him rock back in his chair. "I just thought you might know someone. That's all."

"I knew his victim." Cole's about to point out the woman dancing, but he thinks better of it.

Chase doesn't go down to rescue Leah. She always says he's too protective. Besides, Kate and Leah seem more focused on the kids. *Why shouldn't they be friendly?* After all, Kate helped her get away from Forest. When Leah turns from Kate, though, he sees the tight line of her mouth. He knows that face. He knows the sorrow it fights against. He heads down the far aisle. Kate strides up toward him. "I think I upset your wife."

Gord Bernard whirls into the start of *Pipeline*. Leah leads Max back to their seats. Chase isn't there. She's so busy scanning the crowd that she nearly runs into Cole. He backs up as she gapes at him.

"Are you okay?"

Leah nods, but she's holding back tears. Cole retraces her path to the dancers. He spots Kate walking away. "What did she say to you?" he asks over the swirling staccato of Bernard's guitar.

"It isn't her." Max has toddled ahead, right under Bedard on the elevated stage.

"It's me, isn't it?"

Leah looks in Cole's eyes. Then she steps forward and surprises him with a hug. "I'm sorry," Cole says, putting his arms around her. "I'm so sorry."

"It was a long time ago." Leah pulls away. "And it happened for a reason. You have to believe that."

He studies her face, like he's trying to make sense of a foreign language. Finally, he replies: "I will."

It's only then that Cole sees Chase behind her, waiting with the stroller, midway between them and the dancers. He nods. Chase returns the gesture.

Bernard ends his set. Everyone starts leaving. Jackie straps her younger boy in his stroller and calls to her older boy. He weaves between the chairs, still full of energy. Eventually, he follows Jackie. Cole doesn't catch up to them until they're by the Rackham Building. Ben's still playing his guitar there. Jackie's older boy charges up the sprawling steps.

"You've got your hands full with that one."

Jackie turns without slowing the stroller. "I've given up trying."

"I knew your husband," Cole says before she gets too far ahead.

She stops and studies him in the growing dark. "Oh yeah?"

"I work at Crescendo. He—Grant—he hired me."

"That must've been a while ago."

Cole comes closer. "What I mean is..." *Don't waste this moment.* "I owe a lot to him. He—he took a chance on me... when I didn't deserve one. And I, well... I just thought you should know."

The boy is back. "Mommy, can I have some money for the singer?"

"No, Brandon. Mommy doesn't have any."

Cole fishes a dollar out of his pocket. "Here you are." Brandon snatches the bill and runs off.

"You're Cole," Jackie says. "Grant talked about you." She holds out her hand. "I'm Jackie."

"I know." He offers her a soft grip.

"I guess everyone knows. We're infamous."

"No—" Cole falls silent. He takes a nervous breath. "Grant used to talk about you a lot."

"I didn't know that."

"He had this picture on his desk." Cole talks fast. He's afraid he won't get it all out. "From when you were in college. It was a picnic in the Arb and you were in that valley—I know exactly where it is. And when he talked about you, and I'd see that picture over his shoulder—" Cole stops. Jackie's gazing at him with what he's worried is dread. "I always thought to myself, *he's so lucky.*"

"I was the lucky one."

Brandon bounds down the steps and bounces between them, waving a dollar in each hand. "Look! The singer gave *me* money!"

"That wasn't ours to begin with, Brandon. You need to give it back to Mister…"

"Emory."

The boy deflates but instantly rallies. "But I can keep this one!"

"No. You wouldn't have gotten that one without the other."

"I have an idea." Cole seeks out Jackie's eyes. "How about if you keep those, but you share one with your brother? If that's okay with your mom." Brandon looks up to Jackie. She nods. He takes one of the dollars over to his sleeping brother and jams it into the pocket of his little jacket. It's a small gesture, more obedience than generosity, but it moves Cole, nonetheless. He smiles at Jackie.

Her eyes flutter away. "Thank you."

"Can I walk you anywhere?"

"I'm just parked around the corner."

Well, I'm going that way, too. We might as well…" He trails off.

"Might as well."

She grabs the handles of the stroller and heads away from the mall, going slowly, waiting for Cole. The boy runs ahead. Nobody sees them leave but Ben. And nobody hears Ben change the melody.

But he does.

Top of the Park

Townies

*T*here comes a point, after living here so many years, when you don't have to wonder if you're a townie. You know it. You're the one telling stories about the city. You're the one people come to with questions.

You know that an arsonist burned down Haven Hall in 1950, destroying all the student exams. You know that John Kennedy's campaign speech at the Michigan Union launched the Peace Corps. You know who John Norman Collins is and how his serial murders terrorized the town. You saw Bert Hornback perform his annual tradition of reading "A Christmas Carol" dressed as Charles Dickens. No one has to tell you the town's connection to Robert Frost or Jesse Owens or Gerald Ford or Bob Seger or Tom Brady or Madonna. You remember the blizzard of 1978 and the hurricane winds that ripped through town two years later. You remember when the little Le Dog stand was open and that they never sold coke (ever!) and that Jules would yell at you if you asked for lobster bisque without pre-ordering it. You miss the Wildflour Bakery and the Whiffletree and Turtle Island and Cracked Crab and Sweet Lorraine's and the Rubiyat and Second Chance and Del Rio.

You're a townie. You're a permanent resident. You aren't going anywhere. Everything there is to learn about this world and whatever comes after will happen to you here. There's a certain peace about that, but a responsibility, too. Peace because you're no longer striving or seeking; you're where you're meant to be. And responsibility because you know you're part of something now, even if no one can agree on what that is. Still, it's inside you and every other townie. You feel what anyone feels as a part of something: belonging, obligation, belief.

Let's add another 24 years to our experiment. Look down from Burton Tower again. See how few of the trails from 1977 are still there? All the *people left are townies.* They don't intersect with each other as frequently as they used to, but when they do, they have more history together, and they appreciate the singularity of it more. What they may have once called a coincidence they might now think of as no coincidence at all.

Look at how their paths swarm around together through the days. They're never all that far away from each other, but they don't get that close, either. Except on the rarest of occasions. Stop the action now, on this early Monday morning, April 23, 2012. See how the paths are starting to veer toward a central point, like a tangle of loose knots tightening? What will all these townies do when they're brought so close together that they suddenly glimpse the design in things? Will they just shake their heads and say, "That's incredible," or will they look to the heavens and wonder, "If this *isn't* a miracle, then what is?"

17. Karma

Chase's phone rings in the dark. It's 3:48. The call's from Max. "Everything's okay." There's a breathless edge to his voice. "We just—we've got a problem at the house."

"At four in the morning?" Chase rolls off the twin mattress he's been sleeping on since moving into the abandoned efficiency. He gets to his feet.

"You know that back room in the basement?"

"I told you: the basement's off limits."

"I know, but... someone got into that room. And it's locked."

Chase isn't following. "So have them unlock it."

"That's the thing. The guy—he must've passed out. Do you have the key?"

"So what are you saying, Max? What's really happening?"

There's a long silence, then a hushed response: "We're worried he might be... in trouble."

"What kind of trouble?"

"He might've overdosed."

"Shit." Chase crosses the tiny room and turns on the light above the kitchenette. "Call nine-one-one."

"It's not that bad," Max insists.

"How do you know how bad it is?"

"Are you going to help us or not?"

Chase sighs. "It'll take a while. The truck's in the shop. So I have to walk."

"I can pick you up." Max hesitates before asking, "Where are you?"

"Meet me at Blimpy's in ten minutes."

Of all the properties Chase owns, he pays least attention to the Forest house. It looks about the same as it did in '78, save for the new windows he got installed five years ago and the fresh coat of paint he slapped on the trim. Other than that, Chase only visits to fix damage before new renters move in. And for the last two years, with Max living there, handling upkeep, Chase doesn't even do that anymore.

When he follows Max through the front door this early April morning and takes in the scene across the haze of sparse light and smoke, Chase feels the same dread that seized him the day he rescued Leah. Three guys slouch on a beat-up couch, faces flickering blue from whatever's on the laptop they're huddled around. They don't even bother to look up. At the table where Boz had divvied up weed, two girls sit, gazing into their phones. There's a muffled clamor of voices coming from behind the porch door where Chase first saw Leah naked. And in the kitchen, a guy crouches in front of the fridge. "I'm so tired of everyone taking my food," he says as Max and Chase pass.

"Who are all these people?" Chase grumbles, following his son down the stairs into the basement.

"Can we talk about it later?"

Chase takes in the clutter. It's pretty much how he remembered it—rickety shelving, ancient paint cans and crates full of forgotten tools. A path has been cleared through the junk to a metal door in the far corner. A girl's sitting on the floor there, elbows on knees, head hanging between them. She looks up as they approach.

"This is Maggie," Max says. "She's—a friend."

Chase gives a little grunt as he fishes a keyring out of his coat pocket.

"I heard some moaning," Maggie reports.

"That's good," Max says.

"Nobody should be down here to begin with," Chase mutters. It isn't until the fifth key that the lock turns. Chase pushes in the door, steps over a pile of clothes, and takes in the passed-out kid, sprawled face down on a mattress beside a stain of red vomit. "Holy Hell."

Max shakes the kid. Finally, there's a groan. "Maggie, go get Bruce and Carter. Let's see if we can get him upstairs." Maggie leaves. Chase scans the room. Beside the mattress, there's an empty pint of Jose Cuervo. And under a small lamp that barely lights the room, Chase sees a baggie of powder, a spoon, and a syringe. That's when he notices the gold hose knotted around the kid's arm.

By the time Maggie returns with the two guys, Max has gotten the kid mumbling. They manage to lift him up, loop his arms around their shoulders, and lug him out of the room. "You gonna call nine-one-one?" Chase asks Max.

"I thought I'd get him some coffee and… sober him up."

Chase points at the syringe. "He needs more than sobering up"

"Dad—"

"Don't *Dad* me. Call nine-one-one. Who is he anyway?" Chase kicks at the piles of clothes on the floor.

"Just some guy."

"I'm guessing he's not on the lease."

"He was just hanging here. He—" Maggie calls down to him then. He escapes before Chase can grill him any further.

Chase scoops up an armful of clothes and throws it out of the room. Then he stands up the mattress and files it out the door. After that, he gets the pint, spoon, syringe, and baggie of dope. As he's leaving, he notices a shirt behind the door. He picks it up—and finds a phone and a pistol. Chase slides the pistol into his coat pocket. Then he turns on the phone. One swipe and he's past the lock screen. He checks the contacts. The top name reads "COLE" and the face that grins back at Chase is unmistakable. He taps Cole's thumbnail.

"Brandon?" There's panic in Cole's voice.

"This isn't Brandon. It's—it's Chase Tyson."

"Wait. What? How'd you get this phone?"

"I got it from your son," Chase starts. "I—I just found it now."

"He's not my son. Where is he?"

"He's... he's had some drugs."

"Shit."

"We're calling nine-one-one," Chase says.

"Where are you?"

"I'm in the basement of my house on Forest."

"What are you doing there?"

"That's where he is."

"I'll be right over," Cole says.

Chase comes up into the kitchen to find a broken beer bottle marooned in a puddle. There's a kid with his back to the spill, pondering an open cabinet. "What the fuck?!" Chase barks. The kid turns slowly, dazed, slack-jawed. "Did you do this?"

The kid studies the spill like he just noticed it. "No, man."

"Who are you?"

The kid chuffs out a laugh. "Dude, I live here."

"Well—*dude*—I own this house. Are you on the lease?"

"Yeah." The kid scratches at his hair.

"What's your name?"

"Mark."

"Awright, Mark. Clean up this mess." Chase goes to the sink, yanks a roll of paper towels off its holder, and tosses it on the floor. Then he stomps away, barges through the door to the party room, and flips on the light. Faces turn to him in the smoky haze. "Cops are going to be here in five minutes. If you don't want to meet them, gather up your toys, and head out the back door right now."

Max faces Chase in the hall. "Dad, what the hell?"

"What the hell?" Chase barrels past Max. "This is my house."

In the front room, they've cleared a space on the couch for Brandon and propped him up with pillows. Maggie's trying to get him to take a drink of water. He keeps pitching forward and snapping back. Chase switches on the overhead light.

"We got this now," Max says. "I called nine-one-one."

Chase waggles the phone at Max. "I found this down there. And I called a number. They're coming, too."

"You're making too much of this."

"Outside," Chase orders. He leaves so fast Max has to run to catch up. Chase wheels around in the driveway. "That kid could've died. And you think I'm making too much of it?" Max starts to object, wavers, and sighs. "You told me you'd take care of this house. That you'd be the landlord. You think a landlord would be okay with this?"

"No."

Chase simmers. When he speaks again, his voice is softer. "Son, if you can't do the hard things, you can't do the job."

"I was going to call for help, but one of my friends said—"

"See, that's the problem. You let in friends and you lose control."

"Sorry." They stand together in the cold through a long silence, each shuffling their feet. Max blows on his hands. Chase stuffs his in his coat pockets. The hard fact of the gun shocks him.

"I meant to ask," Max says. "Are you coming tomorrow?"

"To what?"

"That thing. At Rackham. The Hopwoods."

Chase rubs his forehead. "That's tomorrow? Is your mother coming?"

Max looks away. "I didn't ask her."

"You can't do that, Max. You can't."

"Why not? After what she did to you?"

"That has nothing to do with this." He pauses. "Ask her."

"We don't talk anymore."

"Then start." There's more silence. They hear the surge of car engines stuttering down the gauntlet of stop signs on Hill Street. Before long, headlights wheel onto Forest.

"He just got sick," Maggie calls out from the front door. The car turns into the driveway and the lights swing onto them.

"Go get him cleaned up," Chase says.

Max hurries into the house. Maggie closes the door just as Cole gets out of his car. "Where is he?"

"Inside," Chase says. "He's coming around, but..."

Cole takes in the looming silhouette of the house. "You still own this?" he asks like there's fault in it.

"Yeah."

Cole nods, still gazing at the house. "Karma," he pronounces finally, before heading up the walkway to the door.

"Wait."

Cole stops. He takes a long shivering breath. "I know what I'm walking into."

Chase pulls the baggie of powder out of his pocket and holds it out. Cole takes it and lifts it up into a shaft of light coming out of the cracked door. "Goddamn drugs." He unseals the baggie and turns it over. A small plume of mist rises from the grass where the powder landed. It looks like the cloud from a bomb miles below him. Chase tries to think of something to say. But he can't get that image out of his head.

Cole grinds the drugs into the lawn with his shoe, then bounds up the steps and disappears into the house. Chase stares down at the clearing mist. He readjusts the gun in his coat pocket. Then, with what seems like great pain, he climbs the steps to the house his father bequeathed to him when he was younger than Max.

18. Lost

Kip pulls into the handicapped spot near the back entry of the office building at Main and William. It's 7:30 in the morning. Kip doesn't plan to stay long. He doesn't think he'll get the chance. He gets out his phone and calls Asbury Lowe, the law firm on the top floor of the building. Then he navigates through the company directory to Carrie Asbury. She answers right away. He fooled her. "You won't even answer a text? I had to break into the house."

"You broke in?"

"What do you expect? I had more in there than my clothes and records. There was that whole stack of stuff by my nightstand."

"You mean my books?"

"Not your books," Kip says. "Those folders with the song ideas."

"Fine. But you didn't have to break in—"

"There's a lot more I could've taken. The keyboard, the TV—"

"How did you get in?"

"Why are you locking me out anyway?" Kip blusters, in spite of himself. He decided on the way over he wouldn't lose his temper. "Aren't we even going to talk about this?"

"No. We're not."

"So we're just going to throw away twenty-odd years like that?"

"Like what?"

"Like... *this*," Kip says as if the new word describes it perfectly.

"No. I want to know what we're throwing it away like."

"What do you mean?"

"My best friend calls me from Vegas and says you're with another woman—a younger woman—and you're holding hands across a table and there's a little gift box between you. That's what I mean."

"I admitted that."

"That's what I'm throwing it away like. Like I've been cheated on. Like I've been played for a fool."

"Carrie, just give me five minutes. I'm in the lot right now."

"I should've seen this coming. All the trips out west, the pow-wows with your mystery music moguls. How long's it been going on?"

"That's what I want to talk about. I want to be… straight with you."

"It's a little late for that."

"I'm not doing this over the phone," Kip says, as if he had any right to dictate terms. "Just come down and we'll talk."

"You never answered: how did you get in?"

"I broke one pane on the back door. Then I put cardboard on it. It's no big deal."

"No big deal? You cheat on me. You break into my house. Who knows what you really took—"

"I'm paying half the mortgage!"

"God. You're incredible."

"Look. Do you want to talk about this or not? I don't expect to change your mind, but I figure you at least deserve to know the truth."

"A confession," Carrie says. "From the man who can't have a sincere conversation if his life depended on it. This ought to be good."

"What does that mean?"

"It's like you're always playing at life, playing to some great audience in your mind."

"Gosh, Carrie. Tell me how you really feel."

"Don't turn this on me. Don't you dare turn this on me."

"Do you want to hear me out, or not?"

Carrie's answer is barely audible. "I'll be down."

Kip gets out of his car and goes to the security door. It's a brittle morning. Carrie is taking her time coming down. There's nothing to do but watch people walk up William on the backside of town, each hurrying to take their place in the performance of another day. Or so Kip imagines. He blows into his hands, wondering vaguely what part he's playing and how he should practice for it. On the drive over, he actually *did* rehearse what he'd say, how he'd come clean without devastating Carrie. How was he going to start again?

Kip doesn't get the chance to collect his thoughts. "I'm not coming out there." Carrie's glaring through the cracked-open door. He turns with his hands open at his sides, already in surrender. "You can come as far as the lobby."

Kip follows her into the vaulting lobby. She sits in one of the two swivel chairs that face the elevators. Kip slumps in the other. They stare at the numbers above the elevators, as if expecting someone to join them. The lobby walls are museum white and reach up three floors. The space could use artwork. As it is, the "Unraveling Couple in Swivel Chairs" is the only exhibit. "I'm waiting," Carrie says.

"This isn't easy," Kip starts, just as he'd rehearsed. "I never wanted this to happen. Believe it or not, I was trying to make it *not* happen."

Carrie swings her chair around to him. "What the hell are you talking about?" Her voice reverberates in the lobby.

"I don't deny what you heard. But you don't know the context."

There's a gust of traffic noise. A woman bustles in from the entrance on Main. She glances at Carrie, strides past, and goes into the stairwell beside the elevators. Kip gazes out the glass façade that separates them from town. He has a sudden urge to run through it.

"I can't imagine a context that makes it okay to have an intimate dinner with another woman," Carrie says, "and give her jewelry."

"See? It's that kind of assumption that's distorting things."

"So there wasn't a gift box on the table? Because—"

"Yes, there was a box. But *she* was giving it to *me*."

Carrie pushes the lap of her skirt flat. "How does that matter?"

"She thought we were there for an anniversary. I was there to tell her we were done."

"An anniversary? How long, Kip? A year? Or is she still young enough to count in months?"

"That's not the point." Kip stops as the drone of Main Street swooshes in, and another person tromps across the lobby. Kip uses the time to compose himself. "The point is, I told her about us. I told her I was done. And I told her I was moving back."

"Moving *back*?"

Shit. You've said too much. "Yeah, back here." He glances past Carrie to the high panes of the glass entrance.

"So she thought your home was out there with her? Sort of like I thought your home was here with me."

"Yeah."

Carrie's eyes rise up the wall, as if appealing there to some silent jury. "So we were both girlfriends and mistresses at the same time."

"I wouldn't put it like that."

"How would you put it?"

Kip knows he's reached the moment he'd need to face ever since reading Carrie's text in Vegas. He leans forward, elbows on knees, and cups his hands in a single fist. "Margo and I—that's her name—we were…" He props his head on his hands. The silence settles with a kind of finality, like he's already said what he meant to say.

"You were?" Carrie prompts him with a quiet dread.

"We were married. It was a mistake. I knew it right away. And it was wrong to keep it secret. But ten years ago—"

"Ten years?!" Carrie cries out so loud it echoes.

"Carrie. It's over now. Or will be. I told her last night."

"And you kept telling me you didn't believe in marriage."

He opens his mouth, but all that comes out is a weak gasp. Carrie stares at him like she's taking him in for the first time. Her lips curl. Her eyes blaze. Someone comes in from the back door and stops in front of the elevators. Carrie's head begins to shake, not so much in disapproval as with a tremble. "You're inhuman," she declares.

Just then, the bell dings. She springs out of the chair, marches across the lobby, and straight into the elevator. The doors close with her still facing away from Kip.

He sits alone in that swivel chair in the lobby of the building at Main and William through countless entrants, some hurrying up the stairwell, others waiting for the elevator. As still as Kip is, any of them could've mistaken him for the exhibit the lobby seemed to need. But at some point, as if on cue, he rises. It's with the slow deliberation of someone who mistrusts his balance. Then he steps across the lobby, passes a woman pulling her arm out of her winter coat, and disappears out the back door.

It isn't until he's in his car with the engine running that Kip realizes, with a kind of removed curiosity, that he has nowhere to go. "I'm lost," he says out loud. He sniffs and squints like he's trying to read something that's too small. Then he pulls out.

19. Street People

The Beast

Boz climbs the steps from his basement room on Arch Street into the morning sun. That's when he sees the splattered stain on the sleeve of his trench coat. There's a wedge of snow beside the house. He rubs some of it against the stain. The wet sleeve clings to a lump along his forearm. He shakes it until the ridge isn't so defined.

Boz heads toward Packard and State. At the corner is Bell's Pizza, a ramshackle store that looks more like a gas station. Boz goes inside. "The Bozman!" hails a kid behind the counter, stretching dough into a pie tin.

"Where's Art?"

"Back in the freezer."

Boz starts to go behind the counter just as Art, the manager, comes out from the back room. "Let's talk outside." He's holding a box with a blue Bell's coupon flyer taped on top. He takes the lead to the State side of the store, where no one inside can see.

"What the hell?" Boz grouses.

"Take it easy. I just—I didn't want to say this inside."

"I'm doing exactly what you told me to do."

"I didn't tell you to go to the dorms. I got a call from East Quad. They said our flyers showed up in some of the halls."

"What's wrong with that? That's how it we did it thirty years ago."

"Yeah, but it isn't now. Not just because the university has rules, but because that's what your parole says."

"It's all the same," Boz mutters.

"You're getting decent money to do a simple job, Boz. Just stick to the kiosks." Art hands him the box of flyers.

"These are worthless on the kiosks," Boz says. "If you want to stand out, I'd make a big roll that wrapped around the whole thing. Everyone plasters flyers all the way around the kiosks now. It's crazy. You want a law? There's a law: one flyer per kiosk."

"What's wrong with your arm?" Art points at the wet sleeve.

Boz glances at it like he's just as baffled as Art. "Beats me."

"Looks like you broke it," Art says and heads back inside.

Alone now, Boz faces the traffic waiting for the light at Packard. A guy in a Charger peeks at him. Boz yanks up the flyer from its taped end on the box and steps in front of the captive car. The driver pretends not to notice. Boz pulls up the windshield wiper, slides the flyer underneath, and snaps it down. Then he gives the driver a tip of his fedora. When the light goes green and the car rushes away, Boz flips up his middle finger. He can't help himself.

Can't help himself, my ass, Boz thinks—*or did I say it?* To remind himself of the difference, he utters slowly, "Do not fuck with me." He doesn't head off until he's settled himself. *It's important to stay calm*, he thinks—and he knows he was thinking it this time because he's concentrating to keep his mouth closed.

Boz crosses Packard slowly. He passes the Blue Front party store and stops at a traffic pole by a side street that angles into the student ghetto. There's a black flyer on the pole with a gargoyle head below yellow letters that read, "Feast for the Beast: April 28. Blind Pig." A shiver runs through Boz. "This is what I mean," he mutters, glancing around to make sure no one's watching. He takes out a flyer and the roll of tape Art put in the box. He covers the gargoyle poster then hurries away.

A giant monolith of a building, one of the newer university constructions, looms over the intersection of Hill and State. The thing seems to tumble off the hill. "It isn't tumbling off the hill…" Boz argues. Then he slaps his hand over his mouth. *It's charging off of it, down on all these lifeless fools.*

An older woman at the corner peeks at him. "Not you." He makes a gun with his hand and swings it up the sidewalk. "All of them. Look at 'em! Sucked into their phones, plugged into their iPods. They *are* pods!"

A university police car crests the hill and cruises by. The driver stares Boz down. He faces forward and settles himself. "Alright, alright. I get it." He buries his chin below the ridges of his collar. "Keep it to yourself, Boz. Don't act up."

He's passing the new building for the law school, an imposing structure, built in the same Gothic style as the old Law Quad. Boz snickers, at first concealing it, then forgetting himself again and leaning back with an open-throated laugh. "And that's supposed to fool us!" Boz falls silent, but you can tell by the way his hands keep moving, he's still trying to figure something out. *You can still get away with thinking*, he thinks.

"He *thinks*"? I *thought!* See what they do to you? And I don't even go in these buildings. These "halls of knowledge." Knowledge, my ass. These poor kids. Their parents actually pay to put them here. And for what? So they can fuel the machine. Get reprogrammed to perpetuate the system, serve the secret circle. Feast for the Beast. Damn straight.*

At the three-way stop where South U comes into State, there are enough people that Boz either loses or hides his train of thought. He crosses State, avoiding the class buildings, a superstition he's observed since being released from prison in the fall. *Not superstition: preservation. Why go near the mouth of a monster?* An older man in a black overcoat gives Boz a glance as he passes him in the walkway. Boz reaches up in surrender, his one arm bent like a dislodged bone. Then he presses a finger to his lips. *Okay, okay. I'll be quiet.*

Boz stations himself behind a pole so he can see across the whole intersection. He takes a flyer from the box, pulls the tape out, and, as he fixes the sheet to the metal, watches the ungoverned routine. "*Ungoverned*... that's what you'd like us to believe."

Watch. There! And there! Look at how many are glued to their phones, staring into screens, tethered to wires in their ears? They think they're free. They think they're in control, that they can watch whatever they want. But who's watching who? Who's really in charge? That's the genius of the Beast. All these tempting toys, they can't put them down. They keep staring into them. And they never suspect someone's staring back.

"Someone's staring back!" Boz hacks out, pretending to cough. He shuffles up the sidewalk. A woman sitting in a bus shelter raises her eyes as he passes. He winks at her. "Don't let 'em empty you," he warns of the corner of his mouth.

It only makes sense. To fill you up with their shit, they have to take something away. And what is that? "You lose your soul!" Boz barks as he ducks behind a kiosk on the side of the Michigan Union. At the bottom, there are two rows of maize and blue flyers about the Men's Glee Club, taped all around the cement cylinder. Boz rips down one loop of flyers, then glances around for somewhere to get rid of it. *How can there not be a trashcan around here?* A clutch of panic squeezes his throat— "I'm in control!" he blurts out. Then, as if his words conjured it up, a trashcan materializes near the side entrance to the Union. "I'm in control," he repeats with giddy defiance, marching over and jamming the twisted roll of papers into the can.

Boz heads off toward The Cube, the giant black sculpture balanced on a corner. "Bigger than the cell they put you in," Boz points out to no one. *Glee Clubs and spinning cubes. They need something to distract you while they suck out your soul.* Boz raises his crooked right arm as he passes the cube. His wrist clanks when it contacts the metal and gets the cube spinning. *It's all so clear now. I know how to fight it. They can't do anything if you stay strong in yourself.* "Stay you!" Boz bellows at a woman hurrying past. She flinches and scuttles away.

That's the mistake all the bums make who hang around campus. They've got the right idea. They know to resist the Beast. But then they get seduced by drugs. Not just pot or coke. It's the smack. Stand anywhere around the bars, in the arcade, near the Diag. Stand and wait. They'll come begging. Those sad junkies. They need to score as bad as the zombies need to stare into their phones. They're just as lost. But they do serve a purpose. They're the warning: here's what happens when you don't follow the rules. *The junkies are there to make you afraid. You don't think they could round them up if they wanted? Where do you think the heroin comes from?*

Boz casts a cold glare up at the Administration Building, the massive brick block with the tiny glass portals and window strips, a nightmarish Mondrian puzzle. The myth was that it had been built in the sixties to be riot proof. "Myth, my ass," Boz grumbles. He takes an angry swipe at a light pole when he gets past the building. His forearm clanks again. "I did that junkie I robbed a favor," Boz mutters. Then he stops. "I'm giving out mercy!" he shouts. A man crossing Thompson takes out one piece of a hidden earphone. "Are you with them?" Boz jerks his thumb at the riot-proof building.

"Sorry," the man says and rushes off.

A couple knocks on the head. Big deal. He'll get over it. Taking the money was a favor. He just would've used it to score. Boz forgets himself on the quiet stretch heading to Division. He flails wildly with his unhinged rant. "Unhinged?" Boz yells. "*Unhinged?!*" He flings out his arms. Something flies from his coat sleeve. It clatters against the sidewalk. He lunges to scoop it up—a miniature baseball bat. "Our secret," he whispers, sliding it back up his sleeve.

It's impossible to miss the red splotch on the barrel before it disappears. "Shut up!" Boz yowls, eyeing two men in overcoats who stop to stare from across Division. "Just shut up!"

The Ghost

*A*re you here, Ben? Do you see that graffiti across the street? That eye, the Great Eye of Ann Arbor that gazes out from beneath the railroad trestle and straight into your soul? Will you open yourself to it?

Can you feel your soul shifting in your chest, the weakness of your body to contain it? Stare straight into the Eye. Meet its gaze. Pretend you aren't here, that every part of you has flown away in the breeze. Your guitar falls from the ghost of your shoulder and jangles on the pavement. What would the Eye see on the other side of you? The poor and weak and forgotten, all dreaming on their cots in the homeless shelter. Imagine their souls stirring, too.

Hold on to this, Ben. It's time to turn from this fathomless gaze and believe. Believe that it keeps watching, that it follows you, pierces through and shines out of you. Climb the bank to the tracks. Walk out onto the bridge. Stand above the traffic and look down on Huron Street. Watch the cars flow under you. The bridge rumbles. Again and again. Go now to the other side.

Why don't you bury this somewhere else? A purple Crown Royal bag, poking out of these rocks. Down here where the homeless sleep. Do you want it taken? And so what if it was? What is money compared to a soul? Let it go. When you're under the bridge, go and touch the Eye. Feel it burn inside you. Trust that it stays with you. Trust. And be. Be good.

Take this sidewalk up the hill, beside the nightclub that beseeches "LIVE." Now: be ready. That man approaching. Feel his soul. It takes the faith of a ghost. He'll glance up—and when he does, look back. Kindly. Don't turn away. Imagine his body insubstantial, the soul leaking from it, swirling around him. Now this woman. Now these two. Everyone you pass. And the fading trails of the ones you follow. A crosswind of souls. Can you feel the trembling? Always, that trembling.

Up ahead, in the alley. He's there again. Same as every day. Curled up by that dumpster, hard on the pavement. Stop this time. Be with him.

"What the fuck you want?"

"I'll sing for you."

"You'll sing for me? *Shiiit*... You got any money?"

Give it to him. Take the money out of the purple sack. Set it down. Now go. Sing the song of him, the song of every soul you take in, the hundreds wafting through the streets.

If you listen, you can hear it already. In the clatter of those branches on that sapling. In the cry of birds swooping between buildings. Hear the humming din of the city, the unknown, unceasing chant. Listen. Let the song sing. The song of Crazy Wisdom. The song of the workers bantering outside Sottini's. Feel the song go through you. Feel it catch in the hollow of your guitar. Remember the song, even as it plays on, all the way up Liberty to Fifth, right to the moment when you sing. Then forget. Quiet yourself. Imagine the riot of your mind dispersing, all before you flooding in. Without judgment or understanding.

Let time cave in. Let the moments come to one. Here, before this old edifice, this ancient vessel of bricks, once a wealthy man's home, now a lawyer's office; Newbold, who once heckled you. Even here, in this oldest stonework, the song brings the spirits together. See the ghosts of Ann Arbor inside? See them entering and departing? Children of the dusty settlement, artisans in the bustling village, luminaries of the shining city, defenders of justice, wanderers through these unknowable streets. All of them here at once, all of them within.

Take them with you. Take them to Liberty Plaza, excavation site of outcasts and dreamers, endlessly reaped, endlessly renewed. Walk down to the deepest level. Sit. Take out your instrument and play. Play for the children of Ann Arbor, the dead and the living and the unborn, the townies and the transients. The Great Eye sees you. Play!

The Wretch

Not everything is worth seeing. The jeweler whose store on South U backs into the fenced-off alley knows Reese sleeps by the dumpster there. But he doesn't tell anyone about it. What would be the point? It would only bring trouble. Leave him alone. Set a bag of food by the fence if you want to help.

You *want* to watch him? Alright, but we can't get caught. If we keep a safe distance, he'll never see us, not with those eyes of his.

What are you looking for? Nothing has changed. Yes, he's slower and skinnier than the last time we saw him. That's what time does. And he's having trouble climbing that fence. So what? It wouldn't be so hard without the backpack. You try doing it with 50 pounds of books on your back. Yes, he's still stealing books for Kate. Is that so surprising? She pays him well—and even if she didn't, he'd still do it. He loves her. He's loved her since the moment he saw her. You know that. And you know nothing will come of it, either.

Don't worry. He always walks that way. He's been dragging that foot around for the last five years. Yes: he *does* look more hunched over. But, again, it's the backpack. See how full it is, how the straps strain on his shoulders and cut through the thickness of that ratty coat? You'd hunch, too.

Can we move on? We know where he's going. He'll turn on South U and head for the Raven's Call. Maybe he'll stop in the Diag. Sit on a bench there. Rest. But when the campus police roust him out, he isn't going anywhere else but to Kate. If we could help—if we could appear before him and carry his pack a while—that would be different. But we can't.

And there he goes—through the Engineering Arch and into the Diag. See? There was nothing to worry about. He's sitting down on that bench and resting— *Wait.* Who's that kid coming to sit beside him? Look at how pale he is, how dark and haunted his eyes are. Probably some junkie; you see them all the time these days. Now he's talking to Reese, cupping his hand over his mouth. What sort of secret would the two of them have? Alright: we'll get closer.

"This is it. This is my last bag of books," the kid says. "I don't want to get jumped like Riles and have my face all broken up."

"What are you going to do when you can't score?"

"I'll worry about that when it happens." The kid stands. He points under the bench at a bulky laundry bag. "It's heavier than usual," he says. Then he hurries away.

Classes end. Students stream through the Diag. Reese reaches down and grabs the laundry bag. He sits up slowly under the weight of his own backpack. He lifts the bag by the drawstring, ducks his shoulder under it, and stands. And now he's shuffling through the throng, stooped lower as the bag of books swings against his gimpy leg.

Alright, so maybe he's worth watching after all. Something's going to happen. Will he even make it to the Raven's Call?

The King

Ben sits on the lowest level of Liberty Plaza, sheltered by the half wall and switchgrass the city left uncut over the winter. He takes out his guitar. There's a huge black man pacing the level above him. He's wearing a ragged army coat and a grimy Detroit Lions sweatshirt, stained darkest where he wipes his hands on his bulging gut. All the street people call him the King of Liberty. He takes the title seriously. Anyone who sits in the park risks the King's wrath. "State your business," he'll command. Or he'll blurt out, "I ain't never seen you here before." Once every few minutes, he'll yell, "This here's a sanctuary!"

The King peers through the switchgrass at the hidden singer. "Play it cool, Mister Ben. Soft and cool." There's a businessman in sunglasses sitting on the bench in the corner closest to the Raven's Call. It's hard to tell if he sees the King coming, what with the sunlight on his shades. He opens an *Ann Arbor News* newspaper and shields his face. "You mustn't be from around here," the King calls out. "Ain't gonna find what's going on in there."

The man folds the paper down and stares up at the King. "You don't mind if I look, though, do you?"

"Naw. Just trying to be helpful. That's all. That rag don't say nothing anymore folks don't already know."

"I'll keep that in mind." The man looks back down at the paper.

"All good. Ain't no judgments here. This is a sanctuary you at. Understand what I'm saying?" He marches past the benches along

Liberty. When he gets to the plaza's main opening near the intersection, he notices a familiar intruder on the back side of the park, taping a flyer to the picket fence that defends a neighboring house.

"Aw Boz. Now we done talked about this!" He approaches his month-long adversary.

Boz is standing on one of the benches to reach the fence. He towers over the King. "I told you if you ripped these down, I'd be back."

"This is a *sanctuary*!" the King barks, spinning away as if appealing to the passersby on Division. "No agendas! No conflicts!"

Boz goes on taping up flyers. The King watches from a safer distance. "When you go, I'm just going to take 'em down."

"And what am I gonna do?"

"You just gonna put 'em back up," the King grumbles.

Boz steps off the bench. He's the taller man, but not nearly as big. "You keep talking about a sanctuary," he says with a savage grin. "How do we know you're not a plant, some mercenary for the Beast?"

"Mercy what?"

Ben starts to play. Boz groans. He bounds down the steps to where the singer's hidden away. "Don't start singing."

Ben stops mid-strum and closes his eyes. The King comes as far as the top of the steps. "Ben's got every right to play his tunes."

"So this is your idea of a sanctuary," Boz says. "No one's allowed to do anything, but we're forced to listen to this idiot's nonsense?"

Ben puts his guitar away. "Don't you mind him," the King says to Ben. "He can't help he got no heart. Hell, the music you make, you'd be better off uptown anyway. That's where the money is."

Boz huffs. "Nobody's paying to hear you play." He parks himself on the seat across from Ben. "That hippie-dippie shit's over with, even in this town." He leans forward. "You see what's going on. How can you not?"

It's quiet for some time. Boz contemplates how to clinch his point. And it's during this silence that Reese struggles down the handicapped ramp beside them, lugging a bulky bag and bent over under a bloated backpack. "How goes Reese?" the King calls out.

Reese stops and unbends himself as best he can. His good eye swings across the three. "Getting by."

"Just barely, by the looks of it," Boz observes. Reese puts a hawk's bead on Boz. He doesn't say anything, but Boz won't let the silence stand. "You're going to keel over from all those books you steal."

Reese turns to the King. "You hear about the beating last night?"

"Just that it happened. And Riles got his eye broke up pretty bad."

Reese heaves a wheezy sigh. "Ray said they clubbed him in that alley across from Starbucks."

Boz folds his arms. "Maybe if he wasn't walking around with a bunch of stolen books, he wouldn't have gotten jumped."

"Who said he had books on him?"

Boz blusters out a laugh. "Hell, he's one of your boys, right? It's either the books he steals or the smack he buys with what you pay him."

"Fourteen dollars," Reese says.

Ben makes his presence known, humming out a wounded sigh.

"That's all they got?" the King seethes. "That's what they jumped him for?"

"Fourteen dollars," Reese repeats.

"Shit," the King snarls.

"Well," Boz pauses for effect. "Fourteen less dollars up his arm."

The King snaps. "You a motherfucker! You know that?"

"Whoa, your majesty. Hold on. This is a sanctuary. Remember?"

Ben stands and loops the strap of the guitar case onto his shoulder. He pushes his hands into the front pockets of his jeans and stares at the ground. And he stays that way, standing between them all.

Reese continues down the ramp toward the backside of the Raven's Call. "I'll sing for you," Ben calls out to him. Then he starts off the other way, past Boz to the steps that climb a level higher.

"I'm sure that's a great comfort to him," Boz says.

Ben undoes his first step on the stairs. He turns part way to Boz. "I know who you are," he whispers. Then he stares straight at him. "The Great Eye sees you."

The smirk on Boz's face falls. He goes flush.

"What's that you say?" the King asks the singer, but Ben continues up the steps and across the plaza.

"This is a *sanctuary*!" the King reasserts, emboldened to see Boz so troubled. He whirls away in triumph and struts to the middle of the square. But out of the corner of his eye, the King catches the man with the sunglasses, flipping up the top of his newspaper again to hide his face. He slows and meanders off behind the cover of the park's switchgrass. Something's going on. The King's sure of it. He just can't figure out what it is.

20. Raven's Call

Most days, Kate doesn't get to the Raven's Call until minutes before she opens at 10. Even on Mondays, when Reese comes, she shows up just half an hour early. It doesn't take long to unload his books. After 20 years, they have the routine down. But today, she's in before nine. Today's the day she's been working to orchestrate for months. And this time is her only chance to make the call that sets everything in motion.

Kate sneaks down the unlit aisles like a thief. She always carries herself this way when she's in on off-hours. She checks her watch: 9:20, 10 minutes before Reese will be knocking on the door of the closed-off entry on the back side of the building. She slips into her corner office without turning on the lights. She can barely make out anything, but she can see the red phone light. Kate has the number memorized. After the second ring, there's a click and the howling drone of driving. "Tom?"

"Yes."

"This is Kate!" She musters a jaunty lilt in the darkness.

"Well, I'll be."

"You don't sound very excited."

He laughs. "I take it you got my number from Alec. And I'm guessing he didn't give it to you."

"No."

"Well, you're nothing if not resourceful."

"I'll take resourceful then."

"I didn't mean it like that."

Kate laughs. "So I can't hold a famous author to his words?"

"I'm not that famous."

"You're famous enough, Tom."

He laughs. "Famous enough for what? To convince Alec I'm worthy of speaking to literary neophytes?"

"He decided that all on his own." She figures that a plain lie might at least disarm him.

"You know, my first instinct was to decline. Not because of… us. I just didn't want to tarnish memories."

"So you cherish them," Kate says.

"Some, yes. Others…" Tom pauses.

And in that pause, Kate realizes the audacity of the hopes she's nurtured these past months. "Don't worry. Even in Ann Arbor, life goes on. That's why I called. I wonder if you have any time today."

"Why? Are we going to catch up, Kate?"

There's an edge to his voice. She chooses to ignore it. "If you want to. I thought we'd all get a cup of coffee and spend some time."

"All of us? I'll be seeing more of Alec than both of us can bear."

"You know who I mean."

"No, I didn't. But I do now."

"I'm not trying to corner you, if that's what you're thinking."

"I'm just wondering how a mother convinces a young woman to have coffee with an old man."

"As it turns out," Kate says, "Maggie's a fan."

Tom surrenders a long deflating sigh. "How did *that* happen?"

"I gave her some of your early books."

"So you *were* behind it."

"I'm always giving her books. She hardly reads any of them."

"If they were my early ones, I'm afraid I'll disappoint her. I'm not the same man. I've pretty much had the hope worn out of me."

There's a silence, more droning. Then Kate hears thumping from the back of the store. *Reese.* "I thought we could do it a couple hours before the ceremony," she gets to the point. "There's a café in the Bell Tower Hotel where you're staying."

"I don't know. It just doesn't seem like a good idea. For any of us."

This is the response Kate had prepared for. "Why would you think that? You'd get to see who your daughter was, and I'd get to see the two of you together."

"And her?"

"If we ever did tell her the truth," Kate raises her voice over the pounding outside, "she'd at least have this one time to hold onto."

"I would've thought you'd given up on the truth by now."

"Do you want to meet your daughter or not?"

"I just want to do what's right. Can I think about it?"

"Of course."

"Is this the right number to reach you?"

"I'll be waiting," Kate replies.

"Just so you know," Tom says, "I was going to reach out if you didn't." He hangs up. For a moment, Kate thinks she might cry. Then the pounding comes again. She hurries through the unlit aisles to the hidden back door. The comics spinner in front of it takes some doing to move.

"Thought you forgot," Reese mutters as Kate lets him in. He lugs the laundry bag over to the storeroom door and slides it off his shoulder. While he struggles to get his backpack off, Kate wheels out an empty book cart. They work together quickly. Reese passes books to Kate a title at a time. She arranges them on the cart. It's a system they've perfected over the years.

Kate's disappointed in the haul, but she resolves not to say anything. Reese would take it too hard. When they're done, she wheels the cart into the storeroom. It's 9:45. Susan, her day employee, will be there soon. Usually, Reese is waiting at the back door to leave by the time Kate comes out of the storeroom. But this morning, he's right where she left him, propped up on one knee, leaning against a bookshelf. He's hanging his head. There are blotchy sores on his scalp. "Are you alright?"

"Just need to catch my breath. Those hardcovers take it out of you."

"Tell them you don't want any. You're in charge." She holds out her hand. He takes it and works himself up to his feet. She's surprised how much help he needs.

"Riles got beat up last night," he says.

Kate picks up the bag and backpack and holds them out to Reese. "Is that why you only had the two bags?"

"Fourteen dollars. That's what gets me."

"What?" She unlocks the door and opens it. Reese hasn't moved.

"That's what he took off Riles. He lied there in his own blood with a busted-up eye until the cops found him in the morning."

"Come on, Reese. I have to open."

He finally starts moving. "They had to take him to the hospital."

All at once, the story comes to Kate. "The police were there? Did they find any books?"

"I don't know."

"You don't think Riles would say anything, do you?"

"No. He knows he's got a good thing." He swings his good eye to find her. "We all got a good thing."

That reminds Kate. "Oh God! I forgot your money." She checks her watch. "Can I get it to you later today? I'll give you an extra twenty."

"You don't have to do that."

"It's only fair." She tries to make eye contact with him, but he won't oblige. She notices how red his face is. "Come back at two. Not to this door. To the one in the alley. Remember that back hallway where I let you in to wash up?"

"Could I do that again? Just use the sink really quick?"

"Sure." She puts her hand on his shoulder and nudges him toward the outside. "But at two, okay? And don't knock. Just wait."

"Okay."

"And stay out of the stores on campus."

Reese steps out into the daylight. In the sunlight, he seems frail.

"You're not getting into what Ray and Riles are doing, are you?"

Kate sees the trace of a smile quivering on the good side of Reese's face. "I got better uses for my money." The way he tilts his chin, it seems like he's bragging. "I'm saving for a place of my own."

Kate wonders: *After all the books, all the payments, all the years, could he really have enough?* "That's a lot of money. Just make sure—" She's about to tell him to think things through, to be careful. But the phone rings. "We'll talk later."

Kate answers the phone expecting Tom. But it's another old partner's voice, muffled, urgent. "Kate? Kate, this is Hal."

"Hal? What are you—"

"Just listen," he cuts in, hushed and edgy. "I'm over at court, meeting some clients. I was in the hall and I heard something. They—"

"Hal," Kate interrupts, peeved. "I don't have time—"

"Just listen to me. They're watching you."

"What?"

"They're *watching* you. I don't know any more than that."

"Who?"

"I could get in trouble for this," Hal says. "Just—just be careful."

He hangs up. Kate puts the phone back in its cradle. And now she's out of her office, shuffling down the aisles like a sleepwalker.

"Did you want me to clean up the storeroom?"

Sue is at the register. "No. No, I need to—I need to do inventory. Can you open?" Kate doesn't wait for a response. She's already hurrying to the storeroom, her mind racing. She'll put the new books Reese gave her in boxes and label them "Charity." Then she'll push the cart down the aisles and take out every book that came from Reese. There's no way she can remember them all. But if she can get the ones since Christmas, that might be enough.

She turns on the light in the storeroom and finds the tape gun on the worktable. Behind that, there's a stack of flat cardboard boxes on a metal shelf. She picks out the smaller boxes, remembering how hard it was for Reese to push himself up from one knee. When Reese shows up at two, he'll have to make more trips to get rid of them. But at this point, it doesn't matter what he does with the boxes so long as they're away from the store.

Kate starts pulling the new books Reese brought off the cart and packing them into the first box. Then she stops. If they're watching, won't they know about the exit in the alley? It doesn't matter now. It's her only choice. She reaches for another handful of books.

Out in the store, the phone rings. Moments later, Sue pokes her head into the storeroom. "Your daughter's on the phone."

"Tell her I'll call her back as soon as I can."

"She sounds sort of upset."

"Tell her to call her father."

Sue backs out and shuts the door. Kate pulls more books off the cart. It's only as she's folding up the flaps on that first box that she thinks of Tom, on his way right then to meet Alec. Will her husband be taking Maggie's call with Tom sitting across from him? How could this be happening—on this of all days?

21. Visitation

Cole creeps down the long hallway to Brandon's hospital room. It isn't that he can't be there. Visiting hours start at nine and it's well after that. And it isn't the guilt of a healthy man among the sick. *It's the suit,* Cole thinks, as he passes room after room of bed-ridden patients. *I'm so out of place.* One patient, a woman about Cole's age, stares out at him, tethered to some unnamable machine. "Hello?" she calls out. Cole hurries on. *Who does she think I am?*

Midway down the hall, past the nurses' station, there's a crosswalk. Cole spies a bay of elevators off to the side. He stops. Maybe this isn't such a good idea. It's been nearly a year since Jackie told him she couldn't be with anyone the way he wanted to be with her. Now here he is, showing up on the day she always feared, dressed in some slick suit, like he cared more about making an impression than consoling her.

"Are you lost?" A nurse asks behind him.

"No. Just turned around." He points ahead and strides away, feigning certainty.

Brandon's room is the last on the right. When Cole cracks the door open, he sees Jackie first. She's in a chair at the far side of the bed, slumped over, sleeping. Cole quietly closes the door behind him as he enters. How long has it been since these two were so close and so peaceful? Never mind that one's sedated and breathing through a mask, while the other's exhausted with despair. Here they are, together, and for once there's no shame, no anger, no pain. Cole stands with them for a long time, preserving their contorted peace, long enough that his breathing settles in with the orchestrations of the room—the hollow gasp and catch of the ventilator, Jackie's soft snore, a monitor's heaving beep. And now Cole—a measured draw and release. It feels good to conform to this rhythm, like reaching an unspoken agreement. And he would've gladly gone on. But Jackie stirs. And now she's eyeing him across the dim light. Cole holds up his hand without waving. She eases out of the chair and comes to him, pointing to the hallway.

"Sorry about the suit," he apologizes as soon as she clicks the door shut. "I have a meeting later."

"You didn't need to come. I told you—"

"I know. But I said I'd check in."

"He's fine."

"Oh." Cole resorts to slow nodding. "Okay. Good. So…"

"He still needs help breathing. That drug they used to revive him… Nar… Nalc…"

"Naxalone."

Jackie glares at Cole, or so he thinks, but the look is gone as quickly as he registers it. "Right. They had to give it to him twice."

"So… so it was just the heroin, eh?"

"The heroin and the alcohol. And the vomit. And the collapsed airway. Just that."

"I didn't mean—"

"I don't know if I said it, but I'm grateful you were there for him."

"I'm here for you, too," he offers with a downcast gaze.

"I just don't understand why he called you."

"He didn't call me. The guy who found him did. Brandon had my number in his phone. I gave it to him once. If he ever needed to talk."

"One junkie to another."

Cole rocks back like he got slapped. "Something like that."

"Sorry. It's just—it's hard. After all the times he's pushed me away, when he really needs help, he doesn't come to me."

"He probably didn't want to hurt you again."

"He didn't succeed." Jackie's eyes glaze in the hall light.

Cole isn't ready for her tears. "This—this meeting," he stammers. "It's not important. If you need someone… if you needed to talk."

"What is there to say?" Jackie asks like she really wants the answer. But then she turns away. "I need to get back in."

"Okay. I was just checking in. It was on the way, so…" He trails off. She's already on the other side of the door and closing it.

Cole's face goes flush. He wheels around and hurries off, rushing past open doors for the hallway's far escape. He doesn't remember the elevators until the crosswalk splits in front of him. He veers into the bay, slaps the down button, and paces in front of the two doors. *Is that what I'm always going to be to her?* he thinks. *Just some old junkie?* All of a sudden, his shirt feels too tight. He tugs at the knot of his tie, loosens it, then yanks it apart altogether. The elevator opens. He flings the tie aside and steps in.

Moments later, Jackie runs past down the main hall. It's a long time before she returns. If she'd bothered to check the elevator bay on her way back, she would've seen the tie there in front of the doors, twisted like a bright broken snake.

22. Safe Arbor

Leah's been late to the clinic before, but never this late—a good half hour. She squeezes past a group of students coming out the door that leads to Starbucks on the first floor and Safe Arbor in the basement of the building at State and Liberty. She could use a Grande Pike. She hasn't been sleeping much since everything came out. But the line's a dozen deep. How would that look, showing up late, yet finding time to wait for coffee?

She hurries downstairs, into the clinic, and behind the glassed-in reception desk. Luckily, there haven't been any walk-ins. Of course, how would she know? They could've come and gone. A wave of guilt rises from the pit of Leah's stomach. She holds her breath against it. Lately, it seems like all she does is fight against these waves. She switches on the light in the office, starts up the computer, and takes the stack of forms she needs to input out of the inbox on the desk.

"Thank God you're here." Leah gives a start. But it's just Beth, another volunteer. "Kathy won't be in until noon and I've got someone in my office now, plus another appointment in half an hour."

"Did Kathy tell you I'm not counseling anymore?"

"I did hear that," Beth says. "I'm just asking if you could help any walk-ins get started with the intake form while I'm busy."

"I usually just hand them the clipboard. That's what Kathy—"

"I guess I'm used to Peggy. She walks people through the form."

"Oh..."

"But whatever's comfortable." Beth retreats to her office.

Leah scans the form, even though she knows the questions by heart: *How are you feeling emotionally today? Who knows about your situation, and how have they reacted? What is your relationship to God?* She takes down a clipboard hanging by a hook on the wall, presses the clip open, and snares the form with a snap. Then she slides open the window to the waiting room and sets the clipboard on the counter. Who is she to ask a troubled woman such personal questions?

Leah's inputting her third form when the phone rings. She takes a deep breath. "Safe Arbor Pregnancy Center."

"Mom?" Leah is too stunned to speak. "Hello?"

"Max..."

There's a long silence. Finally: "I don't know if you remember me talking about the Hopwoods back in December."

"I remember."

"Well, I found out last week that my short story won."

"Wow. Is that the award you said Arthur Miller won?"

"Yeah. That's... um... that's the one. They—they do this little ceremony, too, where they announce the winners. So if you wanted, you could see that."

"A ceremony? When?"

"Today at five. Sorry for the short notice. But it's right around the corner. At Rackham." Leah's quiet, taking it in. "You don't have to go. Lots of people won. They'll probably just read off the names."

"No, I want to go. I just need to sort things out. Is Dad coming?"

"No."

Leah cups her hand to the phone. "Did you talk to him?"

"I'm not getting into the bullshit with you and Dad."

"I just asked a question."

"Fine. Yes, I saw him this morning."

"You *saw* him?"

"Oh for crissake. Yeah. He didn't want to go."

"Because you told him you were going to ask me..."

"Not really."

"Where did you see him? He told me he was leaving town."

"Mom, I'm pretty sure he doesn't want you to know."

"You don't think I know that?" The door to the center swings open. "Just tell me. Please?" A young woman bustles in holding a large Starbucks. She surveys the room like she's lost.

Max relents. "I met him at Blimpy's."

"I know where he is," Leah says, eyeing the woman as she works her way around the posters on the walls to the reception desk.

"I figured you would."

"Thank you," Leah whispers.

"This doesn't mean I'm on your side. Because I'm not."

"How could you be?"

"What you did—"

The woman's in front of Leah now, sipping her coffee. "I have to go." She hangs up and slides open the glass. "Can I help you?"

The woman pushes a wave of dark hair off the side of her face. "I was told I could talk to someone here about getting an abortion."

"You can talk to a counselor, yes."

"But I take it you don't endorse abortions." She gestures to the side wall, where a poster shows a close-up of a woman her age under the headline "Parenting is Possible."

"We're here to give you information," Leah replies calmly. "We believe that the more you know, the better decision you'll make."

The woman smirks. "As long as I don't decide to get an abortion."

Leah feels a twinge in her cheeks. "That's not for us to judge."

"So if I talked to someone here and I still want to get an abortion, you'll refer me to a doctor?"

"No. We don't give that kind of referral."

"The kind where I make the wrong decision."

"That's not how we think of it," Leah finds her voice rising. She lets out a long breath and goes on, softer now. "We're just trying to help. A lot of women who come to us think they have to make a fast choice. We don't want that choice to be something they regret."

"No matter what I do. I'm going to regret it."

"Maybe. But you might regret one more than the other."

The woman lets out a sigh. "What would you do if you had a loser father who's long gone and a new boyfriend who'd be crushed?"

"People are more forgiving than you think."

"Is that really your experience? That people you hurt can let it go?"

Leah's face crumbles by degrees. "You should talk to a counselor. I'm saying the wrong things."

"I'm sorry. I didn't mean to upset you."

Leah closes her eyes. "I'd hate to think you left because of me."

The woman pushes her hair off her face again. "Maybe it would be good to talk. I keep going down the same ruts." She looks up at Leah. Their eyes meet… and hold. They smile sadly at each other.

"I think we'll have an opening soon," Leah says, relieved now. "Let me check the schedule. And while I'm doing that, can I get you to fill this out?" Leah holds out the clipboard. The woman takes it warily. "Fill out at much as you're comfortable with. All we really need is your name, number, and signature on the back."

"A signature?"

"Just to acknowledge you read our policy."

"I'm not sure I'm ready to sign anything."

"It's nothing you haven't figured out. It basically says that our bias is to support you in carrying your baby to term."

The woman scans the form. Leah looks for the schedule book, but it isn't where they usually keep it. She stands. The two face one another now through the glass. For a second, each is perfectly still, and in that moment, it strikes Leah how alike they seem—same pale complexion, same slight frame and fluttering eyes. The woman nods, as if agreeing. "I'll be right back."

"Alright," the woman says. Leah heads for the back offices. It isn't more than a minute before she finds the missing book. When she returns, though, the woman is gone. On the counter outside the glass lays the clipboard. Hardly anything's been filled out. She reads the name: *Maggie Bucksley*. She unsnaps the sheet and turns it over. No signature.

Then it hits her: *Bucksley*. She thinks of Kate in the backyard of the house on Forest. Those sad doomed eyes. Then she remembers that time at Top of the Park, when she told Kate that she prayed for her. She had her baby with her. Her daughter Maggie. Leah looks out the glass door of Safe Arbor to the stairway that leads to the street. She wants to run after Maggie. But no one would be there if another woman came into the waiting room. She deflates with a heavy sigh, sits back down, and sets the clipboard on the desk. It takes a while for her to accept that she's done the right thing by staying. As soon as she does, she remembers Max's call and how she knows now where her husband is.

23. Masks

Dean stands behind the bar in the shadows of Bar Brio. He has his back to the run of tables that extends the depth of the cave-like tavern. It isn't quite lunchtime. The place is empty. He scans the columns of cassettes housed in wood slots that climb as high as he can reach. He takes out a case with an old Dymo label strip and the embossed words "TROUT MASK REPLICA." A waitress comes out from the kitchen. "What are we playing?"

"Captain Beefheart."

The waitress groans. "For lunch?"

"People are just going to have to deal with it." Dean pops the tape into the dusty player.

"This is still a collective," the waitress points out. "Can we vote?"

A burst of jagged jangling fills the bar. "Sorry, for these last two weeks, it's all decrees."

"That'll go over well." The waitress walks away

Dean goes on gazing at the wall behind the bar. There are bottles on the high shelves he hasn't taken down in years, faded Polaroids of regulars cockeyed on crumbling corkboard, dented plastic masks that were there before he bought the place—Beetle Bailey, Casper, the JFK mask people keep asking to buy. A gash of sun lights up the masks. Dean turns to the door. The visitor is faceless at first, silhouetted in shadow, but her features emerge so fast they catch Dean by surprise. Carrie is standing across the bar. "Dean Harper," she states, as if she's calling one of her witnesses in court.

"Carrie Asbury."

"So this is Bar Brio." Carrie takes in the place with a critical frown. "I've never stepped foot in here."

"I know."

"How would you know?"

He twirls a finger at the ceiling. "I've got this whole place bugged. I watch the tapes every night looking for you."

"No, you don't."

Dean chuckles. "It's not your kind of bar."

"Why not? I'm a townie. I like poor lighting and waitress abuse." She delivers the line as earnestly as everything else she says.

Dean laughs. "We're not really after the business crowd. We're focused on the Ann Arbor hippie elite."

"Not exactly a growing market."

"And that—" Dean throws his arms open to the empty bar—"explains this rousing success." They fall silent, staring at one another. Dean gives in. "How are you, Carrie?"

She makes a show of mulling it over. "I think I'm okay."

"That's a lot of reflection for small talk."

"So you didn't really want to know how I was."

"There's the lawyer I love," he says. "Putting words in my mouth."

"Right where they came from." Carrie grins.

Dean smiles back. "So to what do I owe the honor of our esteemed councilwoman's visit? Here to pay your last respects?"

"Did someone die?"

"Just this old bar."

Carrie settles into a mask of indifference. "Can I sit?"

"Of course. What are you drinking?"

"I don't suppose you have any good wines."

"Just Boones Farm. You know how us freaks fly."

"You're making fun of me." Carrie slides onto a barstool.

Dean wipes down the surface in front of her. "I've gotten defensive in my old age. How about a nice Russian River pinot noir?"

"You remembered what I like."

"Not at all. We just have a bunch of Kenwood to get through."

As he goes to the far end of the bar, two men enter and take the booth in the window. The waitress fills two water glasses beside Dean as he uncorks the Kenwood. "Who's your friend?"

"Just part of the old college gang."

Mel bats her eyes. "*You remembered what I like.*"

"Shh." Dean pours the wine, thinks about it, then adds another splash. Mel leans in to make sure he sees her. "What? We're trying to get rid of it." She smirks and heads off with the waters.

"Employee troubles?" Carrie asks as Dean sets her glass down.

"I own a collective. I have nothing *but* employee troubles."

She laughs. "How many years have you been here now?"

"When it's all said and done, around eighteen."

"I've been down at the law firm about that long." Carrie takes a big swallow of wine. "You'd think we'd run into each other."

"I see you every once in a while," Dean admits.

"Really? I've only seen you once. A few years back at Le Dog."

"Oh yeah?"

"You were at the indoor one. I got in line about five deep and didn't realize it was you until you asked Ilka for Cajun rice."

"Still my go-to."

"It's sounds dumb, but when I saw you, I got out of line and left."

"Why?"

"It just surprised me. I wasn't ready for it."

"*It* being me?"

Carrie holds her glass up by the stem and gazes into the shimmering liquid. "*It* being having to explain myself. Having to face the judgment of the only one around who knows what I wanted to be."

"Seems like you're everything you wanted to be."

"It's not so much what I became, as how I felt about it. I guess I thought you'd see through me. Anyway, I stopped going to Le Dog."

"Because of me?"

"I told you it was dumb."

"No, I get it. Once, outside Conor O'Neil's—" He stops. Mel's leaning up to the bar, a safe distance away. "What do you need?"

"Two Wolverine Ambers." Dean pours the beers and takes them to her. They exchange glances.

"Outside Conor O'Neil's…" Carrie reminds Dean when he returns.

"So I was walking to the Prickly Pear and I saw that guy who helped you in the brawl at Maude's. He was sitting at one of the outdoor tables, facing me. As I got closer, I saw he was with a woman, and even though she had her back to me, I knew it was you."

"Don't be too sure," Carrie mutters.

"The guy saw me, and he gave me this weird look, like we were in on something together. I turned around and hurried away."

"In on something together…" Carrie puffs out a dismal laugh and takes a big swallow of her wine.

"I didn't want to stand there with you and your—what? boyfriend? husband?—and explain that I was still stuck in the same rut."

Carrie empties her glass. "Well, you don't have to worry about that anymore."

"Want another?"

"What the hell." This time, Dean brings the bottle over. "That guy," Carrie begins as Dean pours a new glass. "There's a funny story there. Turns out he's been leading a double life. Had a wife out west."

Dean stops mid-pour. "You're shitting me."

"Nope. I just found out. We've been together for more than twenty years. And I didn't have a clue. How's that for stupid?"

"It's not stupid to trust the person you love."

"Love…" Carrie laughs gloomily. "You were the one who said I didn't know the first thing about it."

"You were the one who said that."

"Was I?"

Dean scratches the back of his head. Now he isn't sure, either. A couple comes in, walks by, and takes a table at the back of the bar.

Mel bustles past with a quick glance. "Well, if I said that, it was just lashing out. How would I know what love was back then?"

"You sure seemed like you did."

"I was certain about everything in my twenties."

"There are times in life when you can go one way or the other. That was my first time." Carrie stares at Dean. He stares back. They keep still, while everything goes on around them—the clatter at the tables, the jangle of the music, the pulsing of sunlight as people enter. Mel interrupts for another order.

"I'm sure looking back on things, you thought you had a choice," Dean says when he returns. "But there really wasn't a choice to have."

"Maybe not a concrete one, but more of a cosmic sort of thing."

"I'm cutting you off. You're starting to sound like a regular."

Carrie laughs, but it doesn't last long. "You never think about it?"

"Not like I used to. At some point, you just accept that everything happens for a reason."

Carrie wags a finger at Dean. "Unless you don't let things happen."

Dean hurries away to a businessman who's parked himself at the end of the bar. By the time he gets back, Carrie's finished the second glass. "Sorry. It's about to get busy now."

"That's why I came early." She pulls her wallet out of her purse.

Dean waves her off. "On the house."

"Oh no." Carrie sets a twenty on the counter. She stands and smiles softly at Dean. "I feel like I owe you enough as it is."

"I don't know what that would be."

She stares at him as long as she can bear, then turns away with a deep breath. "This wasn't as hard as I thought it would be."

"Wine helps."

"True." There's a long moment where Carrie just stands there. Finally: "I think I'll come more often."

"That won't be too hard."

"No. Once in the next decade ought to do it."

"I wish we had that much time," he says. "Just stop down in the next couple weeks. Or come to the closing party."

"I saw something about that on the door. How late do you close?"

"That doesn't mean closing time—" Dean suddenly realizes: *She doesn't understand.* She's looking at him now with a kind of faraway gaze. He sees the trace of the younger Carrie, the scared, hopeful face he pulled close to kiss.

"There's no way I can stay awake past midnight," she says.

"Yeah, that party's probably a bad idea," Dean goes along. "I'll be so busy, there won't be time to talk." He notices Mel standing off to the side behind Carrie. He motions to her. "I better…"

Carrie turns. "Oh. I'm sorry."

"No, please," Mel says. "I'm not that busy."

Carrie turns back to Dean and tips her chin. "See you soon."

"Take care of yourself, Carrie."

He watches her walk out into the April sun. "She didn't get that we're closing for good, did she?" Mel says.

"What do you need?"

"Another round of Ambers." Dean goes to the tap. "You didn't try to set her straight."

Dean yanks the tap open. "She had a rough day. She didn't need to hear my shit." He pushes the tap shut and slides her the first draft. "She'll figure it out soon enough. Or I'll tell her."

"Will you also tell her that we're moving to Portland?"

"Is that important?" When the last beer tops off, he holds it out to Mel. She doesn't take it.

"I thought you said you didn't have any ex-lovers in town."

"I don't," Dean insists. He sets her beer down and turns to pick a new cassette. The battered masks are right in front of him, staring their hollow-eyed stares.

24. Relics

Kip's been meaning to leave town ever since Carrie dumped him. He keeps telling himself, *one last thing*. But one thing keeps leading to another. Now, he parks off State Street and heads for the Diag to stomp on the big "M." If stepping on it when you get to school means flunking your first test, maybe stepping on it when you leave means putting trouble behind you.

Kip stands in the square with students flowing around him. He can see all the way through the Engineering Arch at the far end of the Diag to South U. It comes to him: a fold-out map of the U.S. would be handy for the road trip he's decided to take. He heads to Ulrich's, but the bookstore's changed since he'd been there last; there's nothing but school supplies and textbooks.

Kip decides to try Village Corner, the student ghetto standby. On his way, he thinks of another need for the trip: bourbon. When he reaches Forest, Kip sees that the whole building, including the Bagel Factory, is gone. In its place is a huge pit, surrounded by a chain-link fence. "FOR LEASE" reads the sign on the fence. Kip squints at the artist's rendering of faceless people flocking to the perfect shimmering high-rise. Ulrich's sterilized, Village Corner gone. *What else have they destroyed?* He goes down Forest. The bike shop's been demolished, along with the Mule Skinner leather shop.

Is Rick's still around? He cuts through an alley, and there's the Rick's, same as always, at the corner of the building. Kip is surprised he's so relieved. He looks down toward East Quad. The road's blocked off. He heads there anyway. Along the entire side of the dorm, there's a network of scaffolding. Some workers are milling around a nameless door. Kip steps between the barriers.

"What're you doing?" a worker calls out.

Kip crouches to peer into a window by the door. "Looking."

"Those barriers are there for a reason."

"Is that still a lounge?"

"Whatever it was, it's gutted now."

"Shit!" Kip barks.

"You got a problem?"

"This whole fucking thing's a problem!"

Kip storms away. The workers laugh. *The town's soul is getting dismantled, fixture by fixture, quirk by quirk, and no one cares. Why gut the Halfass? How many singers like Ben got their first chance there? How many will never see that chance?*

Ben…

Kip stops at East U. He could go right, back to his car. Or left, where there's more scaffolding. He goes left. *Why am I prolonging this? I've already got enough reasons to leave—and not a single one to stay.* He finds that Dominick's is still there, the old bar that felt like you were visiting an Italian uncle. What he wouldn't give for a sangria now.

He cuts through the Law Quad, that sandstone sanctuary, taking it in with a kind of detached perplexity. *Why have I never appreciated this until now?* As he leaves the Quad, it occurs to Kip: California's a long drive to make alone. He remembers the rideboard at the Union. Maybe there's a kid looking for a way home, someone who can take his mind off his troubles. But the rideboard isn't there. *Of course not. It's probably just a website now.*

The side door to the Union feeds out to the plaza that surrounds the twirling cube. For the first time in years, Kip thinks about his freshman roommate, Reese; how they stumbled through here with a parking meter on their shoulders. Kip gives The Cube a spin. The last time Kip saw Reese was at the Sunspot, when he hobbled out of the shadows. Kip pretended not to know him. He can still hear Reese yelling his name as he rushed away.

Relics

Kip comes up to the spot where they yanked out the meter. There's still one there, but it bears no resemblance to what they took as a trophy so many years ago. It's an "e-meter"—just a pole t-squaring into thick blue bars with space numbers on either side. It looks like a heavy sword jammed into the cement. Kip gives it a shake, like he and Reese did that night. It doesn't budge.

He heads back to his car. Forty minutes—that's how long his excursion took. And nearly every relic from his college days was gone. It dawns on him: there *is* one thing he can still get done. State Street Liquor is just around the corner. Kip buys two pints of Jack. He puts one in the inside pocket of his coat and carries the other in a paper bag across State, under the trees on the fringe of the Diag. This is where the outcasts of campus hang out—runaways, Hare Krishna, and punk rockers when Kip was in school, drug addicts and derelicts now. Kip sits down, opens the pint, keeping it in the bag, and takes a long draw.

Off to his side, a rag-tag band of drifters laze under a big tree, two girls and a guy. They look like rasta-gypsies. Across State, people weave along the sidewalk in front of Ashley's. Now and then, a red door appears between the streams. It takes Kip a minute before he notices the yellow awning above the door, with black lettering that reads "WAZOO." *What's that doing there?* The last time Kip stepped foot in Wazoo Records, it was on the other side of the State Theater, above the head shops. Kip takes a quick swig and eyes the lazing vagabonds. "You know how long that's been around?"

One of the girls pulls out an earplug. "What?"

Kip points at the red door. "That place. It's been around forever."

"Wow," the girl utters lifelessly.

"What are you listening to?"

"Music," is her snotty reply. It draws a cackle from the guy.

"I didn't figure you for the type that would listen to a lecture."

The guy sits up. "What type do you figure us for?"

Kip waggles the brown bag. "The type I could talk into a drink."

The second girl pops her head off the lawn. "I'll drink."

"Abbie…"

"Relax, Gary," says the girl who froze Kip out.

"Yeah, Gary. Relax." Kip walks over, holding out the bag. The first girl reaches to take it. He pulls it away. "Oh no. You don't get a drink unless you show me what's on your Nano."

The girl gives Kip the Nano. He sits down and exchanges his bag for the device. The girl takes a quick tip. Abbie scoots over for her turn. "So," Kip says. "She's Abbie, you're Gary… and you are?"

"Carly."

"Carly," Kip repeats, scrolling through her Nano. "The Gadflies. You like them?" Carly shrugs. "Gracious Daze?"

"They're solid." She takes the bottle from Abbie, has another drink, and holds it out to Kip. He catches Gary eyeing him.

"Have a drink, Gary. Don't disappoint the ladies." Gary takes a swig and hands it to Kip. "There we go! Now it's a party."

"How old are you?" Gary asks.

"Fifty-three."

"No shit," Abbie marvels.

"I shit you not." Kip puts the bottle between his legs as he cycles through the Nano. "Ah. The Stragglers. What about them?"

"Awesome," Gary breaks in. "Every album."

"I don't know," Carly says. "The last one wasn't so great."

"I hear you. We kind of ran out of songs."

"We?" Abbie reaches out for the bottle.

Kip hands it her. "I produce those guys," he says. "And Gracious Daze. And the Gadflies—who evidently suck."

"Bullshit," Gary cuts in. "What's your name?" He takes out a phone.

"Kip Knight."

Carly takes a swig and wipes her sleeve across her mouth. "So what's a big producer doing drinking alone on campus?"

"Who's drinking alone?" Kip opens the second bottle.

"You know what I mean."

"I'm not here for long. I'm gonna go to Wazoo, buy some CDs, then take off for California."

"Shit," Gary blurts out. "He *is* a producer."

Kip's eyes go wide like he's as surprised as they are.

"You're driving to California today?" Carly says.

"That's right. Wanna come?"

Gary laughs. "We just got here, man."

"I've been here since the seventies," Kip says. "This town's done. Trust me. The romance has gone out of it. It's no Berkeley."

"We're not going to Berkeley," Gary snaps. "We spent all this money to get here. We're going to stay awhile."

Kip slaps his thighs and gets up. "I'm going get those CDs. If anyone wants to come with me, stick around." He gives the second pint to Carly, then heads off toward State. *The day is definitely looking up.*

He bounds up the stairway to Wazoo. It's narrow and steep, encased with swirling day-glo murals. Kip feels himself careening; the liquor's kicking in. The store's packed tight with orange crates full of CDs and records. There's barely enough room for one person to walk around the lone U-shaped aisle. Fortunately, no one's there. Kip works his way around to the front register, where a long-faced man in wire-rimmed glasses solemnly prices a stack of CDs.

"When'd you guys move?"

The clerk peers over his glasses. "About thirty years ago."

Kip gapes in drunken wonder. "Where the hell was I? Hey! I got a long shot. You got local music, right?"

"There's a whole bin under that Stooges poster."

"You remember Ben Hadley?"

"I think I got a *Heaven's Road* in there."

Kip goes slack-jawed. "No shit! I produced that for him."

The clerk glances from Kip's face to his unsteady stance. "Really…"

"Yep. Back in—God—eighty-seven."

"Right around the time he lost his shit at the Sunspot."

"Yeah…" Kip starts thumbing through the local CDs.

"He's still around," the clerk says. Kip pretends he didn't hear.

Kip leaves with over a dozen CDs, all local artists—the Rationals, Commander Cody, the Silvertones, I-tal, the Urbations, the Stooges, the Confessions, MC5, a few bands he'd never heard of… and the album he helped Ben pull together. When he doesn't see anyone under the trees, he figures Gary talked the girls into staying. He turns for his car and there's Carly, slouching across the doorway of Ashley's.

"California, here I come." She holds a hand up for Kip to take.

He pulls her to her feet. "Where are your friends?"

"Chickened out. And Gary took your Jack."

Kip slings an arm around Carly's shoulder. "There's more where that came from."

In the car, Kip gives Carly the bag of CDs. "Pick one." She takes out the Stooges. By the time they turn on Liberty, Carly has the CD in the player. The growling reverb of "1969" gives way to a menacing groove. Carly stays quiet until the singer gripes, "It's another year for me and you, another year with nothing to do."

"Is this what I have to look forward to?"

"This is Ann Arbor's own Iggy Pop," Kip says. "Jim Osterberg."

"Is he that old guy with the twisted-up body?"

"That's the one."

"He should keep his shirt on." Coincidently, Carly leans forward and wriggles out of her coat. She's wearing a tight, sleeveless black blouse with a scooped back that exposes the tops of tucked-in tattooed wings. Kip takes long enough staring at the bright red, orange, and green feathers that he draws a beep at the stop sign in front of the Michigan Theater.

"That's quite the tattoo. How far down does it go? If you don't mind my asking."

"I mind you taking your eyes off the road."

"So?"

"So it goes all the way down my spine and the feathers tuck under the sides of my ass. Is that enough of a visual for you?"

Kip flushes. "That's a pretty scary commitment."

"No scarier than getting in a car with a stranger."

They're stopped at the light just before the old Le Dog shack. "Yeah, but this is just two or three days. Those wings are forever."

"True. But these wings won't kill me."

Kip laughs. "Do I strike you as a dangerous person?"

Now Carly laughs. "I don't know… an old man wandering the streets, plying little girls with alcohol. What do you think?"

Kip glides through the light at Division, past Liberty Plaza, mulling the turn the exchange has taken. "You don't have to worry, Carly. I'm a nice guy."

"I just don't want you trying anything I don't want to do."

Kip looks over, surprised she would even think that. "I probably won't be doing anything you *want* to do either."

"Well, *that's* a disappointment," she says, with an arched eyebrow and a playful grin.

Kip makes a quick right into a driveway. "This isn't a good idea."

"I was joking."

Kip puts the car in park and faces the young girl. "I'm old enough to be your dad. And if I *were* your dad, I wouldn't want you getting in this car."

"I haven't seen my dad since I was eight."

That stops Kip. They sit in silence for a long moment. Finally, Kip speaks. "Look Carly. I'm a nice guy, like I said. But I'm not really a good man."

"So you're kicking me out?"

"I'll take you back to the Diag if you want."

"No," Carly says with a long sigh. "I'll just call Gary."

"You sure?"

Carly smiles at Kip. "It could've been fun, you know? It didn't have to get heavy." She leans over, kisses him on the cheek, and gets out of the car. Kip waits long after the door slams before he looks up to watch her walking back toward campus.

He waits for the line of cars coming from Division. As he's looking that way, he notices the sign for a bar he's never seen before: Mani Osteria. When it's clear to go, he reverses into Liberty with every intention of heading out of town. But as he cruises up to Fifth, he can't remember whether it's the one-way road out of town or not. He sees an open parking space and does his best to parallel park going in front ways. It isn't a great job. The back of his car angles two feet off the curb. Kip doesn't care, and he doesn't even bother messing with the new sword-like e-meter.

I won't to be long, he tells himself. *One last toast to Ann Arbor. One last memory. Then I'll go.*

25. Angell Hall

Tom approaches Angell Hall between the Museum of Art and the red cartwheeling steel beams of a newly added sculpture. Even though noon classes are still going on, he finds it unsettling to be the only one going into the great hall. Formless shadows lurk behind the giant columns as he ascends the steps to the building's entrance. The granite staircases that lead up to the third floor have endured the wear of three decades pretty much how Tom would expect. What surprises him, though, is the flimsiness of the walls encasing the stairwell. He can't shake the feeling that he's backstage on the scaffolding of a fake building.

The receptionist leads Tom through a knot of hallways. He scans the nameplates on the doors. There are only a couple that he recognizes. The receptionist knocks on Alec's office door. A voice summons him in. Alec is standing behind his desk, profiled in the window, hands clasped behind his back. *How long has he waited in that pose?* Tom wonders. Alec turns and smiles. "Tom," he says warmly. You'd think they were friends.

"Hello, Alec. Sorry I'm late."

"We're just happy you could be here."

"I hope I didn't ruin lunch," Tom sets his bag on a nearby chair.

"You're Tom Whelan. They're going to wait."

Yeah, sure. Tom thinks. *They're dying to meet a washed-up novelist.*

"I'll call and let them know we're coming," Alec says. A minute later, he's apologizing. "I'm sorry. Apparently, everyone left about five minutes ago."

"It's okay. I have an errand before the ceremony anyway."

"Oh." Alec's eyes drop to his desk. "Okay. I just figured—"

Tom sees the disappointment. "We've got the reception later. You don't have to go out of your way now."

"Maybe a drink. We can shoot over to Ashley's."

"I don't think that's a good idea."

"No. Probably not. It's just... well... there's something I need to talk to you about. Something personal."

Tom feels himself tense. He thinks of Kate. And the child that might be his—now a woman. "We'll have time later."

"It's not the sort of thing we'd want others to hear."

"What's wrong with now?"

"Okay." Alec sits down and motions for Tom to sit across from him. "Remember the last time we saw each other? At the Michigan Theater?" Tom recalls it all too well. That was the night he broke it off with Kate and urged her to keep the baby. "I told you why you were wrong—about *The House of the Seven Gables*."

Tom clears his throat. "Something about the doors."

"Yes. The doors."

There's an uncomfortable silence. "So?"

Alec snaps out of it. "So, a few years back I reread your paper, and I finally got what you were saying."

"You're going to have to remind me."

"About Holgrave? As the secret narrator?"

"Ah yes."

Alec waits for Tom to say more, but Tom's waiting for him. "Anyway. I started examining the role of the narrator in American novels. And it struck me how much more important voice is than the story itself. Think about Hemingway or Faulkner with *The Sound and the Fury*. Hell, think about Salinger and Vonnegut. Especially Vonnegut."

"Okay." Tom shifts in his chair.

"My thesis is this." He sounds rehearsed. "The history of American literature is defined by increasing narrative intrusion."

"And how is this personal?"

"Because I'm writing a book about it. And I think it all starts with Hawthorne. And because I'd like to use your idea."

Tom leans back. For Alec to ask permission to use his argument after resisting it so vehemently comes as vindication, never mind that he can't recall exactly what he argued. "I don't know."

"I'd give you credit."

"Hell, you could've used it, and I never would've known."

"True. But it wouldn't be right."

"What I'm trying to sort out is if it's right to let my idea support a premise I'm not sure I agree with."

"I assume you still believe what you wrote."

"Maybe I need to reread it."

Alec's mouth tightens. The two men stare each other down in a stalemate of veiled intentions. There's a knock then. And now Maggie is peering around the door. "I'm sorry." She starts backing out.

"No-no-no. Come in," Alec says. Tom turns to behold a sharp-eyed young woman stepping reluctantly into the office. Breathless. Glowing. "Tom," Alec says with a sweep of his arm, "this is my daughter. And Maggie, I'm sure you know who this is."

Tom clambers out of his chair. "You look… just like your mother."

"I'm reading your book," she says.

"Well, I hope you like it."

"Of course she does," Alec breaks in.

Maggie smiles stiffly. Still, her eyes are skittering. "It's okay if you don't," Tom says. "I'm not crazy about it myself."

She laughs softly. "Not your new book. I'm reading your first one."

"My first one? I doubt that."

"*The Gulf?*"

Tom's head rocks back. "That *is* my first one."

"Kate put her up to it," Alec says.

Tom struggles to compose himself. "Well, if you don't like that one, I'd rather you didn't say so. I have a soft spot in my heart for it."

"It's my favorite." Maggie's eyes drift up to his then dart away.

Alec wags a finger. "I think I have a copy somewhere on the shelves. Maybe you could sign it for Maggie."

"I'd love to."

"You don't have to do that." There's an edge in Maggie's voice. "I can come back later."

"No, no. You stay," Tom says. "I have somewhere to be."

"Is there anything wrong?" Alec asks Maggie.

"It's nothing. I was just hoping for—" She breaks off. "I tried to call Mom, but she's not answering."

When Alec doesn't say anything, Tom looks over. He catches the two in some silent exchange. "I'll see you later," he says.

"I was hoping we could… finish." Alec digs into a stack of papers on his desk. "I have something here you can take with you."

"Don't worry about it. Use what you want."

"Are you sure? I'll send you the passage where I give you credit."

Tom waves him off and turns to Maggie. "It was good to meet you."

"I didn't mean to interrupt."

"A daughter coming to her father is never an interruption." He waits for Maggie to meet his gaze. When she does, he smiles. "I'll send you a signed copy of *The Gulf*." He edges past her in the doorway. "Nobody's ever told me that was their favorite."

She looks down and smiles—a small, secret smile Tom isn't sure she meant for him.

Then he's walking back out of the maze of hallways and down that flimsy stairwell behind the façade of the great building. Tom passes between the massive columns of Angell Hall and descends the broad stairway. His shadow goes jagged across the steps like a toppled stack of boards. He doesn't notice.

26. Forgiveness

Chase wakes to knocking. He reaches out from the floor mattress and finds his phone. It's just after one. How did he sleep so long—especially after all the tossing and turning when he got back from Forest? He works his way to his feet. His clothes are still on from the late-night scare, but it's cold because he hasn't turned on the heat. He picks up his coat, feels its heft, and remembers the pistol. The knocking comes again. He pulls out the gun and wedges it under the mattress. Then he throws on the coat and treads to the door. When he peers into the eyehole, Leah is staring back at him, her face a balloon in the lens—now shrinking, as if released.

"Chase?" He backs away. There's a thump against the door. When Leah speaks again, her voice is near the ground. "I know you're there." Chase looks across the room. The back window frames the far hills of the West Side. He thinks of sneaking over there, cranking open the window, and escaping. But he doesn't move. Finally he sits, back-to-back with his wife, separated by the door.

"It's not enough to say I'm sorry," Leah begins. "I know I've destroyed everything. I know I'm unworthy of anything but shame, and there's nothing I can do to deserve more." It's quiet for some time. When Leah speaks again, her voice is trembling. "I know I can't ask anything of you. I just want you to know that I love you desperately. And I'll live the rest of my life hoping, beyond any reason, that you'll forgive me."

There's scuffling on the porch. Leah's leaving. When he figures she's out of earshot, he calls out, "Isn't that what God's for?"

"It's not the same." He's surprised to hear her answer so quickly and so close. "God forgives everything."

"Then he's a better man than I am."

"It's because he knows we're inherently sinful. His is a spiritual forgiveness—for what was, what is, and what will be."

"What a comfort that must be. For you and Pastor Jim."

"He stepped down," she says. "And they asked me to leave."

"Where's the grace in that? They didn't get cheated on."

"In a way they did," Leah disagrees. "They put their faith in a man who let them down. And a lot of them blame me for that."

"Then their faith is misplaced."

"That may be true."

"Of course, I don't have any faith. I just foolishly believed in us."

"Don't do this." Leah knows where he's going.

"We've had rough times, but it was always my fault. It never occurred to me that you were… wanting in that way—"

"Me neither," she whispers hoarsely.

"I should've let you go when you got saved. I should've let you have a Christian man. That's what you wanted."

"No. I wanted you. I've always wanted you."

"It was wrong of me to pretend I'd ever find faith. I tried, Leah. I did. But I never had my heart in it."

"I love you anyway."

"If I had faith," Chase reasons, "I might have a chance of forgiving you. But I don't even know what that means."

"What faith means?"

"Forgiveness," Chase says. "What is it? What am I committing to when I say I forgive you? Am I absolving you? Am I pledging that I'm strong enough to forget—or too weak to muster anger anymore? Am I consigning us to a lifetime of suffering? What is it, Leah? Tell me what you're hoping for." Chase catches his breath with a shudder. "What is forgiveness?"

"It's a miracle," Leah says. She starts weeping.

Chase pitches forward and cups his face in his hands.

"You must've told Max to invite me to the ceremony tonight," Leah says. "He wouldn't have done that on his own."

"Maybe that's the miracle."

Leah laughs unexpectedly. "Maybe it is." There's a pause. "So, are you going to stay here now?"

"I don't know. I might leave town for a while."

"Do you want me to bring anything?"

"That's alright."

"What about the cat food? If you're keeping Cazzie, I don't need it."

"I don't have Cazzie," Chase says.

"Hmm."

"When did you see him last?"

"A few days ago. I figured you took him."

"No."

"Then I don't know where he is," she says.

"He's in the Arb. Every time he gets out, he goes down by the river. Just walk that old road there and call him. He'll come out."

"He won't come for me. He never comes for me."

"Are you asking me to find the cat?"

"I'm not asking you for anything," Leah says, full of anguish.

"I'll find the goddamned cat. Awright?"

It gets quiet, but Chase can tell Leah hasn't moved off the porch. Finally he hears, "I'm so sorry." Then the steps to the porch creak. He peeks out the eyehole. Leah's on the fringe of the fish-eye lens, flattening to nothing as she walks away.

Chase sits down on the mattress and puts on his shoes. Then he pats his pants pockets to make sure he has his keys. It isn't until he opens the door that he realizes what he's forgotten. He goes back to the mattress, picks up the corner, and gets the pistol. He checks the chamber, even though he already knows what's in it: two bullets. He stuffs the gun into his coat pocket and leaves.

27. Deciding

Cole gets a text during his Skype call, just before he's about to give an update on the big software integration project. It's from Jackie: "Brandon OK. Can you visit now?" He turns off the camera, opens his office door, and peers across the cubicles. There's only one person nearby, an intern who started with the group a month before. "Hey Dave. Can you help me with something?"

Dave swivels out of his seat. In the time he's been there, Dave's shown himself to be hard working, but anxious, like he's afraid he'll get fired any second. He's not the best person to cover for Cole. But there's no choice. Besides, the kid deserves a chance. "In five minutes, they're going to ask for my update. Tell them I got a call from GM, and I asked you to report that the project's on track."

Dave's confused. "It is?"

"Just say it is."

"What if they ask what the call's about?"

"What call?"

"The GM call."

Cole looks the intern in the eye. "Dave... there is no GM call."

The intern's mouth opens in a circle. "Oh."

Cole pats his shoulder. "Your first status meeting. You'll do great."

Dave nods nervously. Cole hurries away. He passes Joe Teegan's office on the way out. Teegan catches up with Cole in the parking lot. "Where are you going?"

"Out."

"Aren't you on this call?"

"Dave's all over it." Cole gets on his bike and rides off.

Deciding

Jackie leaves the room to wait for Cole. Brandon's asleep; no point watching a machine do his breathing. Cole's already striding down the corridor. She watches him come all the way down the narrow gauntlet. When he's within a few doors of her, he looks up, a fierceness in his eyes. "Everything okay?"

"He fell back asleep. They're going to take him off the ventilator at three. I was thinking I might like a walk."

When they get outside, they're next to the skeleton of the unfinished children's hospital, across from Markley Hall. "That's my old dorm," Jackie says. "Where were you?"

"East Quad." She gives him a knowing smirk. "And that's why I became a drug addict," Cole jokes.

Jackie looks away. "How *does* it start?" They walk along the sidewalk that slopes down to the entry of Nichols Arboretum.

"Like a lot of things," Cole says. "You try something, and it feels good. You feel free. So you try something else. And that feels better. Then one day, it stops feeling good, and you find you're not free at all. But you can't stop. And now you're trapped."

"That *something* for us was always just pot."

Cole scratches at his wiry greying hair. "Well. It doesn't take a lot of ambition to find something more. All you have to do is ask."

"So Brandon felt the need to ask…"

"Getting hooked isn't a sign of some grand flaw. That's the kind of logic that makes people feel doomed."

"I'd never suggest that to him," Jackie says. "Still, I can't help but wonder. I raised two boys the same way. One has purpose. And the other's… lost. How can you not think that his… darkness… has something to do with seeing his father get shot?"

Cole shrugs. Down where the home for troubled boys used to be, a run of chained-link fencing sweeps around the curve, closing off a lot full of construction equipment. Jackie stops and peers up at Markley. She sighs. "What can I do?"

"Nothing really," Cole says. "Listen. Let him know you're there for him. Hope he works it out."

"Hope is torture for me. I'd almost rather not have it at all."

"I know what you mean."

Jackie starts off again. They approach the entrance to the Arb. Cole thinks of suggesting they walk there, out to where they can see down into the open valley. But he remembers that that's where Grant used to picnic with her. Anyway, Jackie's already striding up toward Markley. It's busy there—students going to and coming from classes, gathering by the entry, goofing around, taking in the warm day. A street person moves between them, taping up flyers on the entry columns.

They stop short of the entrance. Jackie pulls up under the shade of a maple tree that vaults beside a stack of dorm room windows. She rises on her tiptoes and stares into a drapeless window off the ground floor. There's no one in the room. "I'll bet that's the same bed as when I was here."

"You're probably right."

"I fell in love with Grant in that room." She steps back. "It wasn't a decision. It was just a feeling." Cole squints into the sunlight. The number of students has thinned. The street person's closer. "In an instant, I knew: *this is who I love*."

"I guess it happens that way sometimes."

Jackie touches Cole's shoulder. It startles him. When he turns, she's searching his eyes. "I brought you here so you'd know. I'm never very far away from this place. I never will be. And I'll never get away from Circle North."

"I can imagine…"

"I'm not telling you this as an excuse. I'm telling you so you'll know my limits. I'll never be able to love another person the way I loved Grant. I didn't have a choice in that. But that doesn't mean I can't love another way." Jackie goes quiet. Cole allows himself to glance at her. "I've been wondering, does anyone our age ever get overwhelmed by love? At this point, isn't it always a decision?"

"I couldn't say."

"You can't say because you won't or because you don't know the answer?" Cole looks away. "You've been kind to me and the boys for a long time. It's not because you pity me, is it?"

"No!"

"And it isn't out of some sense of... indebtedness?"

"My God, Jackie! You have to know by now! I don't do it for any other reason than... than I love you!"

"Yes, but—"

"I can't help it. And you know it. But you ask me if it's only a decision." He turns away. The street person's just in front of him. Cole can't see through the blaze of the sun, but he figures the bum's watching all this.

"I'm sorry," Jackie says behind him. "I'm not asking you these things to decide about you. I'm asking to decide about me."

"What's that supposed to mean?" He turns back to her.

"How would you feel about my *deciding* to love you."

"Deciding..." Cole echoes with dismal emphasis.

"It's the best I can do."

"So you're talking yourself into loving me."

"Do you have a problem with that?"

He takes a shivering breath. "No."

"Okay," she says, starting toward him.

"O—" Before he can reply, Jackie's kissing him. When she breaks away, Cole opens his eyes. He's dizzy, like he'd been spun around.

Jackie is walking away from him now, down toward the Arb. Cole looks around, stunned, overcome. Only the street person is there.

28. Odyssey

Kate wheels a cartful of boxes back to the door outside her office, near the spinner of porn magazines. When she comes down the aisle, men scatter. Her friends always tease her about carrying so much porn. Kate defends it on the principles of free speech. The truth is, there's profit in it—if she can stop the shoplifting. That's why the spinner's by her office, in front of a one-way mirror.

Kate maneuvers around the spinner and unlocks the door. She enters a short hallway. At the far end there's a door they never open. It's an emergency exit that leads into the alley opposite the plaza. Beside the door, there are three stacks of small boxes. It'll take Reese a lot of trips to move everything, but she saw how much he struggled in the morning. Kate unloads the last of the books she can find that came from Reese. It isn't everything. After so many years, how can she be sure she's gotten them all?

She glances at her watch. Five after two. Kate opens the door and looks up and down the alley. Nobody's there. She takes a box, opens the door again, and places it so she can't be locked out. Then Kate gets another box and hurries down the alley toward the back lot. There's a dumpster enclosure on the far side. Kate opens the gate, hides the box behind the dumpster, then shuts the enclosure. Nobody's going to look in there in the next few hours. She rushes back down the alley and slips behind the propped door.

Where is Reese? It isn't like him to be late. Then again, he only thinks he's coming to get paid. It's probably better that he isn't early, hobbling around the alley, making a spectacle of himself. He looked terrible this morning. What if he really is sick? Would he go get help? Would the hospital even take him in? Why haven't I thought of this before? Kate paces the hallway. She checks her watch again. Her employee Sue must be wondering where she is. She cracks open the door. A man at the spinner jolts and slinks away. A knock comes behind her. She goes and opens the door. Reese is there, head hung so close all she sees is the scabbed top of his balding head. "You're late."

He lifts his face. It's pale and sweaty, smeared with strands of hair. "I got this." He gives her an old book the color of a grocery bag. It has stringy black letters stretched from top to bottom: *ULYSSES*.

"Where'd you get this?"

"West Side Books. They had it behind the counter."

Kate sighs. "What am I supposed to do with this, Reese?"

"You said not to go to the college stores," he mumbles. "The sign said this was five hundred dollars."

"I meant don't take risks." Kate opens the top of the nearest box and sets the old book inside. "I guess we're stuck with it now. Just—no more, okay? We can't be taking chances right now."

"Okay," he murmurs.

"Alright. I know I told you just to come back for your money. But we need to move these boxes."

"Can I get a glass of water?"

Reese's face gleams like melted wax. "Can we move the boxes first? They're not heavy. But if we don't get them out of here…" She stops, unable to reckon the consequences.

Reese swings his good eye onto the boxes. "Where to?"

"Behind the dumpster," Kate points down the alley. "Be sure to shut the gate when you're done."

Reese nods, shuffles around Kate, and picks up the box where she'd put the old *Ulysses*. She watches him strain to lift it. "We'll hide everything there until four-thirty. If you could come back then, I'll park my car right there so we can load it real fast. Can you be there? It's worth another fifty."

"Sure."

Kate is close to Reese now. He reeks—not like sweat or grime, but like something decaying. "I'll move the rest of these outside so it's easier," she says softly.

He swings his face away. "You didn't like the book…"

"Oh no! I liked it. I did. It's a first edition. It's just—I don't want to get caught." Reese sighs and looks off into the fading daylight.

"I'll have that water waiting for you," Kate promises. "It shouldn't take that long. Then you can wash up. Like you wanted."

"Okay." Reese gives her a crooked smile.

29. Authenticity

"I should've left this shitty town years ago," Kip blurts out. He's sitting at the bar in Mani Osteria. It's the dead part of the day. Only two other patrons are there, a man about his age hunched over a stack of papers and a well-dressed woman sitting stiffly at the far corner, sipping a chardonnay.

"Why didn't you?" the bartender asks.

Kip downs his Maker's Mark and points into its void. "It wasn't always shitty. When I first got here in the mid-seventies, it was cool. It had a soul. You could feel it." Kip points to the man at one end of the U-shaped bar. "He knows what I'm talking about." The man shrugs and goes back to inspecting papers.

"Then the shit started happening. All the great bars went down. Bimbo's, V-Bell, Flood's. Hell, even the Blind Pig isn't real anymore. It used to be this hippie cavern, but they sealed it up. And the record stores and bookstores—Schoolkids' and Shaman Drum. Now Borders! Can you believe that?"

"That's a national thing," the bartender says.

Kip scowls. "You realize Borders started right down the road."

"No."

"So you'd think we could hold on to that."

The bartender makes a show of considering the point. Then he turns to the older man. "Another one, Professor Lanier?"

Lanier looks up from his paperwork and nods. "They're closing Krazy Jim's Blimpy Burgers, too."

Kip is making a call. "What? No fucking way!"

"No fucking way what?" A voice comes over the phone.

"Did you know Blimpy's is closing?" Kip asks the voice.

"Yeah. Where've *you* been?"

"Where are you? You said you'd be here twenty minutes ago."

"I'm just about there."

"It's the university," Lanier says. "They needed the space."

"Goddamn university," Kip says. "They're devouring the town."

"Who's devouring the town?" a man calls out from the entry. It's Jeremy Baskin. He's nearly bald now, and what hair he does have is grey and wrapped around the back of his head like a worn-out crown. The old smile is still there, but it's etched deep lines under his cheeks. He's thinner than seems healthy.

"My God, Baskin. You're wasting away." Kip slides off his stool and staggers toward his old friend. They hug, Kip harder than Baskin.

"Prostate cancer'll do that." Baskin withdraws.

"Aw shit." He pulls out a stool for Baskin. "Are you dying?"

"No."

"Then…" Kip shrugs like there's no point in dwelling on it.

"Yeah, let's talk about something else." Baskin laughs and orders a gin and tonic. "I'd much rather hear your theory about who's devouring the town."

Kip wags a finger. "Ah, Baskin. My old comrade. You've heard this rant before."

"Oh shit. You're not going all Tibbals on everyone, are you?"

"I wasn't. But now that you mention it, it's all the same thing. Truman Tibbals would be rolling over in his grave."

"Who's Truman Tibbals?" asks the woman with the chardonnay.

"The old owner of Drake's candy store," Lanier says.

"He was more than a store owner." Kip slams his glass on the bar. "He was the last true merchant, the guardian of a by-gone age when Ann Arbor wasn't just a gentrified street mall. And Drake's was the last great shop."

"Apparently, none of the other stores still around from the sixties qualify," Baskin interjects.

"To Truman Tibbals!" Kip raises his glass. "And the Moon Room."

"The Martian Room," Baskin corrects him.

"I never saw Tibbals smile or utter a single word," Lanier says.

"Exactly!" Kip shoots back. "You weren't going to get a *how can I help?* or *no problem* out of Truman. He didn't go for that shit. The store spoke for itself. And what did the town do in return? They pushed him out for a lousy bagel chain."

Baskin laughs. "That's not what happened."

"The way I heard it," Lanier says, "after his wife died, the strain of running the store got to be too much—and no one in the family wanted to take it on. So they leased the space to Bruegger's. But they still own the building."

"Whatever." Kip motions for a refill. "The family could've waited for the right buyer, someone who would've carried on the Drake's tradition. They sold out poor Truman."

"So it's not the town's fault." Baskin uses his friend's logic against him. "It's the Tibbals's. They started the demise of Ann Arbor."

"All I know," Kip says, "is that once Drake's closed, things went to shit. Bruegger's opens, the Bagel Factory closes, then that whole block starts closing up—Bicycle Jim's, Steve's Lunch. Pretty soon, the soul's sucked out of the rest of South U. Campus Theater becomes a mini-mall monstrosity. Now Village Corner's gone."

"You got all the timing of that wrong," Baskin says. "And anyway, the internet had a lot to do with those stores going down."

"You don't get it," Kip says.

"It sounds like what you're really railing against is progress," the chardonnay woman says in a halting voice.

Lanier punctuates her comment with a hardy laugh. "A hundred years ago, someone like you was sitting in a saloon bemoaning the loss of the town's last blacksmith."

Kip stares him down. "What do you teach?"

"English."

"I'd hate to think a professor of mine was getting soused when they graded my essay. But maybe I'm behind the times."

Baskin grins in spite of himself. "You are something else."

"What?" Kip plays dumb. "I'm just saying this town isn't what it used to be. Am I wrong?"

"You are not wrong."

"I don't know," the bartender weighs in. "Seems the same to me."

"You don't count. You're a child."

"I'm twenty-four."

"Same difference." Kip takes a big swallow of bourbon. "But I still love you because you bring me these."

"Maybe I should stop doing that."

"And maybe I shouldn't give you the big-ass tip I was thinking about." The bartender raises his eyebrows like Kip has a point. "Everything there is to love about Ann Arbor's disappearing—Drake's, Schoolkids', Borders, Pizza Bob's—"

"It's still there," Baskin interrupts.

Kip ignores him. "And everything there is to hate keeps getting shittier. The Art Fair's just a giant flea market now. The Hash Bash is a freak show political rally. And let's not even talk about the football team. Appalachian State? Shit..."

"What about the Water Hill Music Fest," Baskin says. "Or Festifools?"

"What are those?" Kip asks.

"And I suppose Zingerman's no longer meets your standards," Lanier rejoins the debate.

"Nah, they're alright. The lines are too long and the sandwiches are too big. But you gotta admire Ari's passion. He still comes to the store, still talks to people in the aisles. He's trying."

"I'm sure he'd appreciate your endorsement," Baskin grumbles.

Kip shrugs. "The town's become a caricature of itself. Nothing's authentic anymore. No one's pure. No Tibbals. No Santoni. No Sinclair. Hell, there isn't even a Diag preacher anymore."

"Who's Santoni?" asks the bartender.

"Ty Santoni? Only the town's greatest music promoter."

"I'll tell you who he is," Lanier says. "He's a lousy neighbor who won't get the junk off his property."

"So he has a vintage Coke machine in his yard. I think it's cool."

"And a rusty washing machine. And weeds up to your waist."

"See, you don't get it," Kip says. "He's an artist."

Baskin waits until Kip picks up his glass. "I know someone who's still pure. A real Ann Arbor original."

"Oh yeah?"

"Ben Hadley."

Kip sets his glass down. "I told you. We're not talking about him."

"Ben Hadley?" the woman in the corner pipes up.

"He's the street singer you see—"

"Baskin…"

"You said there's no one's real in town. I'm offering an example."

"Is he that skinny guitar player," the woman asks, "with the long coat and the hoodie who hangs out around Burton Tower?"

"That's him." Baskin watches Kip seethe.

"He used to play the Halfass when I worked there," the woman says. "Come to think of it…" She shakes her finger at Kip.

"Kind of a nut case, isn't he?" Lanier says. "I can never understand what the hell he's singing about."

"You've got to stop and listen," Baskin says. "The guy's a genius. He's written a bunch of hits that get played on the radio—"

"Baskin—"

"Fifteen. Twenty. How many would you say, Kip?

Kip springs up off his stool. He catches his foot inside the legs, stumbles, and nearly falls. "You're going too far!"

"Guys!" the bartender shouts. The woman scurries to the restroom.

"He's one of those true townies you miss so much," Baskin keeps at it. "Of course, he could've left years ago, but he never got the chance."

With one quick lunge, Kip is standing over Baskin. "Ben's happy where he is, and you know it."

Baskin stands up to Kip. "So it's okay to rip him off."

"Hey-hey-hey!" yells the bartender "Everybody chill!"

Kip gives Baskin a two-handed shove. He rocks back but holds his ground. Kip jabs Baskin's chest. "You made money off him, too."

"Yeah, and I'm still sick about it." He shoves back. Kip gets tangled on the toppled stool. He doesn't fall, but it gives Baskin time to back away. "Since you're getting all nostalgic, maybe you should pay your friend a visit. He's not that hard to find. You just have to give a shit."

Baskin takes out his wallet, finds a twenty, and tosses it on the bar. Then he walks out. Kip grunts and waves his arms like he's fending off bugs. He picks up the stool, sets it back in front of his drink, and plunks down. Then he finishes the bourbon in one gulp.

"That's your last one," the bartender says.

"Yeah?" Kip holds up the empty glass and jiggles the ice. Then he winds up and hurls it at the mirror behind the bartender. The glass shatters, showering shards down on the bottles under the mirror.

"Dude! What the fuck?!"

Lanier rounds up his papers. Kip stands, takes out his wallet, and starts flinging bills on the bar.

"I'm calling the cops," the bartender says.

"Do whatever the hell you want." Kip walks out.

The daylight blinds him. He tries to shake it out of his head. It takes a second to remember where he parked, then another to focus on his car. He heaves out a long breath. Finally, he swings the other way and starts uptown, swaying as he crosses Division.

30. Last Advice

Tom goes into the Glacier Hills senior center and tells the receptionist he's there to see Harvey Barlow. She asks if he's expecting him. Tom says it's a surprise. She calls Barlow to tell him he has a guest then points Tom to his room. *This might be tougher than I imagined,* he thinks. *If Barlow were well, he'd be striding through that hallway right now, like he used to walk around campus, hands clasped behind his back, jaw jutting out like the prow of a ship.*

The place is like a college dorm, but with wider halls, clusters of fusty furniture, and the faint smell of death. The doors are decorated like freshmen live there, complete with photos, nametags, and dry-erase boards. Barlow's door has one. All that's there, though, is the ghost of a note: "We missed you." Tom feels a twinge of guilt, as if it's his fault nobody's bothered to visit his old mentor. He knocks softly. No one comes. He raps harder. The door finally cracks open. Peering through the slot, Barlow's once hawk-like eyes seem vacant. "Mister Whelan?" His high-flown patrician accent is gruffer than Tom remembers.

"Professor Barlow."

"What a surprise," Barlow states, as if it weren't a surprise at all. He backs into the shadows, making space for Tom to come in. The room's darker than it should be for a sunny day. Tom sees enough to know his old professor is much frailer than when he saw him last. He shifts his laptop bag and holds out his right hand. Barlow shakes it limply.

"I would've cleaned up." Barlow motions Tom to a couch that butts up to the foot of the bed. It's too big for the room. Then again, the place is so small, any furniture would make things seem cluttered.

Tom sits and surveys the accommodations. There's just the bed, a nightstand, the couch, a floor lamp, a card table with dishes on it, and a bookshelf. Beside the shelf is a cramped kitchenette. Near the entry, there's a closed door that must go to the bathroom. Barlow totters over to Tom. There's something about his straight-backed posture that, while once sturdy and dignified, now seems rickety.

Barlow sits on the other end of the couch. Light filters through the blinds. Tom finally gets a good look at Barlow. His skin is stretched tight to his face and his head, that once-solid block that made Tom believe rumors that he boxed in the Army, looks fragile.

Barlow offers a polite smile. "So how are you?"

"I'm good."

"I hear you've made quite a name for yourself." Barlow pauses as though he isn't sure whether this is good or not. "I'm happy for you."

"Well, I had a good teacher."

Barlow rumbles out an odd, mournful laugh. "A friend told me about your recent book. The one that took place in the farmhouse."

"That's *The Outlaw*. I've had two since: *Open Man* and *Holy Road*."

"Really? How wonderful."

"The movie of *Open Man* got an Oscar nomination," Tom can't resist mentioning.

Barlow shakes his fragile head. "I'm sorry. I don't read much or go to movies anymore. I'm afraid my eyesight won't allow it."

Tom looks at the bookshelf. "That must be... hard." He was about to call it a shame. Of course, it's even worse than that.

"I prefer to take it as a challenge to my faith."

Tom never knew Barlow as a man of God. "Have you heard of Kindles? They're little computers the size of a book. You can put a whole library on them and size up the text as big as you want."

"Unfortunately, I have a rather advanced case of macular degeneration." Barlow's eyes flutter. "No matter what I look at, the center's a hazy black hole. But I love when people read to me."

The suggestion catches Tom off guard. He has a draft of his latest book in the laptop bag. He's going to reference it during his speech. But he never dreamed of reading it to his old mentor.

"I always liked your poems," Barlow says.

Tom laughs. "I haven't written a poem in thirty years."

"No? I remember that being your passion. But I suppose now that you're writing for film—"

"I don't write *for* film." Tom hears the edge in his voice and softens it. "They buy the book rights, then someone else does the script."

"So the authors don't write the screenplay? I recall Faulkner—"

"I'm not Faulkner."

"No…" Barlow agrees.

Tom falls silent. He kicks at his laptop bag, scratches the back of his head. "Actually, I might have something." He digs through a pocket in the bag. "I brought a few old papers from college. I was going to use them as props for my speech today."

"You're speaking today?"

"Yes. At the Hopwoods. I'm the keynote."

"Really?" Barlow says like he doesn't believe him.

"Apparently they were hard up this year," Tom jokes. He pulls out some brittle typewritten pages, stapled together and flagged with sticky notes. "One of these was your assignment. But there's a poem here I wrote for that class you got me into with Stanley Plumly."

"Ah yes. That was quite an education for you as I recall."

"That's one way of putting it. Humiliation is another. But I reread the last few poems I did for that class, and they weren't half bad."

"I'd love to hear one."

"Okay." Tom shifts on the couch and begins. "Wake up in an empty house to clocks that do not work and—"

"Did you say *empty house* or *any house*?"

"Empty."

Barlow rubs his jaw. "Except for the clocks."

"Pardon?"

"It's an empty house with some clocks in it," Barlow clarifies. "And a bed, I presume. But go on."

"—to clocks that do not work, and music you cannot find the source of." Barlow clears his throat. "I know. I dangled that."

Barlow shifts on the couch and adjusts his glasses. "I'm afraid I have trouble concentrating anymore."

Tom slips the old papers back into his bag. "I wish I had your concentration when I wrote that."

"I wonder if you'd help me with a more… mundane task," Barlow says. "They're very punctual about cleaning my room. Sadly, I'm no good at having accidents on schedule. A few days ago, I knocked a TV dinner off the back of the couch."

"Oh…" Tom pitches forward like the spill just happened.

"Getting behind the couch is yet another thing I can't manage."

"Let's take a look." Tom stands, offers Barlow a hand, and pulls him up. He's shockingly light. Tom pushes the couch away from the window. The TV dinner is upside down in a pile of crusted glop. That isn't all that's there. Tom discovers a picture frame with photos of three children. He picks up the frame and holds it out.

Barlow takes it warily and sweeps the frame around the fringes of his hollow eyesight. "That's where this went."

Tom cleans up the glop and tosses the tray in a nearby trashcan.

"Are you married, Tom?" Barlow asks out of the blue.

"I was once, years ago, but not for long. It was hell on my writing."

Barlow sniffles. "I've been surprised how little solace my old work has given me in my advanced years."

"Maybe I'll feel that way one day," Tom concedes.

Barlow closes his eyes. "And you don't have any children."

Tom hesitates. "No. No children."

Barlow angles the frame into Tom's line of sight. "My niece and nephews. I haven't seen them in more than twenty years."

"It's easy to lose touch. How far away are they?"

"Not far. I stopped seeing them when they got to the age where I was… difficult for my brother to explain."

"I'm sorry." It's the first time Barlow has ever alluded to what Tom always knew. Here was a man who never hid his homosexuality but never talked about it either.

Barlow lets loose a gravelly sigh. "Just because we don't have a choice doesn't mean others don't. I wish—I wish—" he tries again. "No," he decides at last, putting on a brave smile. "It was so good of you to come." His hand feels for Tom's shoulder. And now pats it.

Tom puts an arm around Barlow, draws his bony frame toward him, and leans his cheek against the old man's head. "Thank you, Professor." He lets go of Barlow slowly, afraid he might lose his balance. "I should be going. They'll be worrying about me."

"Yes. I'll bet they've assigned someone to worry about you."

"Turns out it's Bucksley."

Barlow guffaws. "That's the funniest thing I've heard in ages."

Tom grins. He picks up his laptop bag and slings it onto his shoulder. Barlow makes an unsteady turn toward his old student. "I'll let myself out," Tom says before Barlow tests his step.

"Very well, Mister Whelan." The light from the window flickers in Barlow's glasses. His eyes grope in the shadows. Tom makes a wide wave. When he shuts the door, he sees the message board. He lifts the marker from its holster and writes "We love you."

Tom gets his phone out on the way to the car, finds Kate's number, and clicks it. After the third ring, Kate's voice comes to him. "Can we make this quick?" she asks breathlessly.

"I'm sorry it's taken so long to get back. Busy day."

"Well, it's after two," Kate says. "So I got my answer."

"About what?" He opens the back door of the rental car and tosses his bag on the seat.

"About meeting Maggie."

"Oh shit."

"You *forgot?*"

"I guess it slipped my mind because… well… because I *did* meet Maggie. She walked in on my meeting with Alec."

"And yet I didn't get a call."

Tom opens the driver's door. "This is the first chance I got."

"You, Maggie, and Alec. That's not exactly how I envisioned it."

"Me neither." He pauses. The open car dings at him. "Let's find some time tonight. After the ceremony. I've been thinking. Maybe we should be open about everything. Maybe that's best for Maggie. For all of us."

"You're bringing *this* up? *Now?* I can't deal with this now."

"I didn't mean that we'd tell her tonight. I just meant I'd been thinking about it." It sounds now like Kate's crying. "I don't mean to upset you."

"You're not upsetting me," she whispers. "It's just—I've got to get out of here. I need to think."

"So… can we find some time tonight?"

"Yes, yes. Of course," Kate says. Then she promptly hangs up.

The car's still dinging. Tom eases into the front seat. He's about to close the door when he hears the distant wail of a train. He wonders where it is and how far away.

31. Heart of Jesus

Chase calls Cazzie's name once more before sliding open the glass door and stepping onto his porch. The first thing he notices is how wild the backyard is—the lawn shaggy since the fall, old leaves unraked, fallen branches everywhere. He lets out a mournful mew. Nothing stirs in the yard. He heads back for the fence that divides his yard from Nichols Arboretum, unlatches a gate, and goes into the park. A gravel road winds down the valley to the Huron River. "Caz?" he calls out again, but it's muffled by the clattering of trees. Chase puts his hand in his coat pocket, feels the cold smoothness of the gun, then starts down for the river.

The best place would be way back on the other side of the meadow, up the steep hill in that thicket of thorny brush. Find a ditch, cover yourself with leaves and branches. Then pull the trigger. It could be years before you're found. It took them six months to find that guy who drove off Plymouth Road into a little stand of saplings next to the Wendy's. And there wouldn't be any pain. It would be as quick as turning on a light. One moment there would be the misery of this life, then a flash and whatever came next.

Chase hears footsteps. He turns. A runner hurtles past. Chase watches him round the corner and disappear. He takes a moment to canvas his surroundings. On the low side of the road, the hill slides into the open valley where people go to picnic. On the high side, the Forest Hill Cemetery looms over the road, penned in by a crumbling stone wall. Halfway up the embankment, a drainage pipe stares out like a hollow eye. Chase gets on his tiptoes to gaze into the pipe. Strangely, light comes from beneath the headstones on the other side. He feels heartened to see it.

Chase goes on, down the winding road, under the canopy of clattering trees. *And what would come after that flash? Could there be anything more excruciating than this unceasing torture? What's the worst that could happen? An eternity in the hell that Christianity says you'll suffer? Without faith, I'm doomed to that no matter what. And anything else has to be better than the agony I'm suffering now. Even blinking to nothingness would be a relief. Then there's always the possibility that death brings something wondrous, something unimaginably beautiful.*

Chase rounds a bend and the river appears. There's a yellow call box on a pole beside the dirt road that follows the river to the railroad tracks. Chase has never noticed the call box before. Is it new—or has he actually managed to overlook it on all his walks? The white sign atop the pole spells out "CALL BOX" in big blue letters. Under them, spray-painted red in graffiti style, is a question: "YOLO?" *Do you* really *only live once?* Chase reaches out to open the hinged cover of the box. Then he decides against it. He knows it's a phone and can guess why it's there: no doubt, the university's response to a rash of recent attacks in the Arb. Maybe opening the cover is all it takes to signal distress.

When he gets to the bank of the Huron, Chase is relieved to find himself alone. Even in the dead of winter, he usually comes across someone here. Chase sits down on a nearby bench, pulls his hand out of his coat, and watches the handle of the gun appear. Then the chamber. Now the barrel. He turns the gun to examine the dark hole at the end.

That's when he hears splashing. He isn't alone after all. A hunchbacked man with a long grey beard is walking upstream, the water past the knees of his jeans. Chase stuffs the gun back in his pocket. He's seen the man plenty of times; he just never expected him to be out this early with the water so cold. The man's the creator of a sculpture he calls "The Heart of Jesus," two mirrored arcs of stone that funnel the current from each bank into a narrow channel down the middle of the Huron. Lying just below the surface of the water, the rocks roil the river into a heart shape, but where they converge into the funnel, the water is calm. When kayakers paddle down the channel, it looks like they're steering straight through the top of a split-open, bottomless heart.

The man has tended his stony masterpiece for years. Chase remembers when he was young and he shouted away people who tried to lend a hasty hand, thinking it was just some whim. Here he is, decades later, still channeling the current. *What a comfort it would be to have a passion like that, something without an end.* Chase has always yearned for that, tried over and over to find it, but nothing has endured. That sort of dedication requires faith.

The river artist straightens up at the mouth of his channel and stares over at Chase. Chase stares back, at first wondering if the man really *is* looking his way, then sure of it, expecting some sign of acknowledgement. Nothing comes. Maybe the sculptor is waiting for a sign from him. But it's too late; they've been facing each other for too long. Chase becomes aware of his breathing. Somewhere, geese are squawking. The sculptor reaches into the river, pulls out a skull-sized stone, and walks away to the far arc. Chase rises, adjusts his hands in his pockets, and continues along the river road, heading deeper into the Arb.

Chase could see Leah committing to something as constant as steering a river into an emblem of love. Hasn't she already done so through her work to help women keep their unborn children? No matter what he thinks of that, he has to admire her for it—the courage, the dedication. That's the great power of her faith. If only he could share it with her. Then they wouldn't be so insulated from each other.

A runner bounds out of the woods that widen along the riverside as the road curves into the back meadows. She's coming from the footpath that climbs up to the railroad tracks. She nods as she chugs past. For a moment, Chase thinks about taking the path. Once in the summer, when Caz snuck out, Chase found him down this way, skulking through the reeds along the bank. Chase calls out his cat's name again, but it's a half-hearted effort. Finding him now would complicate matters.

The road narrows as it bends to follow below the rocky berm of the railroad tracks. Soon the path will split—one trail, groomed for runners, heading east to Gallup Park, the other meandering into the forgotten reaches of the Arb. Chase looks back at the river. The trees have been trimmed away from the railroad and there's a clear view of the trestle that crosses over the Huron. There, on the rusty panels between the girders that support the tracks, the word "pray" appears in faded blue paint. Chase isn't surprised to see the graffiti. It's been there since the first time he walked this path. It's the fact that he forgot about it yet made a point of looking back. It's the timing. Leah would've taken the word as a sign, some divine instruction to fortify her resolve. For Chase, it comes as a final, fruitless appeal.

He turns away. It's more important now that Leah has that faith. She'll need it. Between the guilt of her affair and the loneliness of her banishment from church, she'll be tested. But if anyone has the strength to carry on, it's her. His disappearance will add to her pain for a time, but if no one finds him—or at least not for a while—maybe she'll think he just left town, like he said he might. No doubt, she'd interpret it as the consequence of her transgression. Over time, though, she'd move on and finally live the life she was meant to have when he helped free her. But what if they find his body within days, hidden in that thorny thicket, bullet through his head, gun in hand? As shamed and fragile as she was just hours ago, denied his forgiveness, would it overwhelm her? Chase shivers out a breath, but he keeps going toward the meadows.

Then he hears the faint cry of a train. It's east of him, and by the sounds of it, further away than Gallup Park. Suddenly everything is clear. Chase turns and starts running. In a matter of seconds, he's back to where the old road paralleled the tracks at the base of the berm. The train is still a long way off, maybe a couple miles. As he comes up to the footpath that leads to the trestle, another runner approaches. Chase's first instinct is to hide his face. Then he thinks better of it. This new plan doesn't depend on avoiding witnesses; it invites them. It will be an accident, plain and simple. He went searching for his cat and made the mistake of trying to beat the train across the tracks. Maybe he was chasing Cazzie. Maybe he stumbled and fell at the worst possible time. That wouldn't be so hard to contrive, and no one would question it. Trains hit people all the time.

"Caz!" Chase calls out when the runner gets close. "You haven't seen a cat anywhere, have you?" The runner slows, shakes his head, and races away. Chase yowls one more time for effect, then goes quiet. The wailing sounds like it might be as close as Gallup now. He rushes down the path, scrabbles up the berm beside the trestle, and walks out onto the tracks.

Standing on the sloping rocks at the edge of the trestle, with the river racing under him, Chase can't get his breath unstuck. He feels overinflated, unsteady, like his chest is suddenly too heavy for his legs. He backs up, catches the rail with his heel, and stumbles. Somehow, that calms him. He lets his pent-up breath go, laughs at himself, and looks down the tracks to the east. Nothing's coming. He bends down and feels the rail. It's hard to tell if it's vibrating. The train's yowling again, louder now, but still out of sight. Chase turns back to plot out where he'll start and how he'll fall.

Then he remembers the gun. He takes it out, steps over to the edge of the trestle, and tosses it into the river. He watches it splash in the murky swirl. Then he sees the river sculptor out of the corner of his eye. He's gazing up at the trestle. Could he make out a gun twisting in the air from there? It doesn't matter. There's nothing he can do about it now. The sculptor raises his hand, not like he's waving or signaling to stop, but like he's reaching out, like Chase is impossibly small and so close the old man can pluck him off the bridge.

Chase goes and kneels behind the brush by the path up to the tracks. When the moment comes, he'll charge out, seemingly unaware, and play-act a fall too crippling to overcome. He's still getting into place when the train bellows and bursts into view. *Twenty seconds at least. You can't go too early.* He rises up off his knees to check where he'll fall within the tracks.

That's when he spots Cazzie on the other side, lying in weeds beside a few dug-up railroad ties. He's on his back, splayed out to offer his underbelly, staring at Chase upside down.

Damn cat! Chase stands up and turns to the train. It's bearing down on him, still too far away to go, but close enough to see the Amtrak emblem under the windshield on the blue snub nose. A succession of shrieks, louder and more frenzied than anything that came before, rattles Chase. He stiffens and faces the other way, like he's confused where the train's coming from. Across the tracks, Caz is low and coiled, his backside shaking, ready to pounce.

He wouldn't—

Chase races out in front of the screeching hulk—and crosses the tracks. Caz skitters behind the pile of ties. The train floats by, strangely light on the rails, its cry less shrill, almost mournful now. Chase keeps his back to it, eyes shut, hunkering. A blast of wind hits him, kicking up a hail of debris. He stiffens and holds his breath.

Then it's gone. Chase goes slack and collapses, as if his bones were snatched out of him. He falls back against the rocks, staring numbly at the sky. The dizzying blue expanse seems overwhelming. He gasps, convulses, and chokes out his own tortured cry. It comes in waves, wracking his body, inundating every effort to resist. He can't stop. He can't get on top of it.

It isn't until Caz starts kneading his forepaws into Chase's stomach that he raises his head off the rocks. It feels like he's waking to a place he's never been. The trees that face him on the wilder side of the tracks seem foreign. And the way they sway is almost deferential, as if they've been containing themselves to give him this time. He props himself up on one elbow and pets Caz, stroking his back, then using his thumb like a mother cat's tongue to rub between his eyes. Caz purrs and blinks. When Chase grabs him by the scruff, he doesn't resist. And even as he struggles to his feet, zips his coat down, and fits Caz inside it, the cat does nothing more than hum.

Back on the old road that runs beside the river, everything seems hushed to Chase—the high wind in the trees, the soft gurgle of the water, the rustling in the nearby underbrush. He takes it all in, all of it at once, without distraction or discernment. His mind is empty, devastated, powerless to hold a thought. And yet strangely, blessedly, at peace. When he gets to the side road that winds up the hill to his house, Chase sees the sculptor facing him in the river, placing a stone along the near arc. He waves. The sculptor shakes the water from his hands and waves back.

Chase heads up the hillside road. The post with the yellow call box and red "YOLO?" graffiti waits at the first bend. Chase passes it, then stops a few steps beyond and returns. He opens the spring-hinged door of the yellow casing. There's a black phone inside, but no pad of numbers to make a call. The phone's so glossy, he can see his reflection in it. In the top corner of the box, a red button sticks out above two simple instructions: *press button once* and *speak clearly to operator*. Chase picks up the phone, then puts it right back, and shuts the yellow door. He stands there in front of the call box for another moment, then heads for home.

32. Graffiti Alley

To see the multitudes drifting through Graffiti Alley, you wouldn't know the businesses nearby think it's so dangerous they've hired security to patrol it. The passageway beside the Michigan Theater and the Tally Hall parking deck is like a narrow street. Everywhere on the pavement, up the brick walls, and around the piping and fire escapes, there's a Mardi Gras of paint—cryptic tags and lovers' declarations, protest emblems and religious symbols, elaborate murals and slapdash scrawls, slogans, profanities, platitudes, and warnings, surreal cartoons, sinister creatures—all on top of each other, all fighting for the eye.

A few tourists wander through the alley. A handful of Community High kids huddle in the back corner, sharing a joint. An artist stands on a milk crate, wielding a purple spray can. Here and there, in the crevices that pock the alley, street people slump. And up in the shadows of the entry off Liberty, under the low ceiling of painted yellow stars, Ben Hadley sits, twanging his guitar and muttering out a song. Everyone talks over the music like he isn't there.

It doesn't bother him. He keeps on playing, winding his words around aimless flurries of notes. It isn't until a slow clap echoes in the alley that Ben stops and looks up. A silhouetted figure sways in front of him. "Ben Hadley, everybody!" The figure swings his arms as if on stage. "The great Ben Hadley!"

Ben smiles. "Kip."

Kip kicks at Ben's guitar case, lying closed on the pavement. He misses its neck, staggers sideways, and careens into the wall beside Ben. "Open the goddamn case." Kip sinks down the wall and lands hard on his butt.

Ben's head swivels from Kip to his case. "Oh," he says and goes on watching it like it will pop open itself.

Kip groans. "Shit, it's not that hard." He finds the latches and throws open the case. It spins out across the alley.

"I'm not playing anything right now."

Kip looks inside. "And you can't have nothing in there." He takes out his wallet, counts out a wad of bills and spreads it around in the case. "There. A hundred and ten bucks."

Ben glances into his case. "Nobody gives me that much."

"Well they do now."

"I don't need it."

"Bullshit! Everybody needs money." Over where the alley widens out, a behatted shadow peeks around the corner. "What the fuck're you looking at?" Kip barks. The hat retreats. Everyone else is quiet for a second. Then they go back to what they were doing.

"I have some new songs," Ben says.

"Fuck the songs. I don't want anymore. They're your songs. Play 'em here, play 'em in your head. I don't care."

Ben waits for Kip to simmer down. "I heard 'Are You Any Closer' the other day. I was walking down State and a guy in front of me was playing it loud on his iPod."

"You know how much money that song makes me?"

"He was listening to me and didn't even know I was right there. Didn't know I was real."

Kip lets out a tortured laugh. "I make millions. *Millions!*"

"I get it," Ben says with a soft smile. "But who's using who?"

"Don't give me that shit." Ken pulls a checkbook out of his coat pocket. "You know how to cash a check, right?"

"Not really."

Kip scribbles across the book. He tears off the check and holds it out. "Just go to a bank and give this to the teller." Then he pulls it back, writes something else, and holds it out again. "If they give you any shit, have them call that number." Kip jabs the check at Ben. He takes it and drops it into the case. "Did you see what it was for?"

"Money?" Ben answers.

Kip laughs. "Yeah. A shitload of money. Try a hundred grand."

"Kip…"

"Don't lose it." He wags his finger. "And cash it."

Ben sighs. "Okay."

Kip seals the agreement with a slap on Ben's knee and a crooked smirk. Then he starts in on the ordeal of getting to his feet.

"Can I play you a new song now?"

"Play something I know." Ben hooks right into an old riff. Kip closes his eyes and sways. Ben mutters the words at first, but as they come back to him, his voice gets stronger, echoing through the alley.

Are you any, any closer to where you want to be?
Are you trying, trying anymore to let your mind go free?

The Commie High kids file past on their way out of the alley. "Stragglers rip-off," the last kid grumbles through a fake cough.

Kip slams him against the wall. "The Stragglers are the rip-off!"

The kid cowers. "Okay! Okay!"

"Kip… stop," Ben says behind him.

"*I'm* the rip-off!" Kip's eyes blaze in drunken fury. He stares into the boy's terror-stricken face, fuming like some wounded animal. Then he lets him go and stomps off into the depths of the alley.

The kid hurries to his circle of friends. "Crazy fucking drunk!" one of them shouts before they run off.

"This is the real song!" Kip yells. "This is the man!" The energy flushes out of him. He starts to topple over. The guy with the hat catches him. "Careful there." He props Kip up. "They see you like this and you're gone." He turns Kip by the shoulders and points him back to the entryway. "That's how the Beast works."

"Let him go, Boz," Ben says.

Boz lets Kip go with a little push. He lists to one side, rights himself, and sails into the tunnel, pointing at Ben's guitar case as he passes. "Keep that open."

Tom hears the music, checks his watch, and figures there's time for a quick detour. Besides, it's nearly on the way—through the alley to Washington and across State to Rackham, where he's supposed to be an hour before the ceremony. He enters Graffiti Alley. A handful of people stand over a raw-boned, hooded street musician. He's mumbling his words, and his guitar keeps wandering away from the melody. But after a while, Tom senses the pattern to his enigmatic play—and his voice gains clarity and force:

This whole miracle thing,
gonna bowl you over, gonna make you sing.
What if everyone knew,
that miracles blow around like breezes do?"

Tom recognizes the singer. He points at him, the same way strangers point when they recognize his celebrity: amazed, grateful. He sets down his laptop bag and reaches under his coat for his wallet. The song goes on awhile, long enough that Tom starts worrying about the time. He could drop the twenty in the case and leave, but he wants to make eye contact, to see if the singer remembers him. He keeps bargaining with himself, giving it another line, then another. And just when Tom decides he can't stay any longer, some vagabond collapses beside the musician.

The singer stops playing. "Reese. You okay?"

Sweaty and pale, the bum blinks his one good eye. "Just tired."

Tom leans in and shakes his offering over the case. "I saw you at the Sunspot back in the eighties."

"I thought so. Are you listening to the voices yet?"

Tom can't hear him. He's about to ask Ben to repeat what he said, but a pretty coed steps into his view. "You're Tom Whelan!"

He exhales like she brought him to life. "I am."

"I loved *Open Man*," she gushes, digging in her purse. "Would you mind autographing this?" Next thing he knows, Tom is besieged with appeals. He backs against the wall. His laptop bag falls over. The draft of his new book slides out of the pocket. Someone kicks the bag. The rubber-banded stack of papers slips free.

Reese sees the draft there, within easy reach if he can go unnoticed. *Open Man* was on a list Kate gave him once. Reese lies down, head on his shoulder, arm extended out. Anyone watching would think he's trying to sleep. After a few more people crowd in, blocking the author's view, Reese reaches out, grips the corner of the bundle, and slides it under the flap of his coat. Then he curls up and wedges the draft under his body.

He waits and listens, pretending to sleep. Over time, the voices drift away. But Reese doesn't want to move until he's sure. And after a while, he really does doze off. It isn't until Ben jangles his guitar that Reese opens his eyes. Ben's smiling softly at him, the way a parent might to a sick, rousing child. "I was starting to worry."

Reese stifles a cough. "I'm okay." The urge to cough comes again. This time, he exaggerates it as he turns his back to Ben. Facing the wall, Reese keeps on hacking, through the contortions he has to make to secure the bundled papers inside his coat.

"They could check out that cough at the shelter."

"I don't go to the shelter"

"You're smart." Boz emerges from the backdrop of graffiti. "It's full of thieves." Ben clutches his guitar like a shield.

Boz flashes a grin and steps between the two men. He walks out through the sheet of light onto Liberty, looks west toward Liberty Plaza, then turns uptown and leaves their view.

Reese waits until Boz is gone before he stands up straight with a wince and a groan.

Ben lowers the guitar into his lap. "The shelter's a lot better now. I stay there almost every night."

Reese points at the guitar case. "I'd close that."

Ben looks in the case. "I don't want all this trouble. You want any?" He rakes up some bills and holds them out to Reese.

One hand holding the bundle under his coat, Reese reaches with the other and takes the bills. He tips his chin to Ben.

"Careful," Ben says.

The bells of Burton Tower start clanging. Reese listens until he knows the cadence is counting out the bottom of the hour. Then he hobbles away. "See you around."

Alone now in the alley, Ben gives his guitar an idle strum. Shadows are starting to smother the vibrancy of the graffiti. Still, Kip's white check stands out in the case. Ben picks it out of the pile. It isn't the amount that draws his attention or his old friend's wobbly signature. It's the word scrawled in the lower left corner: "REDEMPTION."

Ben folds the check in half and creases it through his long thumbnails. Then he folds and creases it again. Then again and again, like some secret note, until he can't bend it anymore.

Arboriginals

See what's happening? Look at the paths converging. This is the closest all the people we've met will ever be to each other. What will they do when they recognize such a rare coincidence? Some will no doubt think it's a miracle. A few may even wonder, Who's behind all this? What does it mean? Is it good or bad? What should I *do* about it?

Then there are the rarest of people, like Ben, the ones who see that miracles happen all the time—every day, every hour, every second. We just don't recognize them because we don't know all the people involved. It's the knowing that manifests the miracle. The circumstances themselves are typical. "Every moment is a miracle," these uncommon souls might tell you. "You just don't know it."

Maybe, witnessing what you have so far, you've already come to this conclusion. Maybe you understand now that there's something beyond you. You know that whatever happens to you, even if it's the end of your story, it isn't the end of the story. And even if you won't be in it, or you can't follow along, you know that there's a plan to the story, and it's good. You're not in control. You never were. You're just part of the miracle. You're a character, like everyone else, even if you aren't actually here.

You're an Arboriginal.

33. Convergence

They've been silent so long, sitting together on a bench in Liberty Plaza, that anyone passing might mistake them for strangers.

"You could've told me over the phone," Carrie says finally.

"It didn't seem right," Dean explains. "Not after all the years."

She laughs. "And here I had my hopes up."

"Some things just aren't meant to be."

She turns to him. "That waitress. You're together, aren't you?"

"I thought I'd hid that pretty well."

"It wasn't you. It was her." Carrie pauses. "She's young."

"So are we."

"God, you're full of shit." She nudges his shoulder.

"Right up to the end, I can't say the right thing."

Carrie claps her hands on her knees, ready to get up. Dean reaches over and touches her forearm. "Wait." He brings his hand to her cheek. "I didn't want you to leave without telling you I'll never have a greater kiss than the one you gave me."

"I didn't give it to you. You took it."

"You let me take it."

She brings her hand up to his. "I suppose I did."

They lean their foreheads together. Dean's the first to break away. He gets up and holds out his hand. She allows him to pull her to her feet. "I've gotta meet a friend at Jerusalem Garden," he says.

"I need to go myself."

"Can I walk you downtown?"

"I'm going uptown."

"So…" He takes her by the shoulders and leans in. He kisses her on the forehead. "Goodbye, Carrie Asbury."

In a matter of seconds, they're apart, headed opposite ways on Liberty. An old bum comes limping toward Carrie. She reaches into the pocket of her purse where she stashes dollars for beggars who ask for money. As they get closer, the wretch swings a wide eye over to her. Carrie recognizes him but can't fathom how that's possible. She has the dollar ready, but the bum hobbles by without a word.

Kate stands where she can see out of all but one side of her store. Through the high windows off Liberty, legs scramble back and forth. From the floor-length window that runs along the lowest level of Liberty Plaza, she can watch anyone coming or going. What Kate can't see is the alley itself. She's already gone back twice to check for Reese. The last time, she came around the corner so fast, she scattered the sleazeballs at the porn spinner. One was so startled he dropped a *Hustler* and his phone fell to the floor. Kate should've kicked him out. There had to be a law against taking pictures from magazines. But she had more important things to worry about.

She looks at her watch. Quarter to five. This isn't like Reese—late twice on the same day. Maybe after waiting so long this morning, he figured it was better to be late. Any other day and he would've been right. *Maybe I should start loading the car myself.*

"Are you looking for something?" Kate shudders out of her daze. Sue is eyeing her from the register.

Kate blinks. "You ever hurry to get somewhere then completely forget why you did?"

"You've been hurrying a lot today."

Kate's about to make an excuse, then she sees the hobbled gait in the high window. She rushes back toward the porn fiends. The guy who was taking photos turns to the corner. Kate unlocks the door and slips through. When she goes to shut it, the creep's eyeing her. "Haven't you seen enough?" She closes herself in, hurries down the hall, and opens the alley door. There's Reese, shivering and wheezing, his face waxier than the last time she saw him. "I was starting to worry."

"I found something," Reese says. "A book no one's ever seen." There's a bundle of loose pages sticking out of his coat.

"I told you, Reese. No more stolen books."

"But I found this one. I *found* it. On the street."

"We don't have time for this. I'll check it out later, okay?"

"I know the author," Reese persists. "You asked me to get his books a couple times." He fumbles with the loose pages. They shift under his coat. "His name's on the front."

Kate touches his hand. "Reese." She softens her voice. "I'll pay you for the book. But we don't have time right now." Reese looks down at her hand. A smile trembles on the good side of his mouth.

"One quick call and I'll be out to help load the car." She starts to close the door. Reese doesn't move. "Maybe you could wait over there." She points down the alley. "Behind that air conditioner. If you're just standing here, people might wonder." Reese locks his gaze on a squat metal box at the back corner of the building.

"This won't take long. Promise." Kate shuts the door.

Tom enters the Rackham Building out of breath. Alec accosts him before he can get his bearings. "You had me worried."

"Am I late?"

"Twenty minutes."

"I thought you said five," Tom lies. He takes a step toward the auditorium. Alec steers in front of him.

"I thought we'd take a few minutes to finish our talk."

"Our talk?"

"About my book. And your ideas."

"Didn't we settle that? You're welcome to use whatever."

Alec pulls a folded piece of paper out of his sportscoat. "I think we'd both feel more comfortable with something in writing."

Tom laughs. "Come on, Alec. It's fine."

"Let's face it—" Alec's phone rings in his hand. He glances at the screen. "I have to take his." He hurries off.

Tom feels trapped. He needs to get ready to speak. He looks for a way to get backstage. That's when he notices Maggie at the far end of the lobby. He has a wild notion of going to her, but right then, a boy breezes in from the entry and puts his arm around her.

Tom's done waiting. Alec told him they reserved a room for him, but he never said where it was. He needs to think through his speech. There's a door beside the stage. Tom hurries down and goes behind it. There, he opens the pocket of his laptop bag. The draft of his new book is gone. He rakes a hand through his hair. *What happened?* The crowd's humming on the other side of the wall. Then it comes to him; he put his bag down in the alley. *What now?*

Shadows pile up in Graffiti Alley. It's too late to venture in there safely and too early for the security guard. As Ben comes to the end of his last song, a figure materializes at the far end of the alley. Ben starts chanting, a wail so eerie he could be warding off a spirit. Eventually, his voice breaks and he jangles out the final chord. Ben sets his guitar on top of the loose bills in the case. He buckles it shut, gets to his feet, and slings the case over his back. "You think you're invisible," he tells the stranger, "but I've always known you're there."

The stranger doesn't say anything.

"Be good," Ben says. A junkie shambles into the alley. Ben points back into the shadows. "They're watching you." He goes out onto the sidewalk, guitar case flogging his back. Ahead, he sees a police car parked by Mani Osteria. Then another one squawks its siren to get through the intersection and ducks in front of the first patrol car. The cops get out, four in all, and congregate on the sidewalk.

Ben takes a deep breath. He knows the phantom is behind him; he doesn't bother looking back. If he did, he might've noticed Boz rising up off the bench beyond the alley and following slowly on the other side of Liberty.

Kip was doing fine until Denard Robinson came into Bar Louie with his entourage. He was sitting at the bar, nursing his drink, and not bothering a soul. It was just his luck that the Michigan quarterback would get seated behind him. He swivels around and blurts out, "Shoelace!" That's what they call him because he never ties his shoes and is so fast he often runs out of them.

Denard and his crew go quiet. "Don't worry. I'm not going to bug you. It's just—shit—you're the savior of Michigan football!" Kip tips his glass to Denard.

"Thanks, man." Denard leans into his huddle of friends. A waitress comes, takes their order, and leaves.

Before he knows it, Kip's up off his stool and standing over Denard. "I'll say this, though, you gotta get a li'l sharper on the passes."

A hulking behemoth pushes back his chair. "Easy, Mike," Denard says. "Look, man. We're just chillin'."

"I get it! You don't need some asshole saying you're a lousy passer."

All his friends stand up now. Kip backs off. "Sorry. I'm just drunk. You're doing great." He retreats to the bar. Then a thought comes to him. He wheels around. "You 'member Rick Leach?"

Denard shakes his head. "Nope."

"He was the quarterback when I was a freshman. I almost got his autograph, but I fucked that up. If I could just get yours—"

"Then you'll leave us alone?"

"Absolutely."

Denard pulls out a pen. He rakes a coaster off the table, scrawls across it, and holds it out for Kip. "We good?"

Kip examines the autograph. "Hell, yes!"

That's when he feels a tug on his shoulder. "Time to go." The bartender's looming next to him.

"Geez! I haven't even paid up!"

"Yes you did." He clamps Kip's forearm. "You left a twenty."

"My drink was twenty dollars?"

"You tipped me."

That brings a volley of laughter from the football players. Kip spins out of the bartender's grasp and careens into the hostess stand. Next thing he knows, he gets shoved out the door and takes a hard seat on the pavement. He hangs his head between his knees and grins. Then he laughs. *Now* he has his Ann Arbor story. It takes some doing to get up, but he does it shamelessly, ignoring the people swerving by him on the sidewalk. And even when he sees the police gathering near his car, Kip doesn't shrink. He walks toward them at full buoyant stride, chin up, eyes soft, grin unfaltering.

Reese sits behind the air conditioning box and unzips his coat. The sheaf of papers feels hot against his chest. He squares up the bundle, then tucks it under his left arm. He's tired, but he can't sleep before Kate sees what he has. It's unlike any book he's ever gotten her—one of a kind and ahead of its time.

Reese leans against the box, propping himself up on his free elbow. If the book gets big and she keeps the draft long enough, who knows how much it might be worth? Maybe they could stop taking these risks. Maybe she'd thank him for changing her life. Maybe he'd tell her how much he cared for her.

Reese closes his eyes. His head falls back against the wall. The wind seems to be coming from beneath him now, billowing, uplifting. For the first time in years, he sees clearly in his mind's eye who he started to be, that wiry kid from Bad Axe who swaggered into football camp, knowing his speed would surprise everyone. Reese's good leg twitches under the reflex of a running back's fake. He cradles the script like it's a football. *God, I was fast back then. What if I hadn't gotten hurt?*

Lights are swirling in Reese's mind now, gold and blue and red. He has the ball. And he's running. And beyond the end zone, Kate is cheering. She's young again, and everything is ahead of her, too. She's calling his name. When he cuts back to beat the last defender, Reese's head hits the pavement. He lets go of the papers. They fan out on the cement and riffle with the wind. A page with a single word—*Arboriginals*—separates and takes flight.

Brandon's eyes feel like gritty bearings. When he closes them, he gets dizzy, but when he looks out the window of his mom's Forester, the light's excruciatingly bright. He resorts to watching the front wheel of Cole's wedged-in bike, spinning slowly beside him. "So what's the deal again with this program?"

"It doesn't start until Thursday," Cole says from the passenger seat. "We've got to get through three days."

"But why not at our house?" Brandon turns toward Jackie. She's busy contending with the traffic on Glen Avenue, jockeying to make the right onto Huron. "Mom?"

"Because I can't handle you anymore," Jackie declares abruptly, her voice tightened to contain her emotion. "I can't control what you do. And I can't take how it makes me feel."

Brandon blows out a mouthful of air. "Nothing is your fault."

"I know." The monolith of the Power Center looms over them across Huron. "But that doesn't make it any easier."

Brandon sighs. "So it's a weekend with the old junkie, eh?"

"Ex," Cole corrects him.

"I forgot. You're a saint now. Cole, the Patron Saint of Junkies."

"Brandon!" his mother snaps.

"It's okay," Cole says.

The light goes green. They ease onto Huron and cruise past a long backup trying to turn left before the Rackham Building. "What's going on this early?" Jackie wonders.

"It's the Hopwoods," Cole says.

They're nearly to the light at State. Brandon has a wild urge to jump out of the car and start running. His friend Riles told him he was stealing books for his drug money. Maybe he could do that. "So what are you going to do?" Brandon asks. "Lock me up?"

"Nope," Cole says. "Get in the right lane," he tells Jackie. "We'll take Fifth." Still, the traffic's too deep at State to get through the light. They have to wait through another round.

Brandon puts his hand on the door handle. "You know, if I want to leave, I'm just going to leave."

"I know," Cole says. "I'm thinking you won't want to, though. I'm thinking you know what'll happen if you do."

Brandon slumps in the back seat. Jackie noses the Forester through the intersection. The bike wheel starts a slow orbit. "You say it like I'm in control of any of this."

Jackie eyes him again in the mirror. "We're just hoping, Brandon." She reaches for Cole's knee. "Just... hoping."

The ceremony's minutes away. Nearly everyone's taken their seats. Maggie's alone outside the auditorium. She bites her thumbnail. Her mom's late, and Max is off searching for his mom. Now they'll have to rush down the main aisle and make a spectacle of themselves. And this is how the two mothers will meet each other. What a fiasco. If there were a way to sneak off right now, she might do it. But after the ceremony, Maggie's problem will still be there. *I need to tell him. Tonight. Break the news and see where he stands. He said he loved me. And I love him. If only he were the father... Maybe I'm better off getting this taken care of alone.*

The auditorium hushes. Maggie peeks in. Someone's at the podium. "Found her," Maggie hears Max say. She turns.

"I didn't know—" Leah stops short. The women gape at each other, mirrors of shock.

"What?" Max stares between the two. There's a breathless pause. Leah recovers. "I knew your mother. It just struck me how much you look like her—"

Maggie can't find any words. There's a burst of applause. "We better get in there." Max holds open the door. His mom goes in, takes a few steps down, and waits for her son. Maggie follows. "What was that all about?" he whispers. Maggie acts like she didn't hear him.

Kate didn't think her call with Alec would take so long. She expected to tell him she was running late and ask if he'd have Maggie save a seat. She didn't expect Alec to lash out at her. "Damn it, Kate. Are you punishing me for something? Remember: this whole Tom thing was your idea."

"I want to be there more than you do. The truth is, I've been throwing up all day. I shouldn't even come tonight. But I'm trying my best."

It's quiet on the other end of the phone. Kate can hear the crowd stirring, Alec's labored breathing. "I'm sorry. Why didn't you just answer one call and tell me that?"

"I didn't want to worry you. Not today."

"Well, if you're feeling that bad, maybe you *shouldn't* come."

"I don't want to disappoint you."

"I would've thought missing Tom was the bigger disappointment."

"It would've been fun," she says, hoping there isn't a deeper meaning in her husband's words. "But not if I'm sick."

So it's agreed: Kate won't come to the ceremony. When she hangs up, she realizes that nearly 10 minutes have passed. She should've gotten Reese started on loading the car. Hopefully, he's hidden himself from view. Now, there's just one more thing to do. Kate sends Tom a text: "Not coming. Long story. Can you get away later?"

The answer comes before she can get on her coat. "Okay."

"Do you know Bar Brio?" Kate types. She puts on her coat and turns off the lights. In the one-way mirror, she sees the same sad men hovering around the porn, even the guy who took photos. She leaves the office, slips into the back hallway, and hurries down to the alley exit. The first thing she sees outside are flashing lights—gold and blue and red. Two policemen are in front of her, barking orders. She tries to pull the door shut, but one of the cops tugs it open. Now the porn guy is standing beside her, holding a badge up to her face. A dizzying wave of dread flushes through Kate. She staggers. The undercover officer props her up and guides her out into the alley.

They read Kate her rights. She doesn't hear them. They handcuff her. She barely notices. She just keeps gazing up at all the papers swirling in the wind. It isn't until they start leading her out to Liberty that Kate thinks of Reese. She looks back and sees an arm on the pavement, splayed out from behind the air conditioning box. She breaks free and runs through the flurry of unloosed papers. It surprises the police. They can't catch up to her before she falls to her knees and collapses on top of the dead man.

"Oh God, Reese! I'm sorry!" she cries as they pull her off him. "I'm sorry, Reese! I'm sorry!"

A crowd forms beside Liberty Plaza. The police have strung barricade tape from the Raven's Call stair rail out around a light pole by the road, blocking off the sidewalk. They're letting people get by on the other side of Liberty, but hardly anyone is moving on; they want to see what's happening.

Behind the crush of onlookers, Boz stares in a different direction, holding down his hat to secure it against the wind. Across the road, that spacy singer with all that money sits on the steps of the lawyer's office. "Newbold," Boz mutters. *The one they stuck you with who didn't even try to get you free. You're too far away now. If he headed downtown right now, you'd have to fight through the crowd to keep up. What would the cops do if they saw that?* As if to taunt him, the singer stands up suddenly. Boz steps off the sidewalk, between two cars waiting for the Division light. But the singer doesn't make a move to leave. Instead, he holds out his hands like he released a bird. A piece of paper tumbles into them. He reads the page, then looks over in Boz's direction.

Boz ducks behind an SUV. Through the windshield, he can see the singer reach for another fluttering sheet. The light goes green. The driver taps his horn. Boz snaps his middle finger like a switchblade. Then he crosses Liberty, holding out one hand to fend off the traffic he can't bother to check.

Chase knew he'd be late, but he didn't expect it to be so crowded. All the seats in back are taken and the few empty ones he sees as he ventures further down would take climbing over people to reach. He doesn't plan to sit by Max and Leah; they'll be too far in the front. But as he gets closer to the stage, he starts seeking them out. It isn't until he spots them in the second row that he realizes how the curve of the amphitheater has put him beside the stage, competing with the speaker for the crowd's attention. Chase backs up against the wall, glances at the speaker, then out to the audience. The only solution that comes to him is to sink awkwardly into a crouch. He hears laughter and wonders if it's aimed at him. He looks around for an open seat near Leah. Luckily, there's one in the row behind her.

Neither Leah nor Max see Chase until they hear his whispered apologies. He drops into the open seat, wriggles out of his coat, and looks up at the speaker. *What is Alec Bucksley doing up there?* Chase lays his hand on Leah's shoulder and keeps it there. After a time, Leah brings her arm across her chest and puts her hand on top of Chase's. She closes her eyes, and she closes out Alec. And her son. And his girlfriend. And the secret they share. She closes out everything. She thinks only of the sensation in this touch, coursing palpably between her and Chase.

"I brought Cazzie home," he whispers. Leah doesn't hear Alec introduce the author or register the clapping that follows. She just starts crying, quietly, joyfully, because she knows what her husband is really saying. She knows that she's been forgiven.

Kip slouches in his seat, watching policemen come and go. *How much longer do I have to wait?* He's better now. If he were too drunk to drive, he would've passed out. Besides, all he has to do is pull out, ease down Liberty, and turn right on Fifth. Unless he hits a car, the cops aren't coming for him. They have bigger things to worry about. The trick will be merging into the line of gawkers. He'll have to wait for a little break then be bold. He checks the distance to the car in front of him. There's enough room to wheel right out without backing up first. Kip starts the car. When he looks back at the traffic, he sees a group of policemen striding out of the alley. They're surrounding a woman. She's dressed like she was at work, but her hands are cuffed behind her, and Kip can tell by the smeared sheen of the police lights on her cheeks that she's crying. They march her across Liberty, stopping traffic both ways.

Kip puts the car in drive, clocks the steering wheel, and edges past the car in front of him. Now he's free, the last car in a stream driving away from the scene. The traffic's backed up at Fifth, so all he has to do is pay attention and nudge forward. An ambulance hurtles past Kip and swings into the alley where the police caught that woman. *What could someone as polished as her have done?*

By now, the light at Fifth is red again. Kip remembers the CDs he bought at Wazoo. Carly left them at the foot of the passenger seat. He stretches to get one, and as he's rising up with the Rationals CD, he spots Ben walking ahead on the sidewalk, guitar case bouncing on his back. He reaches back down for the *Heaven's Road* disc. A car honks. The light's green and the traffic's separated from him. He lurches forward, fumbling to open the CD case and steer at the same time. It comes as a relief when the light goes yellow again. He ejects the Stooges album, get Ben's CD out, and feeds it in.

Kip's so preoccupied he hasn't seen the traffic passing right to left on Fifth. But he looks up in time to catch Ben crossing the road and turning in front of Afternoon Delight toward the old Ann Arbor 1/2 Theater. He smiles and cranks up the volume on his radio. It blares out the opening of Ben's long-lost album. He rolls down the driver's side window, flicks up his turn indicator, and cocks the wheel right. The music's so loud, he doesn't hear a car honking behind him. And he's so absorbed watching Ben he doesn't notice people waving and pointing at the one-way sign. And there's no way he could see the man in the long coat, hurrying up to the intersection, then turning the same way as Ben on the near side of the road.

When the applause dies away, Tom stays quiet longer than you'd expect from a man accustomed to filling silences. On the podium shelf, he scans the notes he jotted down after discovering he lost his work. He can't make sense of them. He clears his throat. "I was going to read something from my new book," he says finally, just as a wave of whispering begins to run through the crowd.

He takes a deep breath. "But I lost it," he adds like it's a punchline. And it *does* draw a trickle of laughter. "So here I am, with nothing planned to say and no crutch to read from. You should've seen me ten minutes ago, pacing around backstage, mumbling to myself. This moment was almost on me—and I wanted to get my words right." As if to reenact his panic attack, Tom rakes at his hair and gazes up at the high ceiling. When he looks back down, his eyes find Maggie's. "Getting the words right," he says with a gesture toward her that everyone would think was aimed at the award winners. "The young writers we celebrate tonight know something about that. Some of you will work your whole lives trying to get words right—sometimes relishing the pursuit, other times being tormented by it."

Tom pulls out the brittle pages from beneath his scribbling of notes. "In the throes of my stage fright, I remembered that I had in my bag the very first writing assignment I'd ever done at Michigan." He holds the paper up and waves it. The crinkling sound it makes in the microphone is as loud as his voice.

"I wasn't planning to talk about this tonight. After all, it's just your basic freshman paper—and it was pass/fail. The reason I brought it was because I was coming to visit the professor I wrote it for. Some of you know him, I'm sure. His name is Harvey Barlow, and he doesn't have much longer to live.

"I didn't know that until today." Tom drifts away from the mic. His voice gets quieter. "But one look was all—" Behind him, there's a stutter of buzzing. Tom turns to see Alec fumbling with his phone. He mutes it and offers a sheepish smile. Tom taps the old paper against his palm. "Once I saw Professor Barlow's condition," he recovers, "I decided not to bring up my paper. I wish I could say I was being thoughtful, but that's not true. I didn't bring it up because I didn't think he was capable of explaining the comments he wrote over thirty years ago. I still wrestle with them. It was a simple assignment: just go anywhere in town and record what happens. I chose an alley near what used to be Flood's."

Before Tom can go on, a woman sneaks onstage. She kneels beside Alec and whispers. The words rock him back in his chair. He follows the woman backstage. Tom steps back from the podium and looks over where Alec left. A murmur ripples through the crowd. Finally, the woman appears and clocks her finger to signal Tom to keep going. He steps up to the mic again. His eyes drift to Maggie. She's whispering to the boy beside her. Tom keeps watching until she settles back and turns her attention to him.

"This... um... this paper," he stammers to get back to his point. "It was just a disjointed flurry of moments at first. Things I saw. What I heard. The hum out on the street. Light moving up a fire escape. A trickle of fluid from a dumpster. I wrote down everything that was happening as fast as I could."

Tom flips over the page. "Okay. Here's the gist: *I gave myself over to a simple recording of the alley's rhythms. I didn't try anymore to judge what they meant. I simply reported one moment after another in that alley as the night overcame the day. And I felt complete and in possession finally of something genuine, even though nothing of myself or anyone else imposed on the perfect pace of those darkening moments."*

Tom looks up at the crowd. Some faces seem thoughtful, some confused, others bored. "So all these things were happening." He sets the paper down on the podium shelf. "But then something else happened, something… bigger, I guess. Or at least I thought so. Two guys came out the back door of Flood's, and one sold the other a bag of pot. Then, when the dealer left the alley, he saw me, hiding behind a heater or something, pretending to sleep. And he threatened me."

Tom hears a rustle. People's eyes raise to his. He chuckles at their sudden interest. "I jotted down that whole encounter as well. But, honestly, it wasn't all that interesting. I was scared and hid my face, and he told me not to look at him. Within seconds, it was over. So I changed some details for the paper, made it all a little more intense, a little more dramatic. Nothing unbelievable. I wrote it like it was just another thing that happened. At least I thought."

Tom paces away from the podium. "When I got the paper back, there was a red line between the part when I was alone in the alley and when the two guys came out. Above the line, Professor Barlow had written, *This is real.* Below it, he wrote, *This is a story.* That was the sum total of his feedback—other than the fact that I passed."

There's a smattering of subdued laughter. "I never asked him for an explanation. I never found out whether he liked one part over the other, or was just making an observation. For a long time, I forgot all about it. But some years back, when I had writer's block, I remembered the paper and the line Barlow had drawn." Tom returns to the podium. "I was going to talk with him about it today. I was going to find out once and for all what he thought. But the time wasn't right. Fittingly, I suppose, the moment had passed. All he really wanted to talk about was my personal life."

Tom glances at Maggie. "So I'll never know what he was trying to tell me. I *think* I know. We're always told, *show; don't tell*. But is that really true? Doesn't a writer ultimately always have to tell—maybe not in the way he or she records a moment, but in the whole, in the decision of what moments matter? And by telling, doesn't a writer inevitably stray from the truth, casting light on some things, consigning others to darkness? Isn't a story always a lie?" Tom lets the question hang. Finally, he goes a step further: "Why do we like stories so much? Why aren't we content with the truth as it is?"

Tom throws up his hands. "I'm not sure I have the answer. But I know this: stories end; reality doesn't. Stories arrange moments into meaning. Truth just marches on. Tomorrow and tomorrow and tomorrow…" Tom walks slowly across the stage, as if shadowing the petty pace of time. He comes to a stop near the section of Hopwood winners, right in front of Maggie. "So the quandary every writer wrestles with—even the young talents we celebrate tonight—is how best to lie. You can't just tell a tale, like that idiot, full of sound and fury. You have to impose your will on the stream of moments. You have to be a beautiful liar."

There's a hush, then silence, like the whole room's holding its breath together. Tom lets out a sigh. "Don't get me wrong. Lies can be better than the truth. I'm still that kid cowering in the alley. But I'd rather think of myself as someone braver, more noble. Professor Barlow might disagree, but I'd rather tell a story."

Tom walks as slowly back to the podium as he left it. The audience waits for him to go on. He picks up the old paper and scans it. Then he glances at the audience and mutters, "Thank you." As he walks off the stage, hardly anyone claps at first. But the crowd eventually plays their part, applauding politely, if only to move things along.

Dean comes out of Jerusalem Garden just in time to see the ambulance cross Fifth and stop in a swarm of swirling lights. Something's happened by the plaza. Cop cars are there with their lights ablaze. *Probably another beat-up street person*, Dean thinks. Was it him, or was this happening more often lately? The walk sign across Liberty changes to a blinking orange hand. Dean goes anyway.

The first car at the light is blocking the walkway. The driver's oblivious, bobbing to his blaring music. Dean glares at him, but the guy's eyes are trained on the traffic light. It's only after he's gone a little down Fifth, under the looming face of the new Ann Arbor News building, that Dean hears shouting: "One way! One way!" He turns. A man with a hat runs into him. "Watch out," he grumbles, sidestepping Dean. The music from the car is louder now. Dean glances back to the intersection, figures the cries got through to the driver, and moves on.

Kip hears the honking behind him. He thinks it's because he isn't turning right on red. He wheels onto Fifth, taking a wide turn to get into the far lane beside the sidewalk Ben's going along. The window's already down, and the music's as loud as it'll go. It isn't the song Kip wants, though. He looks down to advance the CD, finds the right track, and leans out the window, calling Ben's name.

Ben hears himself singing. *This whole miracle thing...* The words sound foreign to him. He stops and cocks his ear to their source. *Gonna bowl you over...* He finally sees the car barreling toward him.

Then Ben sees Kip's face above the side mirror. He's shouting, but Ben can't make out what he's saying. There's a clamor of horns. Ben turns to them—and immediately recognizes the danger. He throws up his hands. "Wrong way! Wrong way!" But the music's too loud. Kip veers beside him. Ben points frantically down Fifth.

"Listen to *you!*" Kip roars exultantly before Ben gets his attention. He looks ahead to see a wall of traffic advancing toward him. He gasps and wrenches the steering wheel hard right.

Dean turns when the traffic starts honking. The wrong-way car lurches and hurtles his way. He backs up, but out of the corner of his eye, he sees the man who bumped into him stepping off the curb, his focus on the traffic. Dean lunges for him. He might've caught his arm if the man didn't have his hands in his coat pocket. As it is, Dean only grazes his shoulder. The man strides into the street.

Kip turns to a jarring thud. Someone's flipping over his car, limbs splayed, coat bursting open. Kip doesn't see him land, grotesque and formless. All he sees is the wall of the Ann Arbor News building racing toward him. He slams on the brakes and spins the car left. It jumps the curb and crashes into a brick pillar. Kip's head whips against the door frame. Then as the car bounces off the pillar and spins back into the street, he pitches sideways into a hail of glass and the exploding airbag.

When his car comes to a stop, it's pointing south, the way he should've gone—and Kip is facing the lifeless heap of the man he struck. The hood of the vehicle is buckled in. The engine's hissing out smoke. Kip fights to push down the air bag and fumbles for the door handle. Before he can find it, the door swings open.

"Dear lord!" Dean cries, shocked by the accident, horrified by the man's cut-up, blood-smeared face. "Are you okay?"

"No," Kip says. "No, I'm not." His head falls forward.

"Can you move?" Kip groans, twists his torso, and holds out his arms. Dean pulls him out of the seat. He walks Kip away from the car, beyond the Ann Arbor News building, and sits him down, leaning against a light post. Dean smells the alcohol and sees the wild desperation in Kip's eyes. With all the blood, though, Dean doesn't realize that he knows the man.

Ben catches a glimpse of the victim's twisted body, but, mercifully, the coat covers all but a couple pools of blood. He continues past the wrecked car, stepping over the debris scattered on the pavement—broken glass, mangled plastic, CDs, a miniature baseball bat. When he gets to where Kip is, he crouches in front of his old friend and peers into his bloody face. "Are you there?"

Kip's eyes roll, blink, and settle on Ben. "I'm sorry," he moans out.

Dean's further down the sidewalk. When he looks back and sees the scraggly street musician whispering beside Kip, he calls out, "Can you stay with him?" Ben nods. Dean runs for the police.

"I thought this was Division," Kip croaks.

Ben gazes into the blood- and tear-stained face of his old champion. "It's okay."

"No, it's not." Kip wipes at his eyes.

"Yes it is."

Kip shakes his head. "How could it be?"

"Because you're here." Ben lays a hand on his knee. He closes his eyes and winces, like he's trying to absorb the pain.

Cole points Jackie down Fifth to avoid the traffic on Main. But as she's making the turn, he realizes it's a mistake. Every lane from Huron to Washington is jammed. Jackie barely squeezes through the intersection. Then they don't move through two cycles of the traffic signal. "What's going on?" Brandon finally bothers to ask.

A whirl of lights flares in the far windows of the Ann Arbor News building. "It's an accident," Jackie says.

They wait through two more green lights. A few drivers get out of their vehicles and walk up to Washington to see what the trouble is. Brandon reaches for the door handle and cups his fingers around it, glancing from Cole to Jackie. He could be gone in a matter of seconds. The light turns red again. Strangely, that stops him. The next thing he sees, the drivers who abandoned their cars are hurrying back to them. The traffic starts moving. They crawl up to Washington. There, they see a policeman directing cars to split off left and right of Fifth. Then they see the wrecked car and the ambulance and the officials huddled in the street and all the onlookers. Jackie's the last one to turn right before the policeman holds up his hands. The flow of cars going toward Main is backed up now. She has to stop midway through her turn.

"Oh no... it's bad," Cole says, peering out Jackie's window at the accident. Jackie focuses on the cars in front of her. In the back seat, Brandon sees more than any of them. Between the ambulance and the building on the corner, he has this narrow corridor of visibility, and at the end of it, he sees paramedics conferring. They part to reveal a fallen heap of a body, shrouded in black. Brandon starts to cry.

Jackie turns to him. "Why are you crying?"

"I'm so lucky," he says, looking into that corridor. "Just so lucky."

Max and Maggie come out of the Rackham Building and stop at the top of the stairway. "If you need to leave..." Max says.

"No. It's probably just some work trouble my mom's having."

Chase and Leah come up behind Maggie. "Nice to see you again." Chase bows awkwardly. It was just this morning that they met at the Forest house. "I was thinking. Maybe we could treat you to dinner."

The offer takes both Leah and Max by surprise. He opens his mouth to say something then looks to Maggie. She's watching Leah. "Well... there *is* this reception," Max says. "It's just over there, at the Michigan League. I should at least make an appearance."

"After that then," Chase persists.

"Maybe they already have plans," Leah says, getting a hold of Chase's hand and shaking it.

"Oh yeah," Max remembers. "Didn't you say you had some surprise for me, Maggie?"

They're all surprised when the writer, Tom Whelan, steps into their circle. "Congratulations," he breaks in.

"Thank you," Max says.

Tom lingers, shuffling on his feet. Finally, Chase feels compelled to say, "That was a thoughtful speech you gave."

Tom laughs. "I guess that's the polite way of saying I bombed."

"I liked it," Maggie says.

Tom turns to her. "Then I don't care what anyone else thinks."

"Are you headed over to the reception?" Max asks.

"I just remembered somewhere I have to be."

"Sounds like an excuse," Maggie says.

"Don't tell your dad. It's our secret." Tom smiles at everyone. "I'll leave you to your night." He starts to go, then turns back to Maggie. "I was very glad I got to meet you. Your mother has always told me such—such wonderful things about you."

Before Maggie can respond, Tom hurries away. Flushed and flustered, she says, "He and my mom are old friends."

"We knew your mom, too" Chase says. "I mean, everyone did."

There's a long pause. Max jumps in. "Thanks for coming Mom and Dad. It was… it was a nice surprise."

His words ease the tension without him even knowing. "Well, it was nice to meet *you*," Chase says to Maggie.

"Yes." She glances from him to Leah. Their eyes lock for an instant. "It was very nice." Then she follows Max down the long steps and across Fletcher onto the university mall.

Chase reaches uncertainly for Leah's hand. When he finds it, he gives it a tender squeeze.

"Here we are," he says.

"Here we are," she agrees, gazing up at him. Beaming.

Convergence

Above the JFK mask, in Bar Brio's back mirror, Dean spies his girlfriend Mel watching him wipe specks of blood off his face. "What happened?" she asks with a look of dread. "It's a long story."

Reaching for the sheet to uncover the first cadaver, the autopsy director asks his assistant, "What do we have?" The assistant says, "That one's a car accident. The other's unknown." The director frowns at the crash victim. Then he examines the mystery corpse. Its face is twisted in a dreamy grin. "You've got promise," he says.

Before the emergency physician starts his examination, he asks Kip. "What hurts the most?" Kip's doesn't speak for a long time. Then, as if coming to a hard decision, he says, "The heart."

On the trestle that runs across Huron, above the Great Eye graffiti, Ben stands watching cars climb the hill toward town. He should find a better place for so much money, but all he can think about now is the pain in Kip's eyes after the accident. "It's okay," Ben says. "It's always okay." The words rush away in the wind.

Right up Huron, Alec steps out of the police station. He can barely hear his phone in the wind. "So if you're not the right lawyer, Hal, who is?" He listens a while, then says, "I remember that case. But she was a prosecutor. We don't need judgment. We need compassion."

In the interrogation room, Kate hides her face from the two-way mirror. She wonders what Alec will tell Maggie, and how she'll react. She wonders what Tom will think when he finds out. She wonders what she could've done to save Reese—and why she never thought of doing it before.

Going out of the room where Brandon's staying for the weekend, Jackie asks if he wants the door open or closed. "Is this a test?" he asks. Cole squeezes Jackie's arm ever so slightly. "We trust you."

In the Diag, Maggie sits beside Max on a secluded bench. She's studying his shadowy face. And holding her breath. "I don't care if I'm not the father," he says finally. "What bothers me is everyone will think we got married because of this." Then he looks at her. And now he's the one waiting. And she exhales.

Near the back of Madras Masala, the tiny Indian restaurant beside the Maynard parking structure, it finally comes to Chase. "Eden. That's what this store used to be." Leah goes on gazing at him. He's pretty sure she's not listening, but she seems content. "I didn't know it then," she surprises him with a response. "But I know it now."

Away at last from his obligations, Tom checks again for a text from Kate. Nothing. He heads into the Starbucks on State. It's as quiet as a library. All the young people are absorbed in their devices. *I could be anywhere*, Tom thinks. *And so I'm nowhere.* He backs out of line and bumps a woman talking on her phone. He apologizes and goes to leave, but there's something about the way she looks at him.

"Let me get back to you." Carrie's heard the name "Alec Bucksley" before, but she can't recall when. Just then, the guy in front of her backs up and bumps her. She glances at him. He says he's sorry. Then he stops and turns to her. She takes the phone away from her ear and looks harder at him.

"Say, don't I know you?"

Convergence

AUTHOR'S NOTE

I came to Ann Arbor to start my freshman year in August of 1977. My parents dropped me off at the Markley dormitory, said their goodbyes, and drove away. I was 18 years old. I had lived in 10 different homes in my childhood, moving from Iowa and West Virginia to Cleveland, then to Philadelphia and Pittsburgh, then the Detroit area, then Connecticut, and finally back to the Detroit. Little did I know that when I unpacked my belongings in my dorm room that August day in '77, I would never move any farther away from there than 10 miles for the rest of my life, at least so far.

I've spent the last 48 years in and around Ann Arbor. I don't know if this qualifies me as a "townie" or not. That's the name that Ann Arborites apply to long-time denizens of the city, though exactly how many years you need to live here or whether you earn that title only by birthright is unclear. For a town as quirky and enigmatic as Ann Arbor, that seems fair—perfect, really.

I've written before about places that are special to me. My first book, *History of the House Next Door*, was about my childhood home outside of Pittsburgh. *Boiler Beach* was about the Canadian shore of Lake Huron where I've spent more than 60 summers. *Once in Chicago* was about working in a Rush Street bar and learning to love in the summer of 1978. All of them are homages to times and places in my life that I can't visit any other way now but through memory.

Arboriginals is my most extensive nostalgia trip. Think of it as a love song to Ann Arbor. Much of this novel has a basis in reality. All the places in this book were real (though many of the names have been changed). I really did get caught stealing a parking meter and had to do community service at the Wildflour Bakery. And I did work at the Bagel Factory. And there was a guy named Clem who was just as wild as I've portrayed (here's to you, Clem!). I did get fooled into believing that a blind date I was about to meet had gotten killed. I was an English major and I did have an advisor like Harvey Barlow (some of you will know the late Herbert Barrows). I had a dispute with a professor over my interpretation of *House of the Seven Gables*, too. My wife Michelle and I did manage an apartment complex in Ypsi, and there was a shooting. There was also an artist who painstakingly arranged rocks like a broken heart in the Huron River. And there really was a bookstore owner who hired drug addicts to steal books. And it goes without saying, there really was an author who wrote a book named *Arboriginals*.

There's a line in the Beatles' "Penny Lane" that has always struck me. The song is an homage to John, Paul, and George's childhood in Liverpool. It's naïve and knowing at the same time. In the song, we meet a banker, a barber, and a fireman. You could interpret them as innocent characters in a sentimental trifle of nostalgia. But then we meet the final character: "A pretty nurse is selling poppies from a tray/and though she feels as if she's in a play/she is anyway." I just love that line. It implies that, while the nurse *feels* like she's in a play, she knows she isn't. And yet through the Beatles' conjuring of her in the song, she actually is.

Today, we'd call this "meta." I wanted to bring some of the same quality to *Arboriginals*; part reminiscence, part exploration of how we remember, and the blurring of reality and illusion. All the characters you meet in the various threads of the story are composites of real people. Many of them are aware to some degree that their place in the story is a kind of performance. In a larger sense, isn't that true for us as well? Though we may feel that we're in a play, we are anyway. After all, what is fiction or memory or even identity, but the construction of a reality that is only true because we will it to be so?

What exactly is the play that we're in? That's the real question.

ALSO BY PETER TIERNAN

History of the House Next Door
Boiler Beach
Family Trees
Unopened
Once in Chicago

www.ingramcontent.com/pod-product-compliance
Lightning Source LLC
LaVergne TN
LVHW041624060526
838200LV00040B/1420